"Entertaining...Outrageous...The plot is so amusingly complex that one can't help getting caught up by its machinery."

The New York Times

"Levin...has a sense of humor about [his law school] experience and a sharp eye for its absurdities. His novel is lively with the indignation of a bright young man whose time has been wasted."

The Washington Post

"[A] quick-pulsed, sharp-minded and irreverently comic first novel...Levin's verbal humor glistens and...[he] memorably satirize[s] the potential pitfalls of legal procedure."

Publishers Weekly

"At his best, Levin...satirizes the legal education system as effectively as Calvin Trillin satirized newsmagazines in *Floater* and Kingsley Amis did academia in *Lucky Jim*."

People

THE SOCRATIC METHOD

A Novel

Michael Levin

IVY BOOKS • NEW YORK

Ivy Books
Published by Ballantine Books
Copyright © 1987 by Michael Graubart Levin

This book is a work of fiction. Names, characters, places and incidents
are either the product of the author's imagination or are used fictitiously.
Any resemblance to actual events or locales or persons, living or dead, is
entirely coincidental.

ISBN 0-8041-0376-3

This edition published by arrangement with Simon & Schuster, Inc.

Manufactured in the United States of America

First Ballantine Books Edition: November 1988

To Michael Flood, Livonia's finest

Law school is like Korea, it's like Vietnam. You can't explain it to someone who hasn't been.

—GIL SNIDERMAN,
 A REAL-LIFE VETERAN OF ALL THREE

Just because something is irrelevant is no reason to stop teaching it.

—PROFESSOR AARON MOUNTAIN,
MCKINLEY LAW SCHOOL

MONDAY, OCTOBER 1

ONE

Professor of the Year. Sanford Clapp stood before his mailbox and reread the letter bearing the unexpected news. "The students of McKinley Law School have elected you Professor of the Year. Please do not reveal your selection to anyone until the reception in your honor tomorrow, October 2, at 4:30 P.M. in the Thorne Lounge."

Doubt flickered briefly across Clapp's mind. It made no sense, really. He hated the students; they returned his dislike in full measure. He viewed teaching as an unpleasant and unavoidable task incident to his role as a professor of law and was happiest during those rare semesters when he could devote all his time to lambasting other law professors in print. For their part, students looked upon his classes as intellectual muggings. Sanford Clapp's Contracts lecture met three times a week for an hour. He always began the same way, with ostentatious study of the class roster and quick, hostile glances around the room. The morning's prey chosen—but not revealed—he then would turn his back on the class and sketch on the blackboard the facts of one of the assigned cases (after a while they all sounded the same to the students, and even to Clapp). Then he would recite in a singsong voice:

"Buyer orders one hundred tons of concrete to be delivered directly to construction site. Seller attempts to tender the concrete but subcontractor refuses delivery, claiming substantial non-conformance with industry standards and general unmerchantability. Contractor falls behind on construction of building because the concrete was refused. Tenant sues subcontractor, who seeks indemnification from contractor, whose claim is subrogated by insurance carrier. Seller cross-claims against contractor for the cost of the concrete. Mr. Jones, what result?"

The task of untangling the welter of shattered business relationships would fall upon the unsteady shoulders of Mr. Jones, while a hundred classmates would sigh audibly because today was not their turn. The students would listen intently to the ensuing conversation between Clapp and Mr. Jones, torn between sympathy for the morning's victim (known colloquially as the "daily burnt offering") and the overwhelming desire to write down Clapp's every word. "Sometimes I think I'm training not lawyers but stenographers," Clapp frequently told his students, who wrote that down, too. Some even taped his lectures and listened to them on portable headsets while jogging or commuting, fearful of missing the offhand remark that might offer a key to the final exam. One time-pressed couple in the first-year class, both gunning for places on the *McKinley Law Review*, were said to replay the morning's lecture at night in her dorm room after making love.

Complex, multivariable theories purporting to explain how Clapp chose his target swept the class as rumors likely sweep Turkish jails: "He's alternating first row—last row, left to right." "He's picking one woman for every two men." "He's going reverse alphabetical Mondays and Tuesdays, and forward alphabetical on Wednesdays." Most commonly heard was "I don't know how he chooses people—I only know I'm next." Clapp never had to ask for silence at the beginning of the class hour. Nervous laughter, high-pitched conversation, last-minute oral review of the discussion questions, and all other sound ceased when the sweep-second hand on the clock at the side of the lecture hall reached precisely 9 A.M. Few students skipped class or even arrived late. Clapp's habit of deliberately calling on empty seats to recite was well known. He correctly assumed that from two to ten classmates would inform the unfortunate person that his or her absence had not gone unremarked. Even students who lived in the dormitory directly across the street from the law school would arrive fifteen to twenty minutes early. Many brought breakfast.

Clapp's students were obligated to purchase, lug daily to class, and virtually memorize a 1,116-page work, *Clapp on Contracts*. Author's royalties on the casebook and two equally mandatory purchases, the *Semi-Annual Supplement* and *Clapp's Selected Contracts Statutes*, the latter of which was simply a paperbound collection of laws easily obtainable for no charge in the law library, financed Sanford and Samantha Clapp's annual Christmas vacation in the Caribbean. Clapp made a point of so informing his students. Three years ago, Clapp had led a drive to forbid the sale of used law texts at the McKinley University Bookstore. More than half of the faculty supported the move because most of them had also written casebooks and did not like it when used copies cut into their sales. Edward Strong, Dean of the law school and himself the author of a nine-hundred-page treatise on Evidence, vetoed the plan on the ground that it constituted an illegal restraint on trade. For his pains, Dean Strong found himself denounced in a faculty meeting by Clapp as "a traitor to his class." Whether students bought new or used editions of *Clapp on Contracts*, they felt honored to be in the presence, three times weekly, of the person who had written—dictionaries and the Bible notwithstanding—the longest and heaviest book they had ever seen.

Clapp's students knew that he was in fact an author many times over. Like most law professors who write casebooks, he repeatedly cited his own *Law Review* articles, as in *"Compare,* 'Clapp, The Contract as Great Literature,' *Harvard Law Review,* May 1981"; or, *"See also,* Clapp, 'The Only Possible Way to Understand the Writings of Karl Llewellyn,' *McKinley Law Review,* October 1983"; or, *"But see* 'Clapp, A Total Rejection of Professor Sturtz' Life Work,' *Hofstra Law Review,* September 1986." This naked display of academic egotism served merely to increase the students' respect for him. They felt privileged to learn about Contracts from an acknowledged authority. The students did not know that Clapp's casebook was only one of several dozen available on the subject, that it was one of the worst-selling casebooks of all time, and that it remained in print only because the editor of the particular series of casebooks was a former student of Clapp's and was physically afraid of him. At any rate, those who came to McKinley to grapple with the great issues of legal history found themselves, to their surprise, struggling with agreements for the delivery of breadcrumbs, gravel, and telephone wire. No one had time to complain, though. Clapp marched his charges through twenty-five to thirty pages a day of cases, discussion questions, and abject terror.

The grades for Contracts and for each of the other first-year courses, based on single year-end final examinations, established for all time one's place in the legal pecking order. The top ten percent of the class would join the editorial board of the prestigious *McKinley Law Review*, while the remainder, branded the "bottom ninety percent," would accept with stoicism and remorse their places among the great legal unwashed. They would have to scramble for employment opportunities that fell unsought into *Law Review* laps. Even a Mahatma Gandhi could not halt the headlong rush to stratification that first-year law students accepted willingly. Sanford Clapp, by his own admission, was no Gandhi. It would have surprised Clapp to learn that not every student wanted to gain admission to the *Law Review*. Some first-year students were not interested in the endless hours of tedious work associated with the honor. As McKinley graduates, they knew they would do well in the job market, and in all likelihood they would make the same high salaries as their classmates who could append the words *Law Review* to their one-page resumes. Students who possessed, or claimed to possess, no interest in making the *Law Review* could be said to be following in the footsteps of Oliver Wendell Holmes. According to law school legend, when Holmes was invited to join the staff of the *Harvard Law Review*, he declined, saying that "I didn't come to law school to work for a magazine."

When students described Clapp's features to their friends, their families, and on some occasions their psychiatrists, they would invariably mention first his nose. Clapp's large but handsome nose dominated his face. His other features were those of a forty-five-year-old man retaining the strikingly good Anglo-Saxon looks of his youth. His green eyes, shock of graying hair, easy smile, and strong jaw gave him an attractiveness that appealed equally to women and men. There was something patrician about Sanford Clapp, something that vaguely reminded one of Franklin Roosevelt. That nose, though, broad and straight, a nose that might have destroyed the harmony of another man's face, seemed to be the true source of the power that his appearance suggested. Sanford Clapp looked like a man comfortable with the possession and employment of power. Students, rapidly sensing that comfort, could not fail to be ill at ease.

There's no reason on earth for the students to make me Professor of the Year, Clapp thought, rubbing his famous nose, but his willingness to believe quickly got the better of him. There was no reason on earth, he concluded, for them *not* to make him Professor of the Year, either. Clapp went grinning to the elevator.

The McKinley Law School has stood in the same place for over a hundred and twenty years. Here are trained lawyers, law professors, politicians, judges, the occasional Supreme Court justice, and, although one would not read about them in the *Alumni Bulletin,* some of the most successful swindlers, tax evaders, and other white-collar criminals in the nation's history. Most observers placed McKinley among the top three law schools in the country, the other two determined by the geographic location of the speaker. Easterners would include Harvard, Yale, or Columbia; Midwesterners Chicago and Northwestern; and Californians Stanford and Berkeley. The McKinley Law School grew from a Civil War–era entering class of nine, taught by two part-time professors borrowed from McKinley University's history and philosophy departments, to its current size of six hundred students and thirty faculty members. Applications increased annually. Only one student in fourteen who applied was admitted. The only untoward events in the last six months at the law school were two suicides, but both of the students involved had been known to have serious emotional problems, and nobody thought that they were the beginning of a trend.

The University was named not for the late President, as most students supposed, but for John McKinley, a mid-nineteenth-century appointee to the United States Supreme Court. The McKinley campus, now part of the city, was once gently rolling farmland. Around the turn of the century, the original law classrooms, carved into what had been a cowshed, gave way to a handsome six-story redbrick building. The area surrounding McKinley University, once an attractive residential neighborhood, had slowly declined over the last thirty years into something approaching a slum. Such, of course, has been the fate of numerous urban campuses, a process that leads to a fortress mentality on the part of students and faculty. Despite this fact, all branches of McKinley—the college and the graduate and professional schools—remained extremely popular with applicants for admission and with those who sought appointments to teach them. The law school building was renovated during the 1920s and again during the late 1970s in order to meet the demands of the burgeoning student body. The library, the ornate Thorne Faculty Lounge, and some professors' offices were left unchanged by the renovations and today dripped legal tradition from every pore. The rest of the building—the lecture rooms, the hallways, and the other offices—sad to say, was done in Postwar Utilitarian, and was an unpleasant place in which to study or teach. The library was magnificent, though, with its polished marble floors, wooden shelves, and ornate oversize tables. There one could turn one's back on faculty politics and archcompetitive students and contemplate the mystery and infinity that is the Law.

Rebecca Shepard was just now emerging from the law library's glass doors, and Sanford Clapp noticed the assistant professor as he made his way toward the elevator. Rebecca was tall and striking, her hair a reddish blond that came down to her shoulders. Her features—high cheekbones, large blue eyes—gave her the kind of natural beauty that makeup could only obscure. Clapp, not alone among members of the faculty, had developed a strong physical attraction to her the day she first came to teach at McKinley. Rebecca had been twenty-seven then, only slightly older than most of her students, and considerably younger than anyone else on the faculty. At the time, little was known about her aside from a few basic facts —her father was a British judge, she had been first in her law school class, and she came to McKinley from a top Washington, D.C., law firm. For Clapp and for some others on the faculty, her credentials and her appearance created a case of what psychologists call "cognitive dissonance"—they simply did not add up right. In the experience of Clapp and his colleagues, young good-looking women could be secretaries, television reporters, or second wives, but not law professors. This assumption kept them from taking her entirely seriously. For her part, Rebecca found it difficult to take her male colleagues as seriously as they took themselves.

Rebecca was under a lot of strain these days. She taught Securities Law to the second- and third-year students, and Torts to the first-years. In addition to her course load, she served as adviser to the Women's Law Caucus, which was not surprising—she was the only full-time woman professor on the McKinley faculty. Moreover, Shepard was up for tenure this year, and McKinley had never given a woman law professor tenure in a field other than law librarianship. These last few days had been particularly hectic for Shepard because her tenure essay was in final draft at the *McKinley Law Review*. This essay, setting forth her ideas on reforming the American system of legal education, was the last bit of evidence upon which her tenure decision would hinge. Shepard had published several solid articles on Securities Law, but this latest piece represented the fruits of almost two years of research and writing. Today she would receive the page proofs of the article, the last stage in its preparation.

Clapp did not notice that Rebecca was studying his expression, trying to read what was behind his grin.

"Good morning, Rebecca," he said, sounding unusually cheerful.

"Good morning, Sanford," said Rebecca, returning a smile. "You're in pretty good spirits for a Monday morning."

"I might confess to feeling particularly jovial today," Sanford allowed.

"Any special reason?" Rebecca asked.

He gave her a mischievous smile. "A matter of just deserts, shall we say? You'll understand if I can't elaborate, won't you?"

Rebecca bit her lip to keep from laughing.

Sanford noticed. "What's so funny?" he asked suspiciously.

"Nothing," said Rebecca, thinking quickly. "I was just thinking of a story Dean Strong told me about the alumni."

"Oh, yes," said Sanford. "I heard that one." He regained his expression of astonishment and delight. "Now, I know I've never done anything like this before, but, Rebecca, I'd like to ask you to lunch."

It was true. Sanford Clapp, for all his interest in Rebecca, had never intentionally eaten a meal with her during her time at McKinley. She might have joined a group of people including Sanford in the faculty dining room, but that did not count.

"Are you sure?" Rebecca asked, somewhat alarmed.

"I'm positive," he said firmly. "Meet me in the faculty dining room at noon, and it'll be my treat. I've got something to celebrate, that's all. I don't know why, but it just seems appropriate to celebrate with you."

Rebecca did not know how to react. "It's very kind of you to offer," she said. "What's the good news?" She dreaded his answer.

He grinned conspiratorially. "Can't say," he said. He looked around to make sure that no one was listening. He dropped his voice to a whisper. "I'll tell you all about it over lunch," he said. And then, at full volume: "Noon! Now don't forget it!"

"Well, whatever you're so happy about," Rebecca said, "I'm sure it's well deserved."

"You'll get no argument from me," he said as they parted.

Rebecca watched him go. She frowned and shook her head. "This may not have been the smartest thing I've ever done," she said to herself. "What a gullible man."

TWO

Sanford Clapp rounded the corner and reached the elevator, where stood Robert Stanger, at age fifty-two among the older professors at McKinley, but a relative newcomer to the teaching of law. Stanger had been lecturing on Corporations for only three years. His good looks were unlike those of Sanford Clapp, although they also suggested ease and success. Lean, compact, athletic, Bob Stanger was the sort of man one might expect to see emerging from a board meeting, a smart, expensive midtown restaurant, or the section of seats nearest the fifty-yard line of the Harvard-Yale game. Salt-and-pepper captain-of-industry short hair framed his weathered face. His dark eyes constantly darted about. Even friends said that Stanger's eyes read another person not as a book but as a financial statement. His colleagues at McKinley treated him warmly because his move from business to academia reinforced their sense that academia was somehow more important.

Before Robert Stanger came to McKinley, he was president of Blanchard's, a nationwide chain of elegant department stores, the profitability of which he increased ninefold in his eleven years on the job. Blanchard's had been a client at his high-powered midtown law firm until the company's board of directors invited him to step in and run the then-struggling chain. Curiously, the price of its common stock did not keep pace with the rising earnings. After enjoying eleven years of

11

perquisites such as a private helicopter, round-the-clock secretarial staff, and island golf outings with other well-known executives and top politicians, Stanger watched the company he loved become the target of a hostile tender offer, during which outsiders wrested control from Stanger and his team. Stanger's name regularly graced the columns of the financial press during the takeover bid. Speculation mounted as to both the size of his "golden parachute" and what he might do next.

An afternoon of racquetball with the Dean of McKinley Law School, Edward Strong, led to an offer to teach and also to a second childhood for Stanger. Relieved of his heavy corporate duties and confronted with a new challenge—convincing students to think of him as a great guy—he felt thirty years younger. He pitched away his six-hundred-dollar Blanchard's suits in favor of tweed jackets, khaki pants, and Docksiders. With the onset of colder weather, he took to wearing a down parka. Stanger had adopted the prep school dress code of his students. He had one habit that struck students as odd. He liked to drink wine as he lectured, and not just any wine, but a certain 1983 St. Emilion of which he had purchased several cases from the vintner and which he sent home while on a bicycle tour of France. Now he stood at the elevator fumbling through his book bag for a Kleenex. Stanger, unemotional Corporate Man, seemed about to cry.

"What's wrong, Bob?" asked Clapp, still grinning over his award. "Blanchard's stock drop two points?" Clapp dug a handkerchief out of his pocket and handed it to Stanger, who blew his nose and dabbed at his eyes.

"Nothing's wrong, Sanford," he rasped in a voice familiar to viewers of *Wall Street Week* and other financial panel shows. Then the import of the news Stanger had just received affected him again, and a single tear welled forth.

Clapp felt embarrassed. He was so pleased to be Professor of the Year that he could not display the more suitable emotion of concern for his distressed colleague's feelings.

"Something must be wrong, or you wouldn't be looking that way. If you keep this up the students will see you," Clapp said, concerned for his colleague's appearance.

"The students, oh, bless their hearts!" Stanger exclaimed, and he sobbed as quietly as he could. The elevator door opened and Dean Strong stepped out, looking first at the smiling countenance of Sanford Clapp and then at the tearful Bob Stanger.

"Gentlemen," said the Dean, and walked past them without another word.

The pair entered the elevator, Stanger now sniffling quietly into Clapp's handkerchief.

"Can't you tell me what's got you down, Bob? Perhaps I can help."

"I can't tell you, Sanford," said Stanger between sniffles. "Nothing's wrong. In fact everything's right. I just can't tell you—or anyone—until tomorrow."

The elevator opened at the fourth floor and Clapp stepped out, leaving the unhappy Stanger. Poor guy's flipped, Clapp thought, when suddenly Murray Frobisher burst past him, arms outstretched upwards, yelling, "Oh, yeah! I did it!"

"The whole place has flipped," Clapp said aloud. He had never seen the diminutive, portly Frobisher run anywhere, let alone down a corridor of the McKinley Law School.

"What happened, Murray?" Sanford asked. "Did you spring another child molester?"

Murray Frobisher, forty-two, taught Criminal Law and Procedure at McKinley, but he was best known for his legal work on behalf of a variety of clients few lawyers would willingly represent. Frobisher looked less like a professor of law and more like an executive in the garment industry. He stood five feet five inches tall. He carried thirty pounds more than his heart specialist recommended. He was balding all too rapidly. His bushy eyebrows seemed to meet at the bridge of his bulbous nose. There was something appealing nevertheless in his unprepossessing appearance. He was not handsome in the conventional sense, but many women found him attractive—even sexy, although they could never explain exactly why. Part of his charm lay in the fact that he knew how to dress. His vast wardrobe of shoes, ties, made-to-order suits, and monogrammed shirts was the stuff of legend at McKinley. What Nature denied Frobisher, Fashion managed partially to restore.

Frobisher was a defense attorney par excellence. His clientele shared two characteristics: a boundless capacity for antisocial behavior and great personal wealth. Frobisher's reputation, earned through work for the American Civil Liberties Union, among other groups, and a few big scores at the Supreme Court, enabled him to charge two hundred to three hundred dollars an hour for his time. To be fair, his clients received full value for their money and, in many cases, acquittals. Frobisher worked tirelessly for his clients, sacrificing his personal life on their behalf. He had never married, nor was he known to have expressed interest in any woman, or any man, for that matter. Hence his nickname, "the Virgin Murray."

While Frobisher expended most of his vast energy on his clients, he expended none of it on physical exercise. Thus it was all the more surprising to Clapp to see Frobisher galloping past their colleagues' offices.

"What have you done, Murray, win the lottery?" Clapp called down the corridor, but it was too late. Frobisher had run out of earshot. The odd behavior of Stanger and Frobisher by now had blunted Clapp's delight in becoming Professor of the Year. What was so great, he asked himself, about winning an award if A) you can't tell anyone, and B) your competition is a bunch of mental patients? Clapp had concluded long ago that he alone among the McKinley faculty understood what the teaching of law was all about. That others had won the Professor of the Year award in years past—to Clapp's chagrin—reflected, in his opinion, the students' natural affection for professors who ignore the component of discipline that Clapp believed crucial to legal education. He liked most of his colleagues as people and graciously ignored their shortcomings as teachers and scholars. Although Clapp's own attempts at scholarship consisted mainly of attacks on everyone else in his field, his sense of loyalty to McKinley kept him from criticizing his colleagues, but only for as long as they remained on the faculty. After they left, it was open season.

Clapp saw an open door at the end of the corridor, strolled in, and sat down on the large black couch, the most prominent piece of furniture in the office. The office, and couch, belonged to Ronald Blotchett, an exceedingly handsome thirty-five-year-old man and McKinley's Professor of Constitutional Law. As usual when Clapp scanned his friend's spotless surroundings, he could not help but smile. Most law professors' offices, including Clapp's own, were piled high with books, stacks of court decisions, law journals, newspapers, seminar announcements, bluebooks from the most recent examination period, and colleagues' manuscripts, everything competing for attention and almost everything unread. No secretary dared move the mountains of paper for fear of losing something important; for the same reason, no custodian dared vacuum. Most law professors therefore lived and worked in offices choked with information and dust. Not Ronald Blotchett, though. His sense of orderliness kept the unwanted paper flowing out of his office as quickly as the mailroom could pitch it in. Blotchett was simultaneously answering his telephone and reading and disposing of the morning's mail.

"That's true, Karen," Blotchett was saying, "but wouldn't you like to discuss it over dinner sometime? I hear you're a genius with wills, and I haven't updated mine since my divorce."

He acknowledged Clapp's presence by raising his eyebrows and pointing meaningfully at the telephone, and Clapp remained seated on the couch. Blotchett had dark hair, brown eyes, rugged features, a well-muscled physique, and a penchant for the women students of the McKinley Law School. "Better than a singles bar," Blotchett often told Clapp. "You married professors don't know what you're missing." Blotchett was in charge of recommending McKinley students for judicial clerkships, plum jobs that paved the way for prestigious careers in the law. There were whispers in the McKinley corridors that the price of a favorable recommendation, if one was an attractive McKinley woman, in addition to the top grades and *Law Review* status required of all applicants, was a session on the couch now graced by Sanford Clapp. Nothing had ever been proven, but generations of women law students tipped each other off to "the Blotch" and his "clerking couch," and no woman was unconscious of Blotchett's reputation when the handsome professor closed the door behind her for a clerkship interview.

Blotchett was now sliding a letter opener through an envelope bearing as a return address "The McKinley Law School

Student Senate." He unfolded the letter, and as he read it his jaw dropped.

"Karen, I'll call you back. Something's come up," Blotchett said, and he hung up. He looked at Clapp, said, "Excuse me," and stepped quickly out of his office, leaving his guest puzzled and slightly insulted.

"I'll be damned," said Clapp, who wandered into the hall. He saw the door to the stairwell closing, ran to it, and chased down the stairs after Blotchett.

"Ron," Clapp called out, "would you mind telling me what on earth is going on?" Blotchett, not responding, reached the ground floor at a run, charged into the corridor, and bolted out the front door of the law school, with Sanford in hot pursuit. Clapp did not have far to travel, for Blotchett ducked into Pete's, the large, busy discount liquor store conveniently located (from the faculty's point of view) one block down from the law school.

"Champagne!" cried Blotchett as he entered the liquor store with Clapp at his heels. "I want the best you've got," Blotchett announced. By now everyone in the crowded shop turned to see who the big spender was. Among those present were two other members of the McKinley law faculty—Aaron Mountain, known as "Aaron Monotone," and Thomas Oliver Andrew Culpepper. Both of them were also buying champagne.

Mountain, a morose and unloved professor, taught Conflict of Laws, a discipline that endeavored to find principles to guide cases involving litigants from states or countries with different legal rules. For example, if a man bought a Volkswagen in New York City and drove it to Tulsa, where it exploded, injuring the driver, whose law should govern? New York's? Oklahoma's? Germany's, perhaps? If a child on a camping trip in State X crossed the border of State Y and broke his leg there, which state should have jurisdiction over the case? To such questions had Aaron Mountain chosen to devote his entire academic career.

Mountain looked nothing like his name. He seemed too thin for his unvaryingly narrow, dark gray suits. His expression was that of a man who never slept enough. Mountain, thirty-six, had short curly hair that was beginning to recede slightly. His pale, watery blue eyes rarely attempted to make contact with anyone else's. At faculty meetings, Mountain generally restricted his participation to agreeing with opinions that other professors expressed, a means of currying favor held over from his pre-tenure days. Mountain, like Clapp, did not enjoy teaching; he scheduled his classes for 8:30 A.M. in a successful effort to limit enrollment. Early classes also meant that he was free to leave the law school on most days by ten o'clock, and he frequently did so. He was said to spend a lot of time at the Museum of Natural History. He liked the stuffed birds best because, as he put it, "they never ask idiotic questions."

At the age of seventy-five, T. O. A. Culpepper was the oldest professor at McKinley and ranked among the most popular with the students. Culpepper looked, sounded, and acted the part of the Virginia gentleman, a role rightly his by virtue of gentle birth and breeding. He took special pleasure in telling students that Supreme Court Justice John McKinley was born in Culpepper County, Virginia, only a few miles from Professor Culpepper's home town. All the adjectives that applied to vigorous old age applied to him—he was spry, wide-eyed, and above all, calm. Tom Culpepper, his short white hair parted down the middle as it had been since the 1930s, was prone to the occasional mental lapse, but they fortunately never lasted for more than a few moments. Sometimes in the middle of a sentence he would forget completely where he was or with whom he was speaking. This happened in class once or twice a semester. He would smile pleasantly until some kind soul found a delicate way of reminding him that he was lecturing to a group of law students. "So I am," he would say, so sweetly that no one had the heart to complain about him to the Dean, and he would continue from wherever he had left off.

Culpepper was a McKinley graduate who had gone to Washington as a bright young attorney during F.D.R.'s second term and had come back to his alma mater in the 1940s to teach Administrative Law, a field that exploded in importance with the creation of the "alphabet soup" agencies of the Roosevelt years—the F.D.I.C., the S.E.C., and so on. Deregulation deprived Culpepper of much of his syllabus—most of the agencies he taught about no longer existed. This did not matter to him or to his students, whom he kept in thrall with stories about F.D.R. and the good old days. T. O. A. Culpepper's only other fault, aside from a lack of interest about anything that happened in the law after 1945, was a tendency to fall asleep in class. On these occasions, rather than disturb him, the students would quietly slip out the side doors of the lecture hall and go for coffee. Thus he earned the nickname "D. O. A. Culpepper."

Blotchett, Mountain, Culpepper, and Clapp studied one another and the bottles of champagne on the counter. Until now, Mountain and Culpepper had not noticed each other in the large, busy store. None of the four spoke.

"Good morning, Professor Clapp," said Pete, the proprietor, breaking an uncomfortable silence. "I suppose it'll be champagne for you, too?"

"I don't want any champagne," Clapp said heatedly. "The whole faculty has flipped." He stormed out of the liquor store, returned to the law school, made his way to a pay telephone opposite the faculty mailboxes, and called his wife, cupping his hand over the mouthpiece so that no one could hear.

"Samantha?"

"Sanford?"

"Yes, it's me."

"Why are you whispering?"

"I've got good news, and I'm not supposed to let anyone around here know until tomorrow."

"I can't hear you."

"Can you hear me now?" Clapp adjusted his grip and cupped both hands around the mouthpiece.

"Yes."

"I've been named Professor of the Year by the students. They voted for me. There's a reception tomorrow at four-thirty. Can you imagine? I always thought they hated my guts."

"Sanford," his wife said gently, "they *do* hate your guts. There must be a mistake. No student would vote for you for dogcatcher."

"Darling—"

"No, I think someone is pulling your leg. You've been had, Sanford. I'm glad you haven't told anyone else. Please don't be disappointed, but I really can't see you as Professor of the Year. I'm late. I'll see you tonight, Sanford. Bye-bye."

Clapp hung up and watched Rebecca Shepard walk past him and open her mailbox. She stood sorting her mail, unaware of Clapp's attention. In addition to the usual pile of envelopes and legal publications she found not one but two letters from the Student Senate. "That's odd," she murmured. "I hope everyone else only got one." She flipped through the rest of her mail looking for the page proofs from the *Law Review*, but they were not to be found. "Damn," she said aloud, "they should have been here this morning."

"Hello again, Rebecca," said Clapp. "Heading upstairs?"

"Why, yes, Sanford. You caught me by surprise."

"It's been the strangest morning," Clapp said.

"How so?" Rebecca asked quickly. They walked together toward the elevator.

"First Stanger was about to burst into tears. Then Murray Frobisher was running like a madman down the corridor. Then Blotchett—he was reading his mail and then he ran off as though he'd seen a ghost. I followed him into Pete's liquor store, and what do I find but Blotchett, Tom Culpepper, and Aaron Mountain all buying champagne."

The elevator arrived and Clapp and Rebecca stepped in, but she stepped out again just as the doors were closing. "Just thought of something I have to do. I'll see you at lunch," she said quickly.

The doors closed on Sanford Clapp. "You've all gone mad," he said as he disappeared.

"Did you hear that?" Rebecca asked a student standing nearby.

"Sure did," he answered, breaking into a broad grin.

"This may be the best one we've ever done," she said.

"Better than the tuition increase letter on Parents' Day?" he asked.

"Better," she said.

"Better than the letter from the registrar during Orientation?" he asked.

"When we had him ask each student for a urine sample?" asked Rebecca.

He nodded.

"Better," she said. "This might have been too good."

"What do you mean?"

She raised her eyebrows. "Sanford," she said. "He's going to be awfully angry when he finds out it's a joke."

"Aw, don't worry," said the student, whose name was Daniel Conway. "He'll never find out we did it. Hey, how come Culpepper was buying champagne? I didn't put a letter in *his* box."

"So?"

"So if we didn't send him a letter, then what was he doing buying champagne?"

Rebecca thought it over. "Oh, I know," she said. "He must really have won. I guess the real letters came out this morning, too. And I got two letters," she said, flipping through her mail. "That's pretty sloppy work, Saint."

"Hey, I only put one in your box," he responded. "I bet you won, too. Let's take a look."

Conway had come to McKinley after taking a master's degree in theology from Harvard Divinity School and serving five years as coordinator of missionary efforts in West Africa for his church. As a first-year student, he won the annual award for best speaker in the Moot Court competition, a mandatory exercise in appellate argument. Conway's topic, ironically enough, had been public support for private religious schools. So masterful was his presentation that his fellow students, mindful of his past, nicknamed him "the Saint." Conway, now in his second year at McKinley, was twenty-eight years old, stood just over six feet tall, had short blond hair and Midwestern good looks hidden by the wrong sort of tortoiseshell eyeglass frames, and seemed far too thin for his height. Recent acquaintances ascribed the slimness to days of deprivation in Nigeria, but Conway, a long-distance runner in college, had always looked as though he could have used a good meal. Rebecca and the Saint, both of whom found law school a lonely enterprise, fell in love the year before, after meeting in the Torts class that she taught. They kept their romance a secret from all but their closest friends at McKinley, but now she squeezed his hand as she read the two letters ostensibly from the Student Senate.

The first letter was the one that Rebecca had written and that the Saint had photocopied and placed in the mailbox of each faculty member as a prank. The second letter, however, was the genuine article. She and Culpepper had tied in the balloting, it said, and they would share the title of Professor of the Year.

"If they ever find out that I did this," said the Saint, "they could toss me out of here. It's not exactly saintly behavior."

"What do you mean, that you did this? I thought we did it as a team."

"It may have been your idea, but I did all the work, didn't I?" he asked.

"From what Clapp was saying, it worked like a charm," said Rebecca.

"You should have seen Stanger trying to hold back the tears," said the Saint. "I saw the whole thing. You know, I would never have gotten involved with something like this two years ago. Do you see how law school corrupts people?"

"Don't say things like that, Saint. I feel responsible."

"For what?" he asked, as if to dismiss Rebecca's concerns. "Come on, I was only kidding. Hey! Here comes the Dean."

Both Rebecca and the Saint attempted to look serious as Edward Strong, McKinley's Dean, approached. He was carrying his mail under his arm. On top of the pile was an envelope from the McKinley Law School Student Senate, stamped "Personal and Confidential."

"Good morning, Dean Strong," Rebecca said.

"Good morning, Rebecca. Looking forward to reading your article. It's coming out next Monday, isn't it?"

"You had to remind me about it," she said, smiling.

"You write so well," he said. "You could make people believe just about anything."

Rebecca and the Saint shot each other nervous glances. She forced a smile. "That's nice of you to say," she said.

"Why, it's the truth," said the Dean, returning a smile and

walking into the elevator. The Saint watched the doors close on the Dean before he spoke.

"If he ever finds out we did it, we're *pwango kyohi*."

"What's *that* mean?"

"It's Nigerian for 'dead meat.' "

THREE

McKinley Law School, like most schools of law and many other academic and professional settings, is often described as a "male" institution. Rebecca Shepard had spent much time during her first four years at McKinley pondering that expression and attempting to locate the source of the "maleness" of the place. Her first year at McKinley was easily the most miserable year of her life. Nothing that she had done—not her undergraduate studies in psychology, not even her two years of practice at Holyoke and Knout, one of Washington's leading corporate and securities law firms (and itself an unquestionably "male" institution)—had adequately prepared her for the stony silence with which two-thirds of the faculty greeted her. Nor was she prepared for the disrespectful students who mistook Rebecca's kindness for weakness. In her first year, Rebecca had the misfortune to teach Torts—the laws governing accidents, defamation, and other civil wrongs—at three in the afternoon on days when the students had already submitted to Clapp's brutalization, Blotchett's meandering, and Frobisher's benign neglect. (Murray was away so often arguing cases that he taught many of his classes by videotape. He would instruct the audio-visual staff to show various tapes of him lecturing or appearing in court. This practice once led to his being satirized in the annual law school musical as "Murray Tyler Moore," the "television professor," ever on assignment.)

By three o'clock, the students were in no mood for theorizing about the way the law *should* be. They wanted to know only the way it *was*, and the way it would appear on the final exam. Rebecca came to McKinley with an abhorrence of law school professors who called on students at random, as a means of insuring preparation and attentiveness. She had promised herself that she would never do that sort of thing. Rebecca instead sought volunteers to answer her well-crafted questions, which might have provoked thought, or at least some basic level of interest, had they been posed earlier in the day. After 3 P.M., though, few students cared to respond. The results were silences as painful for the students as for the professor.

Rebecca did not take daily attendance, nor did she demand that students sit in the same seat every day, something most law professors required. Sanford Clapp, for example, insisted on fixed seating, and he took attendance every day by means of a class roster, which circulated daily. Each student had to initial it and pass it on. It never occurred to them that if one of them were to slip the list into a notebook while Clapp was drawing one of his unfathomable charts on the blackboard, the system would be destroyed. Such was his spell over them. Even the attendance list reinforced the students' perception of Clapp's awesome power. Rebecca considered both attendance taking and fixed seating vestiges of high school and disrespectful toward the students, whom she, almost alone among the faculty, acknowledged as adults.

But the students, during Rebecca's first year, universally failed to return the compliment. When they spoke up at all, they asked nitpicking questions about meaningless distinctions, offered rambling, pointless monologues, and did everything else they could to derail the discussion. Their purpose, Rebecca concluded, was to prolong the consideration of any given case into the next class hour. In so doing, they reduced the size of that night's homework assignment. Until she caught on to the students' game, she answered even the pointless questions as completely as she knew how, and she devoted so much concentration to following the thread of those twisting student soliloquies that she often forgot what points she originally had intended to make. Once wise to their ploys, though, she dismissed questions she considered irrelevant with a curt "See me after class," and she halted the monologues if half a minute went by without a serious point on the horizon. Rebecca also learned to interrupt any student who did not look at her as he or she spoke—a sure sign of a three- to five-minute speech in the making. "Can you sum up your point in a sentence, Mr. Smith?" she would ask. Mr. Smith invariably could not, and her lecture would continue.

Despite her gentle methods of preserving classroom decorum, Rebecca never managed to interest her students in the subject at hand. As the hour ended, once Rebecca uttered the word "tomorrow," as in "Tomorrow we'll look at the case of *Summers* versus *Tice*," minds and notebooks snapped shut. The students raced out of the room, free at last to take some food or exercise or, most likely, sleep before heading to the library, where they would pass four to six more hours in grim contemplation of the next day's assigned cases. Rebecca, who waited in vain for a few minutes after each class for students who might wish to discuss the finer points of the day's lecture, would stoically make her way to her law school office, a virtual cubbyhole with a window overlooking an airshaft, put her head on her desk, and fight the impulse to sob uncontrollably.

Things improved the following year. Dean Strong took note of her suffering. He assigned her a larger office with high windows affording excellent light, and old-fashioned glass-covered floor-to-ceiling bookshelves. The office most recently had belonged to Dara Sample, the last woman to teach full-time at McKinley. She had been refused tenure in Rebecca's first year and had since moved on to another law school in a distant city. Dean Strong also moved her Torts lectures to 10 A.M. on days when Clapp's Contracts class did not meet. The students, somewhat more alert at that hour, took the class seriously. Rebecca realized that she might still come to love teaching, as she had always hoped she would, the experience of the previous year notwithstanding. Dean Strong, noting her background in Securities Law, assigned her seminars on Insider Trading and Wall Street Today, both of which were attended by the cream of the McKinley student body—those drawn to the best New York corporate and securities law firms. Jackson Ward joined the faculty during Rebecca's second year. Dean Strong had lured him away from a full professorship on the West Coast to teach Ethics and Legal History at McKinley. Rebecca and Jackson quickly fell in love and maintained a passionate if secretive affair, which ended with the school year. In a marked departure from the traditional pattern of collapsed relationships, though, they parted friends.

Rebecca's third and fourth years at McKinley brought added satisfactions. In her third year she accepted the position of faculty adviser to the Women's Law Caucus. Students began to approach her for career as well as personal advice. She was invited to direct the annual student musical. She published several influential articles on Securities Law. And in her fourth year, Daniel Conway, also known as the Saint, enrolled at McKinley, thus ending a relatively dry spell in Rebecca's romantic life.

Despite all the success she achieved as teacher, adviser, and legal scholar—or, perhaps, because of it—many of Rebecca's colleagues curtailed their already limited contact with her. They left her certain that she was not, and would never become, a member of the club. If Rebecca was eating alone in the faculty dining room, for example, few of her colleagues other than Jackson Ward would be likely to join her. If she came upon a knot of McKinley professors standing around the doorway of one of their offices, she would find herself ignored, and if she attempted to join the conversation, the men would look at their watches, mumble something about how late it was, and wander off. At first, she found such behavior rude and inexplicable. She gave more and more of her time to the students, partly in response to the unpleasant reception that her colleagues afforded her. She also developed a taste for practical jokes that she hoped might deflate the pomposity of the faculty. The professors rarely laughed, though.

At one point, Rebecca came close to leaving McKinley and accepting a tenured position at one of several second-tier law schools that were vigorously recruiting her. After much thought and much discussion with the Saint, she concluded that it was more important to risk rejection and attempt to break ground by winning tenure at McKinley, the last of America's top law schools to remain all-male (all white male, it almost need not be added) in its tenured faculty.

Rebecca came to this decision only after the Saint pointed out that the indifference or coldness that her colleagues displayed was nothing personal—they would have treated *any* woman equally poorly. That Rebecca was young, attractive, and successful hardly endeared her to them. Quite the contrary. Rebecca sensed that the animosity of the men of the McKinley faculty was based not in hatred but in discomfort. She worked among men who did not understand women, and who did not want to understand them. At one extreme was the "Virgin Murray" Frobisher, whose interest in women as students, colleagues, friends, or lovers was virtually nil. At the other was Ronald Blotchett, whose two-year marriage had ended when his wife left him for the son of the previous Dean of the law school. Blotchett thereupon entered an "on the rebound" phase, by which it is meant that he embarked on a long string of brief relationships, none of which he took particularly seriously. Those who are "rebounding" from unfortunate marriages or affairs normally resume less frenzied social patterns within a few weeks or months. Ronald Blotchett, who found that he was enjoying life much more now than during or even before his short marriage, had been "on the rebound" for just over six years.

For Blotchett, Clapp, Aaron Mountain, and many of the other McKinley professors, women were some sort of alien beings for which they had no use. Rebecca had never run up against these attitudes in quite such concentrated fashion, and she sought to understand her colleagues, even if she could not bring herself to like most of them. Rebecca believed that men's thinking and women's thinking differed in that most men were happiest when they could look at life in terms of absolutes, blacks and whites, yes-no decisions. Intelligent women, Rebecca believed, took a broader view of things than did men. Women were not necessarily more conservative in their thinking. Indeed, a gathering of men more conservative than the McKinley faculty would be hard to find. Women's thinking, Rebecca believed, involved looking at issues in all their subtle shades of gray.

Rebecca's colleagues had no patience for this mode of analysis. Rarely was she able to complete a thought or even a long sentence at faculty meetings, before she was shouted down. Eventually she gave up trying to speak. When she wished to express a concern about law school policy, she would quietly visit the Dean in his office and make her point without arguing or displaying excessive emotion. For those brief moments of rational discourse the Dean was grateful, although, for reasons of his own, he rarely told her so. Rebecca, who considered even these private visits futile, would have been surprised had she known how seriously Dean Strong took her comments. She enjoyed far more influence than she thought.

If her method of thinking distanced (she might have preferred the word "distinguished") Rebecca from her colleagues, her own sexuality created an unbridgeable gulf. Rebecca rightly sensed that a number of her fellow professors were uncomfortable around her because of their own sense of sexual inadequacy. Rebecca did not go out of her way to emphasize her own sexuality. She did not have to. It radiated from her. She could be unconscious of it but not so her male colleagues. For many of them, to share a lunch table with her, to sit beside her on a couch at a faculty meeting, even to pass her in the hallway, was a searing reminder that they had never been intimate with a woman as attractive, as full of energy, as complex as she, and that in all likelihood they never would have the chance. They fantasized about her, as men often fantasize about the women in their working lives. Once Sanford Clapp even made her a drunken proposition at a faculty Christmas party, while his wife was at another table lecturing the Dean. But the fantasies always ended in despair, because the men feared, not incorrectly, that they would somehow fall short of her expectations. The men of the McKinley faculty— not all of them, just the Sanford Clapp–Aaron Mountain types—might not have been interested in putting the foregoing in words, but they sensed it, and they despised her for it.

There were little things, too, of course. Rebecca had asked Sanford Clapp, ever so politely, a few years back, if he could modify his annual Convocation address. Convocation, traditionally, was the first time that a newly admitted class would be confronted with its tormentors. Rebecca gravely insulted Clapp, or so he later claimed, when she asked whether he might drop his concluding remarks, which were always: "The best advice I can give you about law school is just lie back and enjoy it, which is the punch line of a joke I can't tell you."

Rebecca took a certain amount of indelicate ribbing another time when Ronald Blotchett read aloud in a faculty meeting a *Wall Street Journal* article about a McKinley student who had blown the whistle on a top Atlanta firm's practice of a mandatory wet T-shirt contest for women summer clerks. The contest took place at a party held at a senior partner's poolside. The student who revealed the practice, which had never been mentioned outside the law firm in question, told the reporter that a professor at her law school had given her the courage to complain about something she considered degrading, even though it might hurt her career to do so. Everyone at the faculty meeting assumed correctly that the professor in question was Rebecca. The tenor of the men's comments was to the effect of "Why did you have to spoil everyone else's fun?" and "What's wrong, Rebecca? Got something to hide?" Such episodes served only to reinforce Rebecca's belief in the existence of male menopause.

"Sorry I'm late," said Sanford Clapp, as he stepped off the elevator. He was still beaming. The tip of his nose had gone slightly red, a sign that his celebrating had already begun. "Been waiting long?"

Rebecca Shepard, standing at the entrance to the faculty dining room and hoping that Sanford had forgotten about their date, looked at her watch. She had been waiting almost fifteen minutes. "Not at all," she lied.

"Honestly, I'm sorry," he repeated, and he flashed a warm smile.

Rebecca noticed for the first time that he must have been a very handsome man when young. "Really, I just got here myself," she said. "Shall we go in?"

Sanford gave her a look that said, By all means, and they took places on the cafeteria-style line directly behind Robert Stanger. Sanford gallantly reached for two trays and set one before Rebecca on the metal bars, and equally gallantly provided her with silverware and two paper napkins.

"Feeling better, Bob?" Sanford asked solicitously.

"Never felt better in my life," Stanger rasped, but his eyes were glassy and his expression was vacant. "H'llo, Rebecca."

"Hi, Bob." Him, too, she thought. He must have been drinking since ten this morning.

"What's for lunch?" Sanford asked, examining the menu behind the serving area. "Meat loaf? Meat loaf *today*? Of all days?"

He turned to Rebecca and took her hand. Rebecca began to panic. "Becky," Sanford continued, "I should have invited you to some place nice. Meat loaf, *indeed*."

Becky? Rebecca thought. No one ever called me Becky. Not even my parents. She gently removed her hand from his grasp, as if to point to the salad, which the server, one of her Torts students, then handed her.

"I can't blame you, Beck. The meat loaf's terrible. I'll take it anyway, with extra potatoes. And a bottle—a half-bottle of red wine. You drink red wine, don't you, Rebecca?"

"Yes," she said. It's the award, she thought. He still thinks he won. Her panic deepened and she struggled to retain her composure. Sanford paid for both meals.

"You don't have to do that," she protested, opening her purse.

"Are you kidding?" Sanford asked. "My treat. It's a red-letter day."

Rebecca took a deep breath and picked up her tray. The two meals, including a half-bottle of New York State red wine and Sanford's dessert, an apple brown betty, came to a total of $4.85. The deeply subsidized lunch was a time-honored McKinley faculty perquisite.

"Let's go sit by the window," said Sanford. "It's a beautiful day, and I want to savor it."

They made their way to a vacant table. The view from the third-story windows was of the slum neighborhood surrounding the campus. Meat loaf, domestic wine, and apple brown betty: Sanford Clapp, as his students might have put it, really knew how to party. Rebecca's mind was not on Sanford's limited culinary imagination, however. You weren't supposed to take the letter so seriously, she thought. Oh, well, at least he didn't get champagne.

Sanford Clapp unscrewed the top of the bottle and poured two glasses of wine. As he did so, he explained: "I'm not supposed to tell anyone about this, but I just couldn't keep it a secret any longer, and I wanted you to be the first to know."

"Know what, Sanford?" Rebecca asked. She had lost her appetite.

Sanford handed her a glass, and raised his own in a toast. Rebecca mechanically followed suit.

"To the new Professor of the Year," he whispered. "*Me!* Can you believe it?"

Oh, no, thought Rebecca.

They clinked glasses. Sanford took a well-measured victory sip. Rebecca downed her entire glass. It was not the reaction Sanford was expecting.

"You can't believe it, can you?" he asked. He laughed and took another sip. "Neither can I."

Rebecca felt sick.

"Don't tell a soul. I just had to tell you because . . . because—" He laughed. "I don't even know why. I just wanted you to know. Promise to keep it a secret?"

She nodded glumly. She thought she knew exactly why he had invited her to lunch. The contrast in teaching styles between Rebecca's and Sanford's could not have been more pronounced. Their attitudes toward their students, their roles, and even the way they expected students to address them were diametrically opposed. Rebecca went by her first name in and out of class, while to call Sanford Sanford was to risk a hearing before the McKinley Law School Judicial Board (itself a dumping ground for the most unctuous and vindictive of students). He must think of the award as a vindication for everything he stands for, Rebecca thought. It must be the greatest thing that ever happened to him. She concluded that Sanford had asked her to lunch in order to gloat. Winning meant that his approach to teaching was right and hers was wrong. Wait until he finds out I won and he didn't. I think I'm going to be sick.

Sanford attacked his meat loaf.

"It's by far the greatest thing that's ever happened to me," he said between mouthfuls. "I feel as though I've been right all along. I feel as though everything I've done—all my efforts in pedagogy—" Now he sounded as though he were rehearsing his acceptance speech. "It's a total—what's the word? It's a *vindication* of who I am, of how I teach, of what I'm trying to be. I never expected it, of course. The award usually goes to the professors who, you know, pander to the students, try to be a pal. I don't do that, of course. Spare the rod, and all that, that's my philosophy." His eyes were shining. "I see myself in the great tradition of Contracts professors. Williston, Corbin, Llewellyn, and now Sanford Clapp. It's—it's—well, it's humbling. That's all I can say."

He looked up from his meat loaf and noticed that all the color had drained from Rebecca's face. This isn't funny any more, she was thinking.

"Is everything all right?" Sanford asked. "You've gone pale. Maybe the wine went to your head. Not used to alcohol, is that it?"

Rebecca shook her head. I could drink you under the table, she thought. "I think I'm going to be sick," she said.

Sanford bolted from his chair. "Don't move," he said. "I'll bring you some water." He hastened to the serving line. When he returned, glass in hand, Rebecca was standing.

"Sanford," she said, "I hate to spoil your victory party, but all of a sudden I'm just—"

"It's all right, little lady," he said, putting his arm around her and smiling condescendingly. "You've just got to learn to *sip* wine. It's not Coca-Cola, you know. Why don't I just take a rain check on our little celebration? Shall we continue when you're feeling better? I understand."

Rebecca smiled weakly at Sanford and patted his hand. "You're a gentleman, Sanford. I'll see you later."

"Not at all, not at all. Should I have your lunch brought up to your office?"

Is this the same Sanford Clapp I know? Rebecca thought. "No," she said, "but it's very kind of you to offer. I'll see you later."

"Well, all right," he said, and he watched her leave the dining hall. He returned to his seat, set down the glass of water, shook his head, and thoughtfully sliced up the rest of his meat loaf. Now that she was gone, he could indulge in his favorite epicurean pleasure—ketchup. He applied it liberally, first to the pieces of meat and then to the potatoes. "Professor of the Year," he murmured, and he sipped his wine, all thoughts of Rebecca suddenly disappearing.

FOUR

"I wasn't fooled for a minute," said Sanford Clapp.

"Neither was I," said Murray Frobisher.

"Saw right through it," said Ronald Blotchett.

"Oldest trick in the book," added Aaron Mountain.

"I'm glad that none of you took seriously the prank that was played against us this morning," said Dean Strong, trying to bring the faculty meeting to order. It was 4 P.M. Ten McKinley professors—the "Committee of Ten"—were seated in or sprawled upon the ancient leather chairs and couches of the Thorne Lounge, home to faculty meetings for more than fifty years. Oil paintings of severe professors and deans emeriti covered the room's walls and gave the lounge the ambience of a private men's club. The Committee of Ten was Dean Strong's idea. An orderly man, he could not abide the havoc of full faculty meetings at which all thirty professors would attempt to speak at once. Consensus proving impossible, each fall the Dean would choose seven tenured professors and two nontenured ones to serve with him on a decision-making body. The faculty warmed quickly to the Dean's Committee of Ten because it eliminated their obligation to attend faculty meetings on an average of two out of every three years.

"Although I'm as concerned as the next man for the dignity of the McKinley faculty," the Dean continued, "I'm glad to see that we can stand a little collective ribbing. From what you gentlemen are saying, not one of you was actually taken in by the letter. Just the same, are there any thoughts as to the kind of punishment due the student or students involved, should we ever discover who was responsible?"

"Toss him out on his ass," Clapp said sharply.

The Dean looked shocked.

"Disciplinary charges and a two-year suspension," Frobisher said with equal vehemence.

"Hear, hear," said Aaron Mountain, eager to agree.

"We really can't tolerate this lack of respect," said Blotchett, who, despite his affable expression, was offended by the prank. "We can't let the students try to make fools of us."

Especially when we all do such a good job by ourselves, thought Rebecca Shepard.

The faculty's mood surprised the Dean. "I thought that none of you took it seriously," he said, "and now you want to have the perpetrator thrown out of school."

"If I may speak for my esteemed colleagues," began Stanger, rising to his feet and making a sweeping gesture with his right hand, as if to indicate that he had been authorized to speak for all present. He had been attending Committee of Ten meetings for only a few years but he got the hang of them fairly quickly. "If I may speak for my colleagues, the important consideration here is not whether any given professor was fooled by a fake Professor of the Year letter. I, of course, wasn't fooled for a moment—"

"Then why were you crying like a two-year-old?" Clapp asked.

Stanger ignored Clapp and plowed on. "What matters is the *precedent* we set. If we allow a clearly ineffectual prank to go unanswered today, what will happen next time?"

He paused for a moment to think of examples. "Look," he said. "If we create a, you know, a climate of permissiveness, people might start tampering with transcripts or the faculty personnel files. I, for one, don't want students to think they can go change their grades whenever they feel like it. There's really no limit to what a few determined people can do. Malcontents. They're in every organization, and you can't let them get the upper hand."

"Bob's right," said Mountain.

"Aren't you carrying things a bit far?" asked Dean Strong.

"This could never have happened at Blanchard's," said Stanger. "Our security chief was an ex-Marine, and he could—"

"Please, no more Blanchard's war stories," said Frobisher.

"Gentlemen, please," said the Dean, and he caught a glance from Rebecca. "Members of the faculty, can we stick to the issues and not let the meeting degenerate as usual into—"

No one paid attention to him.

"How have these things been treated in the past?" asked Tony Sloop, at twenty-nine the junior member of the faculty. Rumor had it that he was bisexual, and the young professor did nothing to dispel the rumor. He kept his dark blond hair a shade longer than academic convention dictated. His brown eyes were gentle and expressive. When he wore a tie at all, it was never more than an inch across. Sloop taught Civil Procedure, the course that exposes first-year students to the workings and odd phraseology of the federal court system. Sloop's colleagues wondered aloud, but never in his presence, why the young man ever drifted into the teaching of law. Students were unanimous in their praise and affection for the diffident professor, but they wondered the same thing. In his spare time, Sloop was a member of a post–New Wave performance art group downtown, to the bemusement of his colleagues and to the displeasure of the Dean.

"Tell us, Tom," Sloop continued. "How has the law school treated previous pranks against the faculty?"

Thomas Oliver Andrew Culpepper was the walking repository of all that had happened in five decades at McKinley. He searched his mind.

"In 1941," he began, rubbing his temple as if to jog the flow of memory, "shortly before I came to teach here, two students sent false draft notices to the entire faculty, who were not at all amused. Three of them actually reported for duty and were informed that the notices were forgeries, which was a violation of federal law, of course. The students responsible were discovered and were dismissed from the law school.

"In 1949, four students contracted with a demolition company to tear down the law school building. The four went as far as getting the requisite permits from the city and had chosen a Sunday morning for the actual demolition work. The wrecking crew had arrived and the wrecking ball was ready to fly when the former Dean, Dean Thorne, I mean, walked by on his way to church. He had the devil's own time convincing the wreckers that the whole thing was a joke, especially since the signatures on the permits were really his. I thought it was a fairly harmless prank, just a few students letting off some steam. The students responsible were discovered and were dismissed from the law school.

"There were no pranks of any sort in the 1950s," Culpepper continued. "In 1961, however, three students listed the Dean's apartment—I'm still talking about Dean Thorne—with a real estate broker, procured a set of keys, and invited the broker to show the flat to prospective tenants, but only during the days, when neither Dean Thorne nor his wife was at home. This went on for several weeks until the broker found a tenant. The Dean, of course, was not pleased. The students responsible were discovered and were dismissed from the law school.

"In 1967—"

Dean Strong's patience had run out. "Tom, I'm sure we'd all like to know what happened in 1967, and since then, for that matter, but I'm afraid our time is too short. The pattern is quite clear, though. Are you suggesting that the law school has dismissed every student involved in a prank?"

Culpepper considered the question. "Every serious prank, yes."

"How do you tell a serious prank from a—from a non-serious prank?" asked Ronald Blotchett. About four years ago, Blotchett found a book on "distinction-based thinking" in the seat pocket on a flight from New York to Boston. He became so absorbed in the book's contents that he attempted to apply "distinction-based thinking" to every situation, including this one. Although he often spoke of the concept with his colleagues, he was usually at a loss to offer a definition for the term or to explain how it differed from regular thinking. For a man with a responsible job, Blotchett spent a lot of time reading, absorbing, and applying the lessons of books that purported to change one's life. He claimed to have increased his reading speed, memory, sexual potency, and vocabulary from such books over the past two or three years. He often recommended them to his colleagues, who lacked what Blotchett considered adequate commitment to self-improvement.

"Gentlemen, er, faculty members." Edward Strong had been Dean for eight years, and Rebecca Shepard had been on the faculty for slightly more than half that time, but he could not shake his habit of addressing the otherwise all-male Committee of Ten as "gentlemen." "Let's not start getting bogged down, please—"

"Is it the nature of the prank or the depth of the reaction?" asked Frobisher. "Because then you could have a prank serious in nature which gets no reaction, and so it would not be punished as a serious prank—or the other way round."

"Like the tree that falls in the forest," said Stanger, impressed, as always, with Frobisher's logic. He admired Frobisher's ability to get things done. Efficiency was Stanger's byword in the business world.

"I never thought of that," said Culpepper, who often told his colleagues that there was nothing like the spirited give-and-take of a faculty meeting to keep one's mind young.

If Dean Strong could have been granted one wish, it would be for an end forever to faculty meetings of any sort. It was not that he craved the power for himself alone. He was extremely conscious of the value of consensus and the importance of letting others feel that they were part of the decision-making process. But he could not abide to sit for hours and listen to his colleagues ramble on while pursuing the most trivial of matters. As much as those chosen to serve on the Committee of Ten resented the time-consuming nature of regular attendance, and as uninterested as most of them were in law school policy, they would never have stood for the elimination of the group. The Dean correctly sensed that the faculty found the weekly meetings therapeutic. After all, faculty meetings were settings that allowed professors to speak without the pressure of twelve to one hundred and twenty pens poised to record every word. No student hands were raised to question or contradict. In short, Committee of Ten meetings afforded the McKinley professors the luxury of speaking publicly without the awesome responsibility of having to make sense.

"Gentlemen—members of the faculty, please," said an exasperated Dean Strong. *"You always do this.* Let's get it over with. Resolved that the faculty of the McKinley Law School intends to deal quickly and seriously with the perpetrator of the Professor of the Year hoax, and, in keeping with McKinley precedent, said student or students will be dismissed from the law school. All in favor—"

A chorus of ayes.

"All opposed?"

Silence.

"Resolution carries," said the Dean, alarmed at the stiffness of the sentence but certain that the faculty would forget about the whole matter within days. All of them would forget it, except for Sanford Clapp, whose vindictive side knew few bounds. Sanford caught Rebecca's eye. She looked nervously away and hoped that Sanford did not notice. He noticed.

"On to more serious things," the Dean continued. "The agenda for our meeting this afternoon contains two items, one worthy of serious consideration and the other less deserving of our time. The important matter is this. McKinley Law School has never granted tenure to a woman, except for the law librarian, Miss Pander. We have come under considerable criticism for our failure to hire and promote to tenure level even one woman professor. As you all know, Rebecca Shepard has taught for four years here at McKinley and this is the fifth year, that is, the year in which her tenure decision must be made.

"It is the practice of the McKinley Law School to make its tenure decisions by the middle of October, which gives disappointed candidates, if there are any"—Rebecca suddenly felt searching eyes upon her, and she looked uncomfortably away—"ample time to secure employment for the following academic year. Gentlemen, er, members of the faculty, today is Monday, October first. On Friday of next week—October twelfth—we shall meet to make a decision as to whether we shall recommend to the Board of Trustees that Rebecca Shepard should or should not receive tenure. As you undoubtedly know, the approval of the Board of Trustees is a mere formality. The decision I make—with your advice, of course —is what counts.

"We have virtually all the information we need to decide this matter. We have Professor Shepard's publications, we have the student evaluations, and we have our own impressions. The only piece of the puzzle still lacking is her tenure essay. The *McKinley Law Review* will contain that article in its next issue, which, I believe, comes out Monday."

At that moment a startled Aaron Mountain emitted a "Whua?"

"It is our task today," the Dean concluded, ignoring Mountain, as he always did in faculty meetings, "to choose a tenure committee to reflect on all the evidence relating to Professor Shepard's career—her teaching, her publications, and the intangibles. This committee will sift through the data and report back to us at the Committee of Ten meeting a week from Friday."

The Dean looked from face to face for reaction. None was forthcoming.

"What's the other thing we have to do, Ed?" asked Clapp, in no hurry to see Rebecca Shepard's tenure committee selected.

"No big deal, really," said the Dean. "Two second-year students want waivers of the third-year residency requirement so that they can take their third year at other law schools. It just requires a vote of approval from the faculty."

Stanger rubbed his chin and pondered. "Why do they need to go?" he asked. "Oh, sure. Their wives are in other cities, and so they'll take their third year someplace else, and still get their law degrees from McKinley, is that it?"

"That's essentially it," said the Dean, "but they're not, er, they're not married."

"Well, then, what are they?" Sanford Clapp asked impatiently.

"They're in love," said the Dean.

"With each other?" asked Thomas Oliver Andrew Culpepper. His sudden vehemence caused everyone's head to turn. "Then let them stay here and finish together. Why do they have to go to Los Angeles?"

"Tom, no one said anything about Los Angeles," said the Dean, wondering, as he often did in these situations, what it might take to get Culpepper to retire. "And they're not in love with each other. They're in love with different people."

"Have we ever done this before?" Stanger wanted to know. "What's the precedent?" Stanger had quickly mastered the mode of discourse at law school faculty meetings.

"The precedent," the Dean answered, "is that married students routinely have been granted permission to take their third years in the city where their spouses lived, provided that there was a law school there of academic standards equal to McKinley. I grant that we've never discussed whether students in love with people in other cities should be granted a waiver of the third-year residency rule, but I honestly thought that this wouldn't require formal debate on our part. We still have to choose Rebecca's tenure committee."

"How can you tell if two people are really in love?" asked Ronald Blotchett. He spoke with the urgency of a man desperate for an answer to his question. His colleagues paused and looked at Blotchett. Normally he did not take as active an interest in the discussion.

"How long have they known each other?" asked Frobisher, breaking the silence.

"Come on, Murray, that doesn't matter," said young Tony Sloop. "Haven't you ever heard of love at first sight?"

"I want an answer to my question," said Frobisher heatedly.

"I don't know," said the Dean. "I think both couples met over the summer."

"That's not long enough," said Frobisher, his voice rising. "You can't fall in love over one summer."

"Back off, Murray," said Clapp. "Anyway, what the hell do you know about love?"

"That was uncalled for, Sanford," said Frobisher, hurt. He seemed about to lash out at Clapp but he controlled himself.

Blotchett leaned forward. "What I want to know," said the handsome professor, "is how can you tell if two people are really in love?"

He spoke so earnestly that none of his colleagues interrupted. "I've been . . . infatuated any number of times. Ever since my divorce. Taken with a great many women. Younger women, or women my own age. But the feeling always disappeared after . . . after—"

"After you did them up on your damned clerking couch," said Sanford Clapp, who had heard enough. "I'm in the next office. You should *hear* that thing. When are you going to replace those springs, Blotchett—when one of your victims makes it to the Supreme Court?"

"What's eating you, Sanford?" asked Tony Sloop.

"I'm still smarting over that Professor of the Year letter, if you must know."

"It was just a joke, Sanford. You've got to lighten up," said Sloop.

"I *am* light," Clapp growled. "It's not the letter. It's my wife. I called her to tell her about it and she saw right through it immediately. She said the students wouldn't vote for me for dogcatcher."

"She's right, Sanford," said Stanger, and the committee dissolved in laughter.

"My reputation isn't *that* bad among the students," Clapp retorted. "Some of them actually think rather highly of me." Although he did not care to mention it to his colleagues, Sanford was conducting a romance with a woman in the second-year class. Their assignations took place on the couch in *his* office and, on occasion, late at night in her dormitory room.

"Gentlemen," implored the Dean, "could we please return to our subject."

"You spoke to them, Ed, didn't you?" It was Blotchett.

Dean Strong nodded.

"Well, what did they say to you?" Blotchett asked. "How were they so sure they were in love? I mean, how can people ever tell? How can anyone be sure? Maybe they were just, you know, infatuated. What *is* love?"

Silence.

The Dean shook his head. So did everyone else.

"It is a feeling that comes upon you all at once," said Thomas Culpepper. All eyes turned to the aged professor. "You deny it at first. You think it might be something other than love. But soon you find that you can think of nothing but her. She is the last thing on your mind at night, and when your eyes open in the morning you discover that you are already thinking of her. You eat without tasting, you walk through your day as though in a trance. You simply *know*."

Total silence.

"That was beautiful, Tom," said Murray Frobisher, his tone sarcastic. Inwardly, though, he found himself moved by his colleague's comments.

"Why, thank you, Murray," said Culpepper, who thought that Frobisher had spoken sincerely.

The Dean began quietly. "If there is no further discussion, we might proceed to a vote. We still have the matter of Rebecca's tenure committee."

"Not quite yet," said Stanger, equally softly. "You still haven't told us who the two students are."

The Dean frowned, aware that he could not put off the explosion forever. He spoke the names as quietly as he could. "Andrew Spratt and Katrina Walfish."

Even Rebecca was shocked into speech. "Andrew Spratt is in love? But he's—he's—"

"Gay." Tony Sloop completed her sentence. "Has he converted?"

"No, no, he's still quite homosexual," said Dean Strong. "He worked in Dallas last summer and says he fell in love with another male summer associate."

"Everything's bigger in Texas," cracked Clapp.

Dean Strong ignored the comment. "He wants to take his third year at Southern Methodist, which is in Dallas, and which is where his, er, his lover studies. I was rather hoping this discussion could have been avoided."

"If we approve the waiver for Spratt," Stanger began, chopping the air repeatedly with his right hand, "does that mean that we as a law school are condoning homosexuality as a lifestyle? What kind of precedent would we be setting?"

"I don't know much about homosexuals," said Mountain. "Do they actually fall in love like the rest of us? I thought they tried not to get attached."

"Of course they fall in love," said an indignant Tony Sloop. "And they have the same rights as everybody else."

"Except to get married," countered Stanger.

"Or adopt," added Murray Frobisher.

"I think we've veered somewhat from the topic at hand," said the Dean, "which is whether to grant waivers—"

"We know damned well what the topic is, Ed," interrupted Clapp. "It just deserves some consideration. We're breaking new ground, you know."

Frobisher glared at Clapp. He hated it when Clapp did not treat Dean Strong with what Frobisher considered adequate respect.

"Would they be living together, Spratt and his—his boyfriend?" Aaron Mountain asked distastefully. He was trying to imagine what it was exactly that homosexuals did together.

"I would assume so," said Frobisher.

"Well, in that case," Mountain said, bursting with competence, "under Texas statutes, homosexuals do not have the legal right to cohabit. If we grant Spratt his waiver and let him move to Texas, we would be encouraging him, in effect, to violate Texas law." Mountain was an expert in the laws of the various states, thanks to his Conflict of Laws background.

"I don't mean anything personal, Aaron, but that is the stupidest legal argument I've ever heard raised at a faculty meeting, and I've heard a lot of stupid arguments at faculty meetings."

The speaker was Jackson Ward, Professor of Ethics and Legal History and Rebecca's only close friend on the McKinley faculty. Tall, with thick dark hair, chiseled features, and deep-set dark brown eyes, Ward's bearing commanded respect in the lecture hall, in Thorne Lounge faculty meetings, and in the American Bar Association conferences on Ethics and the Law. Ward's speeches and writings on the importance of adopting and enforcing a strict Code of Ethics—something even *he* admitted was only a pipe dream—made him a nuisance to the legal establishment and a bit of a hero to the McKinley faculty. Most of the other McKinley professors disagreed strongly with his unorthodox views on legal ethics, but they admired his tenacity and his decency. Ward recognized the same qualities in Rebecca Shepard. These traits formed the basis of their year-long relationship. He was the only member of the McKinley faculty not to fall for the Professor of the Year prank. An Ethics professor voted Professor of the Year?

he asked himself as he tossed the letter into the trash. Most of the students don't even know Ethics is in the curriculum.

"We have to keep up with the times," Ward continued. "It doesn't matter whether McKinley Law School recognizes homosexuality as an acceptable lifestyle, because nobody cares about what we think. Look. Spratt's case should be viewed no differently from that of Katrina Walfish, who, I presume, is in love with a heterosexual male. I haven't heard any objections to *her* waiver."

"I was just coming to that," said Stanger. "If only she were engaged, it might be different."

"She's *not* engaged?" Clapp asked, thoroughly surprised. "I assumed for the purposes of this discussion that she was engaged. This puts the matter in a whole new light." He shook his head gravely.

"No, it doesn't," said Dean Strong, hoping to head off still more pointless discussion. "The issue remains—"

Frobisher put up a hand to interrupt. "Maybe she'll become engaged before next September," he said. "Rebecca, you know her pretty well. What are the odds?"

Rebecca did know Katrina Walfish pretty well. Katrina made no secret of her devotion to Rebecca. Katrina had been in her Torts class last year and was the chair of the McKinley Women's Law Caucus. Indeed, Rebecca had promised to attend a Caucus meeting to begin at four-thirty. Now she would be late, if she could make it at all.

Despite nearly five years of experience with Murray Frobisher's brusque manner, Rebecca was surprised at the personal nature of the question. "Murray," she said, "I honestly don't know whether she intends to become engaged before next September."

Fifteen minutes later, the conversation still focused on the issue of Katrina's status as an unengaged woman.

"Could we make her waiver contingent on her becoming engaged?" asked Frobisher.

"Don't you think that's putting a lot of pressure on them?" asked Aaron Mountain in a rare burst of sensitivity. "They only met last summer."

"What about Andrew Spratt?" Stanger wanted to know.

"Homosexuals have to pay taxes just like the rest of us," said T. O. A. Culpepper.

"I don't think you fully caught our drift," the Dean told Culpepper. "We're talking about Andrew Spratt going to Texas."

"I'm not standing in his way," Culpepper announced.

"Please," implored the Dean. "I *hate* it when all of you do this. *Yes,* this is a big step for us. *No,* I don't think we can ask Katrina to marry her young man. Look, you know and I know that nothing important ever happens during the third year. We waste the students' time almost as much as they waste ours. I see no reason to deny the two of them a chance for a little happiness. Resolved: The faculty votes to grant waivers of the third-year residency requirement—"

"Hold it," said Stanger. "Here are the issues." He ticked them off on his fingers. "First. Precedent. What's the precedent? Are we deviating from past practice? If so, how much? Answer—yes, we're deviating, but not enough to make a difference. Second. Are the other schools involved as good as McKinley? Think of this law school as a factory. We produce widgets. McKinley widgets have a certain reputation for quality. If we allow two of our widgets to, uh, to be finished in somebody else's factory, will they be as good as widgets produced here? McKinley has to protect its good name. Same as any other manufacturer. If people find out our widgets are inferior, they'll go elsewhere."

"Must you refer to our students as widgets?" asked Tony Sloop. "It's so dehumanizing."

"Huh?" said Stanger. "It's just a metaphor, Tony. Keep your pants on. Answer. Yes, there'll be some drop-off in quality. McKinley is one of the best law schools in the country. But will it affect Katrina and, um, the other fellow—"

"Andrew Spratt," said Aaron Mountain. "I didn't know we even admitted homosexuals."

"Yeah, Spratt," said Stanger. "Will it affect their education? Marginally, if at all. Maybe a little bit. Hard to say. Third issue. And most important. Money. Bucks. If we let these two students go away their third year, either we lose their tuition, or we have to take two transfer students from other schools. We can't afford to give up two tuition-paying students."

"Are either of them getting financial aid?" asked Murray Frobisher. "If we replace them with a couple of rich kids, we could come out ahead on the deal."

The Dean rubbed his temples and sighed.

"Good point, Murray," said Stanger. He paused and laughed. "That reminds me. Last year, my kid David—you know him, I've brought him around—he took his, uh, his junior year abroad. Went to Spain. Art major. Don't ask me what he'll do with it. Anyway, it cost me a helluva lot less to put him on a plane to Madrid, and pay his tuition at the University of Salamanca, or wherever the hell he went, and even fly him home for Christmas, than it ever did for me to send him to Dartmouth for a year."

"Was he in Salamanca last year?" asked Culpepper. "I lectured in Salamanca last year. You should have told me, Robert! We could have had dinner, David and I."

"I've never really cared for Spanish food," Frobisher confessed. "I get heartburn."

"Same," said Aaron Mountain.

"Bob, where were you half an hour ago with your clear thinking?" asked Dean Strong. "We could have avoided— Oh, never mind. The admissions people tell me we've got plenty of excellent transfer applicants. We'll have no trouble filling those spaces. It's a good point, though, and I thank you for raising it."

Bob Stanger nodded.

"Blotchett hasn't said a word this whole time," said Sanford Clapp, "and we've been talking about his favorite subject, romance. All that lovey-dovey stuff. Cat got your tongue, Ron?"

"What? I—oh, what were we talking about?" Blotchett's mind was elsewhere. Culpepper's oratory brought home to him what he had been suspecting for days. For the first time in his life, Ronald Blotchett thought that he might be in love.

The Dean took advantage of the lull in the discussion to attempt another vote. "All in favor of granting a waiver of the third-year residency requirement to Andrew Spratt and Katrina Walfish say aye."

Ayes filled the air.

"All opposed?"

Silence.

"Motion carries," said the Dean with much relief. "Finally. Rebecca Shepard's tenure committee. I propose Clapp, Frobisher, and Culpepper. Comments? Debate?"

Silence, broken at last by Stanger: "Sounds all right to me."

"No problem with that," said Clapp blandly.

The rest of the faculty nodded their assent.

"I can't figure you people out," said Dean Strong. "You nitpick me to death on trivial issues, but then you don't think twice about important matters."

Welcome to law school, thought Rebecca Shepard.

"All right, that's it, then. Sanford, Murray, Tom, you've got the job. Meeting adjourned."

Rebecca looked at the Dean and shook her head slowly as she considered the men who constituted her tenure committee. Clapp and Frobisher, she knew, would never vote in her favor. She assumed that Culpepper was on the committee either to make the vote seem close, or because he would not interfere with whatever the others wanted to do. I'm dead, she thought. The game is over. Still, she admired the smoothness of Dean Strong's approach. He was sending Frobisher and Clapp, his twin hatchet men, to do his dirty work for him.

She checked her watch and started for the door on her way to the Women's Law Caucus meeting, but Jackson Ward called her over. "You did it," he whispered.

"Did what?" Rebecca's expression registered fear.

"The letter."

Rebecca gave him a knowing smile. "What letter?"

Jackson smiled back. "Don't get cute with me," he said.

"Actually," she said, her voice low, "I'm in no mood to get cute with anyone. Did you see who Ed put on my committee?"

Jackson nodded. "Graceful move," he said. "They turn you down and he gets none of the blame. He's nobody's fool. He could still surprise us all, though."

"I wouldn't bet on it," said Rebecca. "Anyway, how did

you know about me and"—she looked around to make sure that no one was listening—"the letter?" she whispered.

"I recognized your handiwork. But don't worry. Your secret's safe with me."

"Promise?"

Jackson nodded as they left the Thorne Lounge. "Rebecca," he asked quietly, "why would you do something like that just a week before your tenure decision?"

Rebecca looked at Jackson Ward, her lips parted slightly as though she was about to speak. Then she hastened down the corridor.

FIVE

"Where were you?" asked Katrina Walfish. "How could you *do* this to us? I *told* you this would be an important meeting."

"I'm sorry," said Rebecca. "The faculty meeting ran late, and I couldn't just walk out on it."

"It seems like you just don't care about us. We needed you at the meeting today."

"I apologize," said Rebecca. I'm not in the mood, she thought. "I didn't miss your meeting on purpose—you know that. Do you think I can be everywhere at the same time?"

Rebecca and Katrina stood glaring at one another in the hallway outside the classroom where the McKinley Women's Law Caucus meeting had just broken up. It was half past six and the hallway was empty. Katrina ran a hand through her dark blond hair and stared reproachfully at Rebecca. She stood five feet six inches tall, possessed brown eyes, high cheekbones, and even, white teeth. She favored blue jeans and white button-down Oxford shirts, and she utterly worshipped Rebecca. Her reverence added to her sense of betrayal when, as now, Rebecca's actions did not correspond with Katrina's high expectations.

"You don't have to look at me that way, do you?" Rebecca asked. "Come on. Walk me to my mailbox. I've got to check my mail. And please don't be upset with me. I know this isn't the first Caucus meeting I've missed this semester, but I've got a lot of other responsibilities around the law school. How about a little sensitivity to my problems?"

"*Your* problems?" Katrina Walfish asked with surprise. "What kind of problems do *you* have?"

Rebecca changed the subject. "I have good news. You and Andrew both got your waivers."

"That's great!" Katrina, said, but her expression was reproving. "I *told* you it would be no big deal! I can't wait to tell Paul!" Her excitement turned quickly to apprehension, though. "You know what, Rebecca? I think he's going to propose to me."

"If only I'd known that an hour ago," said Rebecca.

"Rebecca, if he proposes, I don't know what I'm going to do. I mean, I like Denver—that's where he goes to law school, and that's where the firm is that we both worked for. But I'm not sure I'd want to live there forever. And I'm thinking about a clerkship, and chances are I couldn't get one with a judge in Denver. And even if I could, it's not the same as clerking in New York or D.C. You know, law firms really sit up and take notice if you clerked in New York, but Denver? I mean, who's going to care? Of course, I could ski at Vail every other weekend, and Paul's family has a condo there . . ."

Katrina's voice trailed off as they reached the professors' mailboxes. Rebecca opened hers and found, to her relief, a large package from the *McKinley Law Review:* the page proofs. She could proofread them tonight. Katrina was waiting for an answer. Since Rebecca was the only younger woman on the faculty (the librarian, Miss Pander, was sixty-four and not at all sure that women should be studying law in the first place), women students looked to Rebecca as a combination of role model, mother-confessor, and instant best friend. They sensed her distance from the power structure. They knew that she was ill at ease around Dean Strong and Professors Clapp and Frobisher, who among them made all the decisions that governed the law school. To be a woman at McKinley was to assume that one had a legitimate claim on Rebecca's time.

Rebecca gave of her time not only to the Women's Law Caucus but to several other student groups as well. As the only woman professor, she had been asked to serve on a wide range of faculty committees in order to provide what the Dean called, without conscious condescension, "a woman's perspective." Women students were constantly dropping by her office for advice, or to describe some latest indignity suffered in a classroom or male professor's office, or merely to chat. Rebecca thoroughly enjoyed her contact with the students, but their reverence at times made her uneasy. The view from a pedestal is pleasant, but not for long. Sometimes their affection actually angered her: "You stand for so much," a woman student once gushed. It's not fair, Rebecca remembered thinking. The men professors don't have to stand for anything.

"Engagement does seem awfully sudden," Rebecca answered, and she thought Frobisher might have been right about the unlikelihood of falling in love over a single summer. "You just met him, didn't you?"

Rebecca had prepared for and taught two classes today— both Securities Law and Torts—in addition to attending the Committee of Ten meeting and spending two hours helping a terribly nervous first-year student named Susan Garrett work through an arduous Contracts assignment from Professor Clapp. Suddenly she felt tired.

"Are you sure he's going to ask?" Rebecca asked. "He wouldn't ask you to marry him over the phone, would he?"

"I guess not," Katrina admitted. And then, quickly: "But what if he does?"

"I really doubt that he's going to propose to you over the telephone," said Rebecca. "I tell you what. Put your answering machine on. He's not going to ask your answering machine to marry him, is he?" she teased.

Katrina thought it over. "I don't know," she said. "I don't know him well enough."

"If you don't know him that well," Rebecca asked, "then why are you thinking about marrying him?"

"Huh," said Katrina. "I never thought of it that way."

"I've been in your position, believe me," said Rebecca.

"Really?" Katrina looked into her eyes.

"I know what it's like. But you really don't have to worry about it tonight."

"That's good," said Katrina, visibly relieved. "Because

I've got to get ready for what's happening tomorrow morning."

"Why? What's happening then?"

"If you'd been at the Caucus meeting you'd have found out," said Katrina, regaining the offensive.

Wrong thing to say, thought Rebecca.

"It's the Blotch," Katrina explained, using the women students' diminutive for Professor Ronald Blotchett. "He's been running wild lately. He tried to seduce each of the last four women who went to him for clerkship interviews. The women were in tears when they described it at the Caucus meeting. Something's got to be done, but it's only our word against his. We need proof, and tomorrow morning we're going to get some."

"How do you plan to do that?" asked Rebecca, remembering the faraway look in Blotchett's eyes at the faculty meeting.

"I have a clerkship interview tomorrow at ten," said Katrina, referring to the session Blotchett required of each McKinley student who wished to spend his or her first year after graduation clerking—doing legal research and writing—for federal or state judges. The lag of nearly two years between applying for a clerkship and actually starting to work never seems to bother law students, for whom delayed gratification rapidly becomes a way of life. "You know Marlene Feight? The tall woman in Securities? Well, her father works in electronics, and he's going to lend us a bug—a little wireless gizmo. It's really a transmitter. It broadcasts to a receiver, which you set up in another room. We're going to hook the receiver up to a tape recorder. I'm going to wear that bug to my clerkship interview tomorrow and we're going to get the goods on Ronald Blotchett."

"I'm impressed," said Rebecca. "Very high-tech. But you can't do that without risking a lawsuit. Didn't you learn about wiretapping in Constitutional Law?"

"I have Blotchett for Con Law," said Katrina, "so if I don't know it's unconstitutional, I can always blame him. Seriously, that did come up at the Caucus meeting. But I can't imagine Blotchett daring to report it to anyone."

"Katrina, it's only your legal career that's at stake."

"His, too. I'll take my chances."

I can relate to that, thought Rebecca. "Where are you going to set up the receiver?" she asked. As if I didn't know, she thought.

"Your office?" Katrina asked.

Rebecca smiled. "Anything for the cause."

"I'll stop by around a quarter of ten to set up the equipment," said Katrina Walfish. "Expect a big crowd. The whole Caucus wants to listen in."

Her expression grew serious. "Rebecca?"

"Uh-huh?"

"Can I ask you something, and please don't tell anybody? I'm really embarrassed by this."

"Sure, go ahead."

"Do you think Professor Blotchett is—you know, sexy? Handsome? Whatever?"

Rebecca smiled. "Yes, of course I do. So do a lot of women. *That's the problem*. But it's nothing to be embarrassed about."

Katrina looked considerably relieved. "Thanks, Rebecca. I really needed to hear that. Listen, do you have a couple of minutes right now? Could we go over to the Blue and White and maybe get a cup of coffee? I need some advice."

"Do you think it can wait until tomorrow?"

"Not really."

Actually, I don't have a couple of minutes right now, Rebecca thought. She wanted to go home and clean up the apartment before the Saint turned up, and, more important, have some time alone.

"I'd be delighted, in that case," Rebecca said, half hoping that Katrina did not notice her annoyance. "I suppose I could use some coffee."

"Good," said Katrina, turning away from Rebecca and walking ahead of her through the corridor and down the steps of the law school, talking all the while.

"I'm really under a lot of stress right now," Katrina announced. "It's just a very difficult time."

Rebecca juggled her mail, locked the mailbox, and took some long steps to catch up with Katrina.

"In a way I think this is the most stressful time I've ever gone through," Katrina was saying. "I mean, it's very exciting being here at McKinley, and there are so many possibilities open to me, but how am I supposed to know what to choose?"

The packages and papers in Rebecca's arms had disorganized themselves as she hastened to keep up with Katrina's long, purposeful strides. Katrina did not notice. She walked on, explaining her problems to the cool evening air.

"But the thing that really bothers me," she said as she reached the entrance to the cafe and found, to her surprise, that Rebecca was twenty paces behind her. "Is something wrong?" she called out.

Yes, thought Rebecca. Your attitude.

Rebecca, her possessions finally in order, caught up with Katrina on the steps of the Blue and White Cafe, a basement restaurant five doors down from the law school. The Blue and White was a McKinley institution. Its staff consisted mainly of McKinley undergraduates and unemployed actors and actresses, most of whom would conclude, after listening to endless conversations about cases and classes, that they would never go near the study of law. A few envied the law students' sense of purposefulness, though, and one or two occasionally applied for admission. In the narrow confines of the Blue and White, McKinley students found decent food, real tablecloths, and a management that would never chase them from their tables, no matter how many refills of coffee they demanded, no matter how little they were likely to tip. For the students of McKinley Law School, the Blue and White was their sanctuary. It was home.

Rebecca Shepard, unlike most of her colleagues, frequented the Blue and White, either alone or in the company of students. Few other McKinley professors cared to venture into what was clearly students' territory. The waiter greeted Rebecca with a slight smile. His expression grew somewhat more grave when he noticed Katrina. The Blue and White was a favorite haunt of the McKinley Law School Women's Caucus, and Katrina had developed a reputation for speaking at length and tipping lightly. Katrina and Rebecca chose a table after acknowledging greetings from other students having dinner, not because it was the best restaurant in the vicinity (the owner, Andrew Kefalias, had no such pretensions) but because it was the closest meal to the library. The coffee happened to be unusually good, though, not that it made a difference to most law students, who would drink motor oil as long as it contained caffeine. Coffee was the lifeblood of McKinley Law School, as it is wherever human beings must force themselves daily to face the unpleasant.

They ordered coffee. Katrina absentmindedly played with a packet of sugar. "I'm really confused," she said.

"Why? What's up?" Rebecca asked.

"I'm trying to make up my mind about too many things at once. Where do I want to work? Do I really want to take a clerkship? What kind of law should I practice? Do I want a big firm or a small firm, or a public interest job, or what? I go on these interviews for summer jobs and I feel like—well, I don't exactly feel like I'm lying when I say I want to work in these places. I feel like I'm telling half-truths. I mean, how am I supposed to know what kind of law I want to practice? Or what size firm I want to work in? And then there's Paul."

"What about Paul?" Rebecca asked. "I thought we had him taken care of for now."

The coffee arrived.

"You're right," said Katrina, nodding quickly. "I forgot. Look, this whole job thing is driving me crazy. Between flying around for interviews and the Caucus work, I'm missing half of my classes. I'm three weeks behind on my reading, and the semester is only five weeks old."

Rebecca sipped her coffee and nodded. Rebecca remembered well from her own days as a law student that the job hunt, which begins as early as some students' first semester at law school, often takes more time and attention than does schoolwork.

"Instead of studying or going to class," Katrina continued, "I'm spending half my time trying to get information about the firms I'm interested in. And I've gotten a *lot* of information. Which firms have the best summer programs. Where you can get the best training. How fast they're growing. What they pay. What perks they give. Even which firms have showers in the offices so that the lawyers can go for a run at lunchtime."

"And?" Rebecca asked.

"And I've turned into a walking encyclopedia of law firms. The other women in the Caucus know how much time I've spent learning about the firms, and they all come to me for information. Which is fine, although I really don't have the time to help other people with their problems. Which is something none of them can understand."

I can relate, Rebecca thought.

"I mean," said Katrina, "everybody knows about Paul, but nobody ever asks about him, or about how *I'm* feeling. But to get back to the question of jobs. I've done something I don't think most law students ever do." More than a hint of pride was evident in her tone. "I've actually *spoken to lawyers*— McKinley graduates—at the big firms. I got their names out of the *Alumni Register*. It wasn't that hard, really. The hard part was convincing them that I wasn't looking for a job. I asked them whether they enjoyed what they're doing."

"And what did they say?" asked Rebecca, genuinely curious.

"Most of them didn't like their jobs, which really surprised me. They liked the fact that they were good at what they did, and they liked the money, although they said they worked as hard as investment bankers but they didn't get nearly the same pay. But they hated the hours, and they thought that the work was mostly really boring. They felt they had given away the best years of their lives just so they could, you know, make a lot of money."

Katrina shrugged. She continued: "And they thought that law school, except for a few courses, was almost totally irrelevant to what they were doing on the job. And I heard this from a *lot* of people. So this is what it comes down to. I'm working my butt off getting an education that barely prepares me for something I don't even think I want to do."

Katrina's expression implored Rebecca to say it wasn't so, to say that the practice of law could be a fulfilling endeavor, to say that legal education was worth the time and trouble.

"It sounds like you did a thorough job," said Rebecca, sidestepping the larger issue, as Katrina downed her coffee in three gulps. "But tell me. Why did you come to law school in the first place?"

"Oh, I'm not really sure," Katrina admitted. "I ask myself that all the time. It was a combination of things, I guess. I thought I might want to get into politics, and I thought I could, you know, save the world. And I guess I didn't have anything better to do."

She paused for a moment. "I didn't realize how important the business world was to law school. I always thought law was about issues and people and stuff. I mean, most of the courses are geared to corporate law and not anything else. Even *you* teach Securities Regulation. Only people who want to work on Wall Street take Securities, and you know it."

"I'm part of the problem, is that it?" Rebecca asked, smiling.

"No, that's not what I meant," Katrina said. "It just seems like if I want to save the world—if I want to do anything in public interest law—it'll cost me thirty or forty thousand in salary in just the first year, and even more after that."

"You don't have to violate your conscience to do corporate law, though," said Rebecca. "Most of what corporate lawyers do is pretty much morally neutral. You're just helping business people solve their problems, and a lot of people find that very interesting."

"It just sounds kind of empty to me," said Katrina.

"It was for me, too," said Rebecca, "but a lot of people thrive on it. It's a game for them, being tough in negotiations."

"I don't know whether I could ever get motivated to care about other people's money."

"In that case," Rebecca asked, "why are you even interviewing with corporate firms?"

"It's a funny thing," said Katrina. "It's because everybody at law school knows that those are the toughest jobs to get. Everybody makes such a big deal out of who's going to what firm. It's like rushing fraternities. It's a real status thing. But also, well, this is hard for me to say. It's because of, well, it's because of the *money*. I want to be able to afford nice things, and buy a condo, and have a nice car." Her eyes met Rebecca's. "Is that wrong? Sometimes I think I only care about material things."

"No," said Rebecca. "Of course it's not wrong. Life is very expensive, especially if you've got a lot of student loans to repay. If you take a job in public interest law, it can be almost impossible to make ends meet. I remember when I was in law school—"

Katrina did not hear. "I saw the most beautiful condo last week," she said, her eyes bright at the memory. "It was a two-bedroom duplex, about eleven hundred square feet, and it had parquet floors and a lot of light, and I know I'm going out to Denver this summer, but I could rent it out to other law students, and I could make back the mortgage payments and the condo fees. I think it could be a good investment. I could make the down payment from my savings, and my folks would help, but I haven't even had time to think because— What's wrong?"

Rebecca shook her head and took two dollars from her purse. "This one's on me," she said. "I've really got to get home. I understand your dilemma, Katrina. It's not easy figuring out what to do with your life. I'm almost thirty-two, and I still don't know what to do with mine."

"What are you talking about? You're a law professor! You're all set!"

Rebecca nodded. "That's right," she agreed. "I'm all set." She stood up. "I'll see you first thing in the morning in my office. And I'm sure you'll figure out what to do about the job thing."

"Well, okay, I'll see you then," said Katrina, unwilling to let her go. "Oh, look. There's Marlene Feight, by the door. I've got to talk to her. I'll see you tomorrow, okay, Rebecca? Hey, Marlene, have you got a minute?"

Marlene turned in Katrina's direction. "Oh, hi, Katrina," she said. "Hello, Rebecca. Can you stay and talk for a moment?"

Rebecca gave an embarrassed smile. "I've really got to be getting home," she said. "I'm sorry I wasn't at the Caucus meeting."

"So were we," said Marlene. "It's okay, though. You can't be everywhere, I guess."

Rebecca looked gratefully at Marlene. "At least someone understands," she said. "Have a good night."

Katrina and Marlene both said goodbye and Rebecca left the restaurant. She walked the three blocks from the McKinley campus to her apartment, which was not unlike the apartment

Katrina had just described. Rebecca lived in a two-bedroom condominium with parquet floors and a southern exposure. She had spent far more time filling the apartment with books than with furniture, though. The tables, chairs, and couches Rebecca had chosen were rather nondescript, as though she had spent no more than a day or two picking out enough things so that the living room, kitchen, and bedroom could not be considered ill-equipped. There was no designer's touch in evidence, but the books made the apartment a home. Rebecca was a passionate reader and an equally passionate buyer of books. She spent much of her leisure time, especially when her work took her to other cities, prowling used book stores for new prizes, and she owned a respectable collection of first editions of American novels. On nights when the Saint did not sleep there, the books comforted her. They made her feel less alone.

Once home, Rebecca put dinner on, and found a note propped against the telephone. The Saint had written that he would be studying late because he was leaving for job interviews the following evening, and that he could not spend the night with her. "Damn," she said aloud, and then: "It doesn't really matter. I've got these page proofs to get through."

After a brief, unsatisfying dinner—a frozen entree, vegetable lasagna—Rebecca went upstairs to her bedroom, undressed, and climbed into bed with a mug of hot chocolate and her page proofs. It always excited her to see her legal writing laid out in neat columns on the printed page. She liked seeing the footnotes most of all, perhaps because they made her thoughts appear so solemn, or perhaps because they took so long to produce. Rebecca quickly found herself absorbed in the arguments her article contained. She read slowly and carefully, searching for misspellings and other typographical errors. She finished shortly before midnight.

Rebecca had felt tired when she had arrived home several hours before. Now she was exhausted. She suddenly burst into tears and sobbed quietly into a tissue from a box on her night table. Then she remembered that she had been named Professor of the Year along with old Culpepper, and she brightened a bit, then fell asleep.

TUESDAY, OCTOBER 2

SIX

Murray Frobisher, like most people, tended to put off unpleasant tasks for as long as possible. Registering his opposition to Rebecca Shepard's tenure bid was, to his mind, one such unpleasant duty. Frobisher had always assumed that she would tire of teaching, marry, have a baby, move out of the city, or be fired long before she might be considered for tenure. So certain was he that she would not last into her fifth year at McKinley that he had never made his feelings about her known to the Dean. As far as anyone on the McKinley faculty could tell, Murray had no feelings whatsoever about Rebecca. In fact, Murray was filled with antipathy toward anyone who threatened to rock the boat. Anyone who wanted to change the system that gave him status and a high salary, while demanding little if anything in return, was Murray's enemy. Murray knew that Rebecca wanted to change things.

Murray's duties at the law school took virtually no time from his law practice. Certainly, there was the matter of classes to teach, but by videotaping his lectures Murray had that one licked. Murray actually enjoyed faculty meetings of any sort and never viewed them as a burden. Whenever things bogged down, someone was bound to ask him about his latest case and Murray was always delighted to oblige, telling the story in great detail. Murray relished discussing his cases and usually came away with a few good ideas from his colleagues about trial tactics or arguments to make on appeal. Murray's secretary was fiercely protective of him, especially when students attempted to take up his valuable time with questions about his Criminal Law class. She had the unfortunate habit, though, of divulging information about his cases to anyone who asked about them. Murray often told her not to do so, and he patiently explained the importance of protecting the confidentiality of his relationship with his clients. She believed no harm could come, and the stories were too interesting not to share with others. As a result, Murray's colleagues sometimes knew about his clients and their cases even before Murray did. Aside from this minor annoyance, however, Murray Frobisher's professional life was in perfect balance. And anyone who threatened to disrupt that balance, to Murray's mind, had to go. Rebecca Shepard, he believed, was just that sort of disruptive force.

The selection of a tenure committee for Rebecca at the Committee of Ten meeting the afternoon before caused Murray to realize that time was short. If he wanted to affect the outcome of the tenure decision, he decided, he could not wait even for the deliberations of the committee to which Dean Strong had appointed him. Murray looked at his watch. Nine-fifteen A.M. He knew that Ed Strong taught Evidence at ten. The time had come. He gathered up his suit jacket—a slate-blue double-breasted Italian job—and he walked down the corridor from his office to that of Dean Strong. He found the usually good-natured Dean in an uncharacteristically foul mood.

"What's wrong, Ed?" he asked, by way of greeting. The Dean motioned him to a chair.

"I just got a call from Tony Sloop," said the Dean, frowning. "You know how he's involved with that crazy performance art group downtown."

"Foaming at the Mouth," said Frobisher.

"That's the one. Well, last night Foaming at the Mouth was giving one of those recitals in the basement of a loft building, performing, if that's the right word for it, in total darkness."

"Not even the usual black candles this time?" asked Frobisher, grinning. Sloop was a protégé of Frobisher, who had attended a few performances of Foaming at the Mouth.

"I guess not," said the Dean, who saw nothing funny in the

entire episode. "Apparently Sloop's role was to have himself tied up by members of the audience and suspended from the ceiling while the rest of the group chanted Aztec death prayers. To make a long story short, the rope broke, and poor Tony came crashing to the floor. He was quite shaken up. I think he broke his arm. The audience applauded like mad—they thought it was part of the performance. The whole thing got written up in the *Times* this morning. Imagine. A McKinley Law School professor mixed up with the likes of that."

"But he'll be all right, won't he?"

"He's resting. He's coming in around one. I had to cancel his nine o'clock Civil Procedure class. Anyway, Murray, what's this I hear about your latest client? A child pornographer?"

Frobisher turned red. "An *alleged* child pornographer."

"Don't you have any shame, Murray?"

"Everybody's entitled to a lawyer, Ed," Frobisher snapped.

"But why is everybody entitled to you? You don't have to take every case that comes your way."

"You know I don't do that," Frobisher said stiffly. "In the first place, I haven't met him yet. He's coming to my office in an hour. I just wonder how the whole law school knows about my clients before I even take them on. It's got to be Carmen. I'd fire her if she wasn't such a good secretary."

"Look, Murray, I'm sure he's a terrific guy, and I'm sure his child pornography is first rate. What brings you to my office?"

"Rebecca Shepard," said Frobisher.

"What about her?" asked the Dean, quickly growing serious.

"Let me be blunt," said Frobisher, rubbing his hands together.

"I can't imagine you any other way," said Dean Strong.

"Cute. Look. You can't give her tenure, Ed," said Frobisher. "You just can't do it."

"What are you talking about?" asked the Dean.

Frobisher sighed. "I'm absolutely serious," he said. "Under no circumstances can you give her tenure."

Dean Strong tried to hide his alarm. "Murray, you've got to

explain this. Did she insult you? Has she done something to offend you?"

"No," said Frobisher. "She hasn't done anything to me personally. It's what she *would* do to the law school." He took out a handkerchief and mopped his brow. "I don't know where to begin. First of all, you must understand that I'm not opposed to the idea of a tenured woman, per se. In fact, I think there should be several tenured women here."

"What about Miss Pander?" the Dean interrupted. *"She* has tenure."

"Miss Pander isn't a woman, she's a librarian. I'm talking about a woman who teaches, who goes to faculty meetings, who sits on faculty committees. Women in the abstract are fine. But giving Rebecca Shepard tenure would be an utter disaster for the law school. I don't know how else to describe it."

"Murray, this is serious," said Dean Strong. "You've got to explain to me what's troubling you about Rebecca."

"I'll try," Frobisher said. "I'm as liberal as anyone—I've represented the A.C.L.U. in the Supreme Court, for crissakes. I'm on the board of CORE. So don't get me wrong when I say this, but Rebecca just *doesn't know her place.* I mean, there are certain fields that are okay for women to teach. Wills. Employment Discrimination. Family Law. Those are marginal fields that women lawyers drift into in practice, and if you have to have women law professors at all, then let them teach that stuff. I checked into the figures, you know. Most of the women law professors anywhere in the country who have tenure are either law librarians, or professors of Trusts and Estates or Employment Discrimination. Why do we have to be the pioneers?"

"I'm glad you did your homework, Murray," said the Dean, but Frobisher rolled past him.

"It's not good enough for Rebecca Shepard to teach Employment Discrimination. No. She has to teach Securities! That's *man's law,* Ed! Men *teach* Securities, men *practice* Securities Law, it's a man's field, and she's encroaching!"

"Segregation now, segregation forever?" asked Dean Strong, not quite believing what he was hearing.

"Well—well—yes!" Frobisher stammered. "The tradition

has always been that women taught some things and men taught others, and that's how it should remain."

"Murray," the Dean said gently, "thirty-five or forty years ago there were hardly any women law professors. There was no tradition of women teaching *anything* before 1950."

"But there's no *precedent* for a woman Securities professor," wailed Frobisher.

"If I may paraphrase Dr. Johnson, precedent is the last refuge of a scoundrel," said Dean Strong, who liked to think of himself as a literary sort of chap.

"I see my appeal to logic is getting nowhere," said Frobisher.

"Is this your idea of logic?" asked Dean Strong.

"Let me try another approach," said Frobisher. "If she gets tenure, it's going to ruin the homogeneity of the faculty. Our Committee of Ten meetings will turn into free-for-alls. We'll bog down over petty details, and we'll never be able to reach a consensus on anything. You'll see! That's what happens when you let outsiders join the club!"

"First of all," responded Dean Strong, who had heard enough, "our faculty meetings have been free-for-alls for years! And we always bog down over petty details and we never reach decisions without my having to cajole the faculty like a—like a kindergarten class! And second of all, Rebecca has already been attending faculty meetings for the past four years."

"That's just my point," said Frobisher, triumphant. "You see? It's all her fault. We haven't been able to make a decision since she got here."

"Come on, that's nonsense. Rebecca never even opens her mouth at faculty meetings. I think she's just disgusted by the whole lot of us and the way we carry on. I can't even look her in the eye. I'm too embarrassed by the way the male professors behave."

"That's just what I'm trying to say," said Frobisher. "She's not one of us. We have to watch our language around her, we can't tell jokes, we can't be ourselves. Her presence puts a damper on things."

"Murray, what do you mean by 'one of us'? Who *are* we? I've never met a more disparate group of people in my life.

What does T. O. A. Culpepper have in common with Tony Sloop? What do you have in common with Ronald Blotchett, or Sanford Clapp?"

"I'll tell you one thing we all have in common," said Frobisher, leaning forward. "We all feel the same way about Rebecca Shepard, and I wouldn't be surprised if more than one of us decided to leave McKinley if she got tenure."

"You must be kidding, Murray." The Dean tried to hide his alarm.

"I'm not kidding in the least. This can't come as a surprise to you, Ed. You know we've never really liked her. There's something else about her. She's a— She's a—" Frobisher could barely get the word out of his mouth. "She's a reformer!"

The Dean sighed. "I know that, Murray."

"She wants to change things. Scrap the Socratic method. The case method. Make law school two years instead of three. And that's just the beginning. She wants to get rid of *entire fields of study*! She wants to totally remake American legal education! And you want to give her a—a platform! That's what tenure would do!"

"How do you know so much about Rebecca Shepard's ideas on legal education?"

"One of my student spies on the *Law Review* told me all about her tenure article. Ed, it's potential dynamite."

"Aren't you overreacting, Murray?"

"No, I'm not! That's how it could all begin. A law professor publishes an article in a law review. She gets tenure. She gets a say in faculty appointments and she brings in people who feel the same way she does. She influences students. They become professors at other law schools and start to spread her gospel. And before you know it, you've got a revolution on your hands. It'll be—it'll be—legal nuclear war!"

"Murray, you're getting carried away."

Frobisher struggled out of his chair. "I am not getting carried away, Ed. I won't stand for Rebecca Shepard getting tenure, and neither will half the men on this faculty. Do you understand?"

"Sit down, Murray," said an exasperated Dean Strong. What a week, he thought. First the Professor of the Year hoax, then the fight over Katrina Walfish and Andrew Spratt. Then Tony Sloop embarrasses the law school and nearly breaks his neck. Now Frobisher is threatening a mass resignation if I give Rebecca tenure. And it's only Tuesday.

"Let me explain things to you from my point of view," said the Dean. "It probably comes as a shock to you that I even have a point of view."

A chastened Frobisher resumed his seat.

"I'm not sure you remember Dara Sample," the Dean began.

"Of course I remember Dara. She taught Trusts and Estates here until four or five years ago. Very good-looking. I liked her a lot."

"It was until exactly four years ago," said Dean Strong. "And you liked her so much that you directed the campaign to deny her tenure."

"I might have done that," Frobisher admitted, looking at his hands.

"You did, Murray. You did such a thorough job that no woman, except for Rebecca, has taught here full-time since Dara was asked to leave. Do you remember what happened after she left?"

"Something about a lawsuit?" asked Frobisher, not looking up.

"Yes, that's right. Something about a lawsuit. Dara was a first-rate teacher. Her publications were excellent. She even taught Trusts and Estates, a 'woman's field,' as you would put it. She was denied tenure the same year that Aaron Mountain received it. And we knew, and she knew, that Aaron Mountain was a bozo. A poor teacher and of no consequence as a legal scholar. And Dara Sample went to court.

"Do you remember the outcome of her case, Murray? You should, because you argued against her on behalf of the law school. We lost. It's not your fault that we lost. *No one* could have gotten us off. The District Court found us in violation of Title VII of the Civil Rights Act of 1964. That's the statute that makes it illegal to discriminate on account of sex. A statute the passage of which you no doubt opposed. But do you remember what happened next, Murray? We signed a consent decree. That means we promised the District Court to hire and grant tenure to at least one woman in the next five years. We persuaded the court to seal the records of the case, to avoid a black eye for the law school. You and I are the only people around here who even remember that Dara sued.

"But word got out to women law professors about you and Blotchett and Clapp and your, shall we say, antipathy toward the idea of women teaching at McKinley. And Rebecca is the only woman who's taught here full-time since Dara Sample. Murray, this is the fifth year of the consent decree. We haven't offered any woman tenure in all that time. Rebecca is the only woman up for tenure this year. We don't want a repetition of all the ugliness we had during the Dara Sample lawsuit, do we? Do we, Murray?"

Frobisher slumped in his chair. "I was trying not to think about Dara," he said. "I guess this means we're stuck with Rebecca." He looked up. "It all hinges on the tenure article," said Frobisher. "If it's clearly no good we can go to court and say, Look, she's just unqualified for tenure here, and we'll keep searching for a better woman candidate. I'm sure they'll give us an extension—keeping Rebecca around all this time will look like a good faith effort on our part. And from what I've heard about her tenure article," Frobisher continued, brightening, "there's no way anyone could take it seriously. Imagine abandoning the Socratic method. It's heresy. The world will laugh at her, Ed. At least, I *hope* it will."

"I'm not so sure," said Dean Strong. Murray's description of Rebecca's tenure essay had whetted the Dean's curiosity. "Is there any chance that your 'spy' on the *Law Review* could get you an advance copy of Rebecca's article?"

"I guess so," said Frobisher. "I'll see what I can do. Anyway, I've told you how I feel. I'm glad it's your problem and not mine. I have to get out of here. I've got to get ready for my child pornographer."

"That's *alleged* child pornographer," said an offended Dean Strong.

"Innocent until proven guilty." Frobisher smiled. "How silly of me to forget."

SEVEN

By the time that Rebecca arrived at her office—moments after Murray Frobisher had finished denouncing her to the Dean—a crowd of twenty-five women students had gathered in the corridor outside. Among those present were Katrina Walfish, dressed provocatively in a short skirt and a man-tailored shirt, and Marlene Feight, who carried a threatening-looking attaché case.

"Where have you been?" asked Katrina. "It's five minutes to ten."

"I'm sorry." Rebecca gave a wan smile. "I overslept."

"It doesn't matter," said Katrina. "At least you made it. Let's get started."

Rebecca unlocked the door to her office, and the women students pushed in behind her. Rebecca's office was not unlike her home. It was neat, orderly, inviting, and filled with books. She hurriedly cleared her desk of papers, hoping that she could find things later. Marlene opened the attaché case and quickly set up the listening device and a tape recorder. She affixed the bug—a pea-sized black microphone—to the inside of Katrina's shirt pocket and gave Katrina a switching mechanism the size of a pack of cigarettes to keep in her purse.

"As soon as you're ready, you just turn this little button 'on,' and the bug will transmit. Here, like this. Why don't you go into the hall and try it?"

Katrina stepped into the empty corridor and closed the door behind her. She switched the transmitter on.

"Why, Professor Blotchett," she said, and her slightly muffled voice echoed through the receiver, "what big eyes you have!"

Laughter filled Rebecca's office. Katrina came back in.

"What you're doing is really amazing," one student said.

"I wish I had your nerve," said another.

"Katrina, I'm really proud of you," said a third. "Risking your legal career for the Women's Law Caucus."

Katrina smiled bravely.

"Wait just a minute," said Marlene Feight, who leaned over and undid the second button on Katrina's shirt. "If you're going to be an undercover agent, you've got to look the part."

Rebecca said, "Good luck," and Katrina took one last look at the gathering and headed down the stairs to Professor Blotchett's fourth-floor office.

"Well, here I go," she narrated to a breathless audience. "I'm walking down the stairs." In Rebecca's office, they could hear her footsteps echo in the stairwell.

"Now I'm opening the door and I'm on the fourth floor, and— Good morning, Professor Frobisher."

"Huh? Oh, morning," they heard Frobisher reply.

The crowd in Rebecca's office were struck by the clear reception.

"Now I'm walking down the hall to Professor Blotchett's office. I'm knocking on his door."

The women could hear Professor Blotchett say, "Come in," when suddenly the transmission went dead.

Marlene paled. She turned every knob on the front of the receiver and shook the entire apparatus. "What happened?" she asked. "I can't understand! It was working fine a minute ago!"

The women were crestfallen.

"Isn't there something you can do?" one asked.

"It might be in the bug—but I just replaced the battery this morning!" Marlene was ready to cry.

Rebecca put her hand on Marlene's shoulder. "It's not your fault," said Rebecca. "I'm sure it'll work. Maybe if we just wait a minute."

A devastated Marlene Feight turned off the tape recorder and the women sat in silence. Poor Marlene, Rebecca thought. I hope this thing starts working again.

The night before, sleep had come slowly and fitfully to Ronald Blotchett. Under normal circumstances, this was the sort of morning that Blotchett adored. It never occurred to him that others might view his lovemaking with women clerkship applicants as an abuse of authority. Blotchett subscribed to the theory that people never did anything they did not want to do. He knew very well that women found him attractive. He simply assumed that women students, alone with a handsome professor who happened to have a large couch in his office, were simply overcome with desire for him, and where was the harm in that? He never actually demanded sex; it just seemed to happen. These encounters left him in such good spirits, of course, that the dazzling recommendations he wrote immediately afterwards were much more likely to win clerkships than those that followed more prosaic interviews during which both parties remained fully clothed. But trading sex for a clerkship? The idea would have shocked Blotchett, whose capacity for self-deception was boundless.

"Come in," he repeated, and a nervous Katrina Walfish entered the office. "Please," he said, motioning to the chair opposite his desk. Blotchett was not his charming self this morning. Under normal circumstances he would have opened the door and ushered Katrina directly to the couch, locked the door, and then sat himself down in the easy chair facing her. He would have fixed his large brown eyes upon Katrina, run his hand through his thick brown hair, smiled, and said, "So you'd like to be a judicial clerk. Well, well, well."

"I suppose you'd like to clerk in Denver," Blotchett began, his tone matter-of-fact.

"Why, yes. How did you know that?" Katrina asked, thinking that he was as telepathic as he was good-looking.

"Isn't that where your boyfriend is?" Blotchett asked.

"I suppose that came up at the Committee of Ten meeting," she said, wishing that he did not have to mention Paul.

"Now, how did you know that you were serious about

him?" Blotchett asked. "Did it hit you all at once, or was it a more gradual sort of thing?"

Katrina wondered what he was driving at. This interview was nothing like those the women students had described at the Caucus meeting yesterday. And she felt guilty enough about what she was doing without Blotchett's mentioning Paul. Katrina shifted in her chair.

"Professor Blotchett?" she said, trying to nudge him back to reality.

"I'm sorry," he said, "I guess my mind is elsewhere." He tried to bring the interview back to solid ground. "Tell me, Katrina, why are you interested in clerking?"

"Well, I'm thinking about teaching law one day, and I think that the experience of working for a judge would give me unique insight into our judicial processes."

Katrina wondered what made Professor Blotchett ask why she wanted a clerkship. Every student wanted a clerkship for pretty much the same reasons: It was a chance to learn about the courts from the inside; it put off for a year or two the decision of which firm to select; and it was a relatively undemanding job. The story was told around McKinley of one judicial clerk who did almost no work for the entire year, secure in the knowledge that he could be neither fired nor reprimanded for his laziness. He viewed his clerkship as a paid vacation between law school and working for a firm. As his clerkship ended, he had the nerve to ask his judge for a recommendation. The judge thought it over and wrote to the law firm in question: "You'll be very lucky if you can get So-and-So to work for you."

Katrina wanted to know why Blotchett asked the question, because none of the women at the Caucus meeting who described their clerkship interviews mentioned any such question. Now Katrina wondered whether they had been telling the truth. At this point she did not know what to believe.

"Yes, I see," said Blotchett, not even attempting to appear interested in her answer. "Would you prefer a trial court or an appellate court?"

"An appellate court," Katrina Walfish replied in perfectly convincing interview fashion. "My Moot Court experience, writing an appellate brief, convinced me that my interests lie . . ." As she spoke, she found herself wondering whether he was trying to make the interview *seem* on the level, so that if anything happened between them he could claim that she started it. "My interests lie in the field of appellate review of trial-level matters."

"I see," said Blotchett, playing with a paper clip. "Are you more interested in civil or criminal cases?"

"Civil cases," she answered quickly. Like most second-year law students, Katrina had suffered through sixty or seventy half-hour interviews with lawyers, either at McKinley or on "callback" interviews at the firms themselves. She believed that she could give the same unvarying answers in her sleep. According to her boyfriend Paul, she frequently did.

Katrina went on. "I'm taking Professor Shepard's Securities class right now and I feel that I would like to make a contribution in the same field because—" Suddenly Katrina had another thought. She feared now that Blotchett did not find her attractive enough. The idea made her furious, because she prided herself on never having been turned down by a man in her life. "—It's important that there should be participation in Securities Law by women and other groups."

"Other groups," repeated Blotchett, his tone devoid of sarcasm, his eyes on his desk. "Um. Yes. Other groups are also quite important. I think society underestimates the contributions of other groups. Would you—would you like to clerk for one year or two?"

"I think just one year, and then I'd like to practice for a few years, and then use that experience as a basis for a teaching career." Katrina decided that the situation called for immediate action. If he did not find her attractive, she feared, she would never get a good clerkship recommendation. She undid another button on her shirt.

Blotchett failed to notice. He pushed the paper clip around the desktop. "If a federal court clerkship was not available in Denver, would you be willing to clerk in some other city?"

Katrina froze. She assumed that he was toying with her, waiting for *her* to make the first move. "Why, yes. I'd be willing to clerk just about anywhere—any decent city, I mean. I don't have my heart absolutely *set* on Denver. I understand the importance of a federal court clerkship to my career, and I would be willing to go almost anywhere."

Katrina knew what she was talking about. A federal court clerkship was the legal equivalent of a college athlete's getting drafted in the first round. It meant that one was among the most select law graduates in the country, and it was a stepping-stone to a teaching position at any top law school.

"I'm glad to hear that you're open-minded," said Blotchett.

Her heart was pounding. She wondered how to understand the term "open-minded." She saw her chances of securing a clerkship slipping away. She feared that he would conclude the interview any minute, at the cost of her clerkship and her teaching career.

Katrina stood up and ran her fingers over the top of the couch. "Looks comfortable," she said.

Blotchett did not hear her.

I've never met a more stubborn man in my life, Katrina thought. "I said your *couch* looks *comfortable*. May I sit here?"

Blotchett's mind was elsewhere. To be precise, it was in the Trusts and Estates department of the downtown law firm of Gregory and Peterson, where worked Karen Conner, thirty-two, fifth-year associate attorney and McKinley Law School's Adjunct Professor of Wills. Conner had taught Wills at McKinley for two years, but her class met at 8 A.M. so that she could be at her office at Gregory by nine-thirty. Blotchett, a late arriver, had seen her for the first time only the previous week. In her presence he felt something that he had never felt before. He wondered whether it might be love. He wanted to know for certain.

Blotchett called Sanford Clapp at home on Saturday to find out who she was and where she worked. The weekend could not pass quickly enough for the lovesick Blotchett. At his desk on Monday morning he called her, on the pretense of needing some legal advice about his own will. He was in the process of asking her to dinner, ostensibly to discuss estate planning, when he read the bogus Professor of the Year letter. Later he realized that he had hung up on her, and he spent much of Monday, including the faculty meeting, trying to fabricate a suitable explanation for his rudeness. He slept poorly Monday night, unable to think of a good apology. At this moment, seducing the attractive Katrina Walfish was the furthest thing from his mind.

Katrina could not know any of this.

"Yes, it is a rather comfortable couch," said Blotchett. "Please, have a seat."

At last we're getting somewhere, thought Katrina. She sat, smoothed her skirt on her lap, and placed her handbag on the floor beside her. Blotchett walked to the door and locked it. His mind was still on Karen Conner. As an actor might repeat a performance that he had given countless times before, he sat himself in the easy chair opposite Katrina, fixed his large brown eyes on her, ran a hand through his thick brown hair, smiled, and said, "So you'd like to be a judicial clerk. Well, well, well."

"What big eyes you have, Professor Blotchett," said Katrina, waiting expectantly.

Nothing happened.

Katrina continued to wait.

Blotchett came out of his trance. "I do?"

"You do what?" Katrina asked, confused.

"I have big eyes?" he asked.

"It's just an expression."

At last he noticed her unbuttoned top. "Your shirt is open," he said.

Katrina did not know how to react. "Yes, it is," she said, drawing in her breath. Her hand moved involuntarily to the opening. Had the big moment arrived?

"Great," he said, looking relieved. "Your timing is perfect. Just what the doctor ordered."

She did not understand.

"Katrina," Blotchett began, "you obviously know a lot about the human heart. You must. You're in love with Paul. Now, I've had a certain amount of, you know, experience with women—I was married once. I guess you know that."

Katrina nodded. She wondered what on earth he was driving at.

Blotchett continued. "And I'm not the kind of person who's afraid to take advice from people who know more than I do, you know, about a given subject."

Katrina was aware of Blotchett's devotion to self-help books. He had a shelf full of them behind his desk. Katrina also knew that he had spent a year between college and Harvard Law School in an ashram in India, where he claimed to have met Mia Farrow.

"I know this might seem a little unusual," he said, "but I was hoping that you might be able to help me figure something out."

As Blotchett spoke he unlaced his shoes, took them off, and placed them carefully by the side of the couch. "It's funny," he said. "I've gone to bed with more women than I can count. I'm not saying that to boast or anything, it's just a fact." He took his socks off, folded them neatly, and placed them on top of his shoes. He rubbed his feet together. "Women go for me. It's not a good thing or a bad thing. Like I said, it's just a fact. I mean, I'm in good shape, and I work out a lot, and I guess I know I'm kind of good-looking, and I meet people easily." He unknotted his tie. "I've never done that singles-bar thing. I mean, who do you think you're going to meet in a place like that?"

Katrina was speechless.

"You won't meet someone you can talk to," said Blotchett, answering his own question. "I mean, I *am* a law professor, after all, and I need a certain level of intellectual stimulation, and I'm not going to find it in a singles bar." He laughed. "You know where I meet people? Aside from the law school, of course. I love this place. Eighty to a hundred new women in each freshman class. And that's not even counting exchange students, foreign students, and those dental assistant students who are always using our library." He unbuttoned his shirt. "There's also the whole McKinley campus. Although I'm not as interested in the undergraduates any more. What I'm trying to say is—oh, yeah. You know where I meet women most often?"

He took his shirt off. He went to his office door, took a hanger from a hook on the door, hung up his shirt, buttoned the collar button, and smoothed out the wrinkles. He eyed the shirt critically, picked a loose thread from the right shoulder, and returned to his seat opposite Katrina.

"In the supermarket! And not just anywhere in the supermarket! In the meat section. No pun intended, of course. I just wait for someone attractive and intelligent-looking to come along with one of those little baskets you can carry in your hand. Anyone pushing a wagon has a husband and kids, and I'm not going to get involved with something like that. I'm no home wrecker." He took off his belt and examined the holes. "I haven't gained five pounds since college," he said.

Katrina, stupefied, gazed at the barefoot, bare-chested Ronald Blotchett. "You *are* in pretty good shape," she murmured.

"Huh? Oh, thanks. Okay. I'm in the meat department. I wait for someone to come along who might be fun. I'm just standing around, like I'm comparing cuts or something. Once I see her, I pick up a piece of meat—anything, a pork chop, a roast, some ground chuck—and I say, 'Does this look okay to you?' And the joke's on *them*, because I'm an excellent cook."

He draped the belt neatly over the back of his chair. "And we get to talking, and since she's got nothing special to do for dinner, I invite her to my place, and then, well, bingo! All right. This was always okay, always pretty satisfying. Although I have to switch grocery stores a lot because, you know, you just don't want to keep running into the same faces."

He grinned. "Once I hit on the same woman twice in two weeks. It wasn't my fault. She got this haircut and I didn't recognize her. I mean, I don't have a photographic memory. Although there *are* books that can help you improve your memory. I have several, if you'd like me to recommend one." He unzipped his fly. "So I'm no, you know, babe in the woods when it comes to women. But this Karen Conner. She's just in another *category*. I've only seen her once. I've only spoken to her on the phone once. And I hung up on her. I was reading that stupid Professor of the Year letter. I could *kill* whoever sent it to me. But Karen. She's just *done* something to me. It's been, let me think. Saturday, Sunday, Monday, today's Tuesday. It's been four days since I first saw her, and I haven't thought of another woman in all that time." He stepped out of his suit pants and folded them neatly along the crease. He stood now before Katrina, wearing starched white cotton boxer shorts, and nothing else.

Nice legs, Katrina found herself thinking.

"I just don't understand how I feel," he continued. "I actually called Sanford Clapp at home to find out who she was. I've never done anything like that before in my life. She intrigues me. I mean, I don't know anything about her aside from where she works when she's not teaching here. She could be married, for all I know." Blotchett endured a moment of panic, because the thought had not crossed his mind before. "I hope not. She could also be completely opposite everything I'm imagining her to be. But somehow. . ."

He went to the office door and carefully hung his pants on a second hanger.

"Somehow I feel as though I just *know* her," he said, walking back to where Katrina sat. "I just have this crazy feeling that we could be right for each other. I think maybe I—" He stopped. "I can't believe I'm saying this. Ronald Blotchett. All right, here goes. I think maybe she's the one I could get, you know, serious about." He stripped off his boxer shorts and tossed them on the chair behind him. He smiled good-naturedly at Katrina. "Ready?" he asked.

He stood completely naked. He seemed to be very proud of himself for having fallen in love. "You're still dressed," he said, somewhat concerned. "Is everything all right?"

"The window shade," said Katrina, pointing to the shade behind his desk.

Blotchett turned to look. He had forgotten to lower it. "Oh, don't worry. No one can see in. We're on a hill."

Katrina attempted to maintain her composure. "Professor Blotchett," she began, "may I ask you a question?" Her tone was as polite as she could manage.

"Sure, anything," he said.

"Please don't take this the wrong way," she said.

"Of course not. What's up?"

"'What's *up*?'" Katrina repeated, trying to maintain eye contact. "Um, Professor Blotchett—"

"Call me Ron."

She forced a smile. "Ron, is there some sort of division in

your brain between . . . between love on the one hand and sex on the other?"

Blotchett looked confused. "I don't think I follow you," he said.

"Let me try it another way," said Katrina. "You look like you're ready to have sex with me. In fact—" She paused. Her glance dropped momentarily. "In fact, you look *very* ready. You look more ready than any man I've ever seen."

"Thank you," said Blotchett.

"Now," said Katrina, "physically, you're ready to have sex with me, is that right?"

He nodded expectantly.

"But mentally, you're thinking about being in love with Karen. Do you see what I'm driving at?"

Blotchett rubbed his chin. "Oh," he said. "I guess I do." He sat down opposite Katrina. "*You're* not insulted, are you?" he asked.

"No, no, not at all," said Katrina, reaching under her seat for her purse. She felt for the transmitter and pushed the switch to "on."

"You still would like to—to have sex, wouldn't you?" Blotchett asked. "That's why you started to unbutton your shirt, right?"

Suddenly, a fragment of a videotaped Murray Frobisher lecture on criminal procedure came into Katrina's mind. The lecture involved the unconstitutionality of entrapment—that is, of enticing people to commit criminal behavior. In Rebecca's office, the women let out a whoop of jubilation as they heard Blotchett's voice over the loudspeaker.

"Um, sure," said Katrina. "Can we talk first, though?"

"Oh, of course," said Blotchett, crossing his legs and making himself comfortable. "I love to talk."

"Why don't you just call Karen back," said Katrina, regaining her composure, "and apologize for what happened, and offer to buy her dinner? Whatever you do, don't try to rush things. I think Paul is about to propose to me, and we've only known each other a few months. My advice to you is just let things happen naturally. Haven't you ever been in love before?"

"No," said Blotchett. "Never. Not even with my wife, that

ungrateful— You're right. I'll just call her and apologize for yesterday morning and invite her to dinner."

"That sounds good to me," said Katrina. I am sitting with a stark naked professor of Constitutional Law, she thought. This is not normal.

Blotchett looked thoughtful. "Katrina?"

"Yes?"

"Do you think Karen knows about my reputation?"

"What kind of reputation is that?" asked Katrina, playing dumb.

"My reputation for—for sleeping with students."

"You have a reputation for sleeping with students?"

"Don't you know about it?" Blotchett sounded a bit hurt.

Katrina remained silent.

"I've slept with every McKinley woman who's gotten a clerkship for the last four years."

"I don't believe you," said Katrina, horrified.

"No, it's true. *Every single one*." He paused for a moment. "Well, I'll be honest with you. Not every one, but at least half. Most of the federal clerkships, anyway. At least six to eight a year. I never intend it to happen, but the interview gets started and somehow we end up making love."

"This happens in your office?" Suddenly Katrina felt as though she was getting what she came for.

"Right here on this couch. Do I disgust you?" he asked hopefully.

"No, no, not at all," she said. "How does it happen?"

"I really don't know."

"Do you always lock the door?"

"Yes."

"Do you usually keep your shades drawn?"

"Most of the time. I just forgot today."

"Do you always invite the woman to sit on the couch, and do you always sit opposite her on that chair?"

Katrina was drawing upon the testimony of the women at the Caucus meeting the day before.

"Yes, I do," said Blotchett.

"And somehow you end up making love?"

"That's right."

Katrina frowned. "Do you take me for a fool?"

"Of course not!" exclaimed Blotchett, sitting up straight and uncrossing his legs.

"Professor Blotchett, people don't just 'end up' making love. Well, maybe sometimes, but not every single woman who comes into your office. Whether you admit it or not— whether you *can* admit it, I really don't know—you use your position as head of the clerkship committee to extort sex from women students. If you didn't have tenure—if you worked somewhere in the real world instead of in a law school— you'd get bounced in a minute. I nearly went through with having sex with you just so that I could get a good recommendation myself. I'm disgusted with myself, do you understand?

"And another thing, Professor Blotchett. I've got news for you. I'm wired for sound. Every word you've said—well, every word in the last minute or so, anyway—it's all on tape. And if you ever seduce another clerkship applicant and the Women's Law Caucus hears about it, we're going straight to Dean Strong with the tape. And you and your damned clerking couch will be out in the street.

"And if you don't write me the strongest recommendation you've ever written for anybody, and if I don't get that federal clerkship in Denver, I'm going straight to Dean Strong. Do you read me?

"Good day, Professor Blotchett."

Katrina grabbed her handbag and stepped past the dumb-struck professor and into the corridor. She ran for the stairwell and did not stop running until she burst into Rebecca's office. The women students let out a deafening cheer and hugged and kissed the exhausted Katrina.

Rebecca smiled. "You deserve an Academy Award," she said.

"I'll never do anything like that as long as I live," said Katrina. "If only Paul knew what I went through to be with him."

Then she remembered how close she came to willing infidelity. "On second thought, maybe it's better that he doesn't know." She slumped into a chair.

"Oh, no!" It was Marlene Feight. "I forgot to turn the tape recorder back on! We didn't get a word of it!"

There was silence. For a full minute the women merely looked at each other, at Katrina, whose performance seemed wasted, at Marlene, ready to shoot herself, and at Rebecca.

Rebecca grinned. "Nobody tell Blotchett, okay?"

EIGHT

Forty minutes after Katrina's conference with Ronald Blotchett, Rebecca had to pull herself together and attempt to give a coherent lecture on Securities Regulation. It was not easy, especially because Katrina, Marlene Feight, and a large number of the students in the Women's Law Caucus all took the class. Few of the women present actually intended to go into Securities Law. They attended only because Rebecca taught it. Their loyalty to her was such that they would have taken seminars in ancient Greek, had Rebecca been the professor. This morning, though, every time Rebecca's glance came to rest on one of the participants in Blotchett's comeuppance, she had to bite her lip to keep from laughing. The other students must have wondered what Rebecca found so funny about the morning's subject, the definition of "underwriter" in Section 2(11) of the Securities Act of 1933.

Rebecca could not tell them, of course, and she could only hope that none of the students would reveal her role in the Blotchett affair. She would be in enough trouble if her authorship of the Professor of the Year letter ever came to light. Then she remembered the way that Sanford had been looking at her in the Committee of Ten meeting. The thought of Sanford learning that she had written the letter—especially after their lunch date—sobered her, and she finished the lecture in relatively professional style. She stopped at her office to drop off her lecture notes and she walked home. The Saint was to meet her there for lunch.

On the way home, she thought about Sanford Clapp and their lunch together. It brought to mind one of her favorite stories about law school, which involved an incident said to have taken place thirty years ago at the University of Chicago. A blizzard struck one February evening, and the next morning the streets were impassable. One student who lived two miles from the campus and who normally commuted by elevated railway heard on the radio that even the el was not running. Dutifully he trudged through the snow-filled sidewalks, arriving twenty minutes late for his Contracts class. There at the podium the professor was holding forth to an audience of one. Instead of taking his regular assigned seat, the student slipped into the seat next to the other fellow. The new arrival listened to the lecture and after a while leaned toward the other student.

"What's he talking about?" he whispered.

"How should I know?" came the reply. "I got here five minutes before you did."

Rebecca liked the story because, to her mind, it symbolized the total disregard of many law professors for the needs of their students. Whether a law professor would lecture to an empty hall is a matter of conjecture, although there are those who will swear that the story is true. What mattered to Rebecca was that even on days when there were no blizzards, too many law professors still failed to live up to their roles as educators. This belief on Rebecca's part drove a further wedge between herself and many of the men on the McKinley faculty, who saw nothing wrong with what they did in and out of class.

Rebecca felt that law school was more concerned with molding people than with teaching them. Graduates, of course, come away with certain skills. They can find things for you in a law library; they can read a case and tell you what it stands for; they can perform certain (but by no means all) tasks of basic legal writing. But, as anyone who ever practiced law will agree, a law school graduate has virtually no idea how lawyers serve clients. If there were a school for, say, sheet metal workers that after three years left its graduates as unprepared for their careers as does law school, it would be closed down in a minute, and no doubt by *lawyers*. In addition to their Juris Doctor degrees and their meager package of skills, law school graduates carry with them the sort of gnawing doubts about their own worth as human beings that only three years of complete powerlessness can provide.

Students admitted to top law schools like McKinley were outstanding performers, by and large, as undergraduates. They applied to law school for a variety of reasons. Some read books like Anthony Lewis's *Gideon's Trumpet* in their political science classes and saw themselves carrying the banner of civil rights, or human rights, or some other equally important cause. The world was filled with Clarence Gideons—honest men and women rotting in jails for crimes they did not commit. Evil, corruption, and greed were everywhere. To many young people, a law degree was the sharpest sword available with which to cut them down. If in the process of uplifting the downtrodden and winning justice for the widow and orphan one were to become rich and famous, so much the better. Thus the doctrine of Doing Well by Doing Good.

Other law students came with different motives. Some needs were purely financial. Certain sectors of the economy, of course, are prone to lean times. A typical entering class at McKinley includes former teachers, nurses, doctoral candidates, filmmakers, and civil servants. One McKinley College graduate with a degree in sociology found herself, to her surprise, in the same Contracts class as her undergraduate thesis adviser, who had just been turned down for tenure. Still others came to law school because they wanted three years of structure and a three-year absence from the nagging question of what they were going to do with their lives.

Most of these students, whether impelled by idealism, the cost of living, escape, greed, the desire for power, or some combination thereof, quickly become putty in the hands of their professors. To a first-year law student, a law professor's power seems equal to that of God, but far more visible. God speaks in general terms about His expectations for human behavior; law professors post lengthy, complex, and tedious assignments on bulletin boards, and God help the student who fails to complete them. God is full of loving kindness, even to the third and fourth generation; a first-year law professor dismisses incorrect answers with a withering glance. God waits for Man, yea, until the day of his death; first-year law professors wait about twenty seconds before they give up on one student and call on someone else. God loves all His creatures equally. First-year law professors grade on a curve.

Law professors know well that the early trajectories of legal careers depend in large part on first-year grades. Law students hoping to launch themselves into summer internships with top firms, judicial clerkships, important Washington posts, and extortionate starting salaries must avoid at all costs the stigmatization of falling within the "bottom ninety" percent of the class, those who are not admitted to the *Law Review*. The students recognize that their fate rests in the hands of their professors, who will issue grades and, for a lucky few, give recommendations or make telephone calls to important people on their behalf. Recognition of the professors' seemingly absolute power provokes different forms of behavior. Some students—the lucky few—look at the whole process as a silly game. They maintain their perspective on law school, do their schoolwork with some minimal degree of diligence, and carry on their lives with an enviable amount of balance. Most students, though, can no more maintain this sunny disposition than can infantrymen in battle. There exists in law school a foxhole-like mentality, a "We're all in this together" feeling, a sense of "If we ever get out of here alive we'll look back and laugh." Of course, even soldiers in battle are not dependent on doing better than ninety percent of their comrades.

Some law students therefore seek ways to distinguish themselves from the pack. Some become "offensive rebounders"—at the first sign of a classmate's hesitation, they thrust their hands into the air to indicate that *they* know the answer. Some students (fortunately, no more than a few in every class) announce that they have gone to the library and read the entire case from which the editors of the casebook have excerpted only a small portion, and based on a consideration of all relevant factors, the answer is clearly such-and-such. These students are known as "gunners" because they are said to be "gunning" for *Law Review;* to no one's great surprise, in most law school cafeterias they eat alone. It might surprise these students, who willingly accept the enmity of their classmates as a cost of doing business, that even the professors do not respect such tactics. If students could eavesdrop on candid faculty conversations, they would hear things like "That asshole So-and-So spoke out in every class this week. I couldn't shut his mouth with Scotch tape. Just wait until he sees what I do to him on the final."

Other students purchase packs of multihued felt-tip pens and mark their textbooks in six colors: red for the facts of the given case; yellow for the judge's holding; blue for the reasoning; green for key obiter dicta, or judicial asides; pink for the procedural history of the case; and black for the most important footnotes. Textbooks so marked fetch premiums when sold as used, and rightly so, because three-quarters of the new owner's work is already done. Still other students sit in the front row of every class and stay after, or drop by the professor's office to ask still more questions and thus demonstrate a keen interest in the material. Often these students' curiosity far outstrips that of the professor, who may not have given thought to the underlying issues in the many years since he first taught the class. Another tactic, usually employed by at least one and as many as two male members of every incoming class, is to wear a tie, or a jacket and tie, every day, on the theory, one supposes, that neatness counts.

One strange thing about law school is that students are never informed about some of the most important things that they should know. For example, students are not told that they will find assignments for the first day of class on a bulletin board the day before. Nor are they told where this bulletin board might be found. It thus comes as a rude shock to a small percentage of students attending their first law lecture—the first day of their important new career—that they were already responsible for reading and digesting twenty to thirty pages of judicial decisions for each of four or five courses that day. When such students have the misfortune of being called upon to recite ("Ms. Jones, would you tell us the facts of *Palsgraf* versus *Long Island Rail Road*?"), their confusion and subsequent ignominy can take weeks to live down. Such embarrassment is occasionally recalled at the tenth and twentieth class reunions (as in "I'll never forget the first day, when old Professor Fussbudget nailed your ass"). Even if they escape all four tense class hours without hearing their name called (itself an experience as sudden and unpleasant as crashing one's car), they find themselves starting law school a hundred and twenty pages behind.

A law student lives with constant tension. Will I be called on today? Will I embarrass myself? Can I get through tonight's assignment even though I'm exhausted? Will I freeze on the final exam? Will half the exam be on material I didn't understand, or from the lecture on the *one day* I missed class? Does the professor think I'm an idiot? Do my classmates? *Am* I an idiot? If I'm not an idiot, why can't I remember all these Latin phrases? Will my boyfriend understand if I cancel him for a fourth straight weekend? Is it unhealthy to go this long without sex? And so on, without cease, for three long years.

Part of the role that Rebecca assigned herself at McKinley was to pour oil on the troubled waters of McKinley students' souls. For one thing, she was in her office from eight o'clock in the morning until six or seven at night. Students learned quickly that she looked forward to their visits and that she gladly tutored them in homework assignments for her own Torts or Securities Regulation classes, or for any other lectures. This practice baffled many of Rebecca's colleagues, who were rarely available to students even during their posted office hours, who otherwise made themselves as unavailable as possible, and who were no more likely to assist students with their course work than to carry their books to class.

Rebecca was of the opinion that law professors did all they could to increase the pressure on law students because they believed living with tension was an excellent form of training. After all, they reasoned, this is how they themselves were trained, and it didn't hurt *them* any. She considered the substitution of stress for education fraudulent and representative of an abnegation of a teacher's duty. On the other hand, she did not believe in spoon-feeding information to students or otherwise conveying the false and damaging impression that the legal and business worlds beyond the gates of the McKinley campus were warm and gentle places. Rebecca simply believed that living with constant tension was demoralizing and ultimately psychologically damaging. She viewed her role as tutor and counselor to all comers as an effort toward reducing the level of tension in her students' lives.

Her colleagues were not unaware of the steady stream of visitors to her office. They were resentful that she did not play the game by their rules. Any professor who sought to decrease the distance between professor and student diminished the power of all the other professors. At the same time, they were jealous of her popularity. Certainly Rebecca was not carrying on a one-woman war against her colleagues. There were others at McKinley who also sought, where possible, to give the students a fair deal. Jackson Ward and Tony Sloop were such teachers. So were Griffin, the associate professor of Corporate Taxation; Gertler, who taught Roman Law; and Parnell, the lecturer in Copyright and Trademark Law. None of these professors, except for Ward, had tenure, though, and none of them set the tenor of the law school as did Clapp, Frobisher, Stanger, and Mountain.

Rebecca's teaching style was unlike that of anyone else at McKinley. Law students normally spend eighty percent of their time out of class "briefing" cases. This involves poring over a judicial decision and extracting information about the facts. It is a tiring, repetitive process that must be performed as many as a thousand times during one's first year of law school. It has nothing to do with analysis of issues, of grappling with questions of right and wrong, or fairness and unfairness. It also has little to do with what most lawyers actually do for a living. Rebecca did away entirely with the process of briefing cases for her Torts class, assuming as she did that her students' experience in briefing cases for Contracts, Criminal Law, Constitutional Law, Civil Procedure, and Real Property was more than sufficient. Instead, Rebecca prepared and distributed her own briefs of the cases, although she still expected the students to read once or twice the cases themselves. In addition to the facts of the cases, she appended questions that became the basis of the discussion in class. These questions, which Sanford Clapp thought irrelevant to the study of law and altogether too "touchy-feely," attempted to focus a student's attention directly on the ethical and societal issues that each case presented. Rebecca's warmth and intensity allowed students who trembled at the thought of speaking up in other classes to venture their opinions as if they were at home by the fireside.

Rebecca had a way of making her students forget that the class was a lecture to one hundred or more people. She could give a student the feeling that he or she was the only other person in the room. For many students unaccustomed to public speaking, Rebecca's class was the first time that they had ever found the courage to speak before a large group. Moreover, Rebecca innovated relentlessly. Some days she divided the class into eight "juries" of approximately twelve students each to debate the outcome of the day's assigned cases. Some days she asked for volunteers for role playing, and students would be cast as a surgeon, a patient, close relatives, a medical insurance company executive, and a hospital director in a drama centering on the decision to undergo potentially dangerous elective surgery. Not all of Rebecca's experiments succeeded, but the students, released from the opprobrium of case-briefing and warmed by her obvious concern for their well-being, did not mind. From Clapp and the others they learned fear, self-doubt, and obeisance. From Rebecca they learned law.

NINE

The anti-Blotchett conspiracy had given Rebecca's spirits a lift, but her mood quickly sank back into the same dismal state it had occupied since her lunch with Sanford Clapp. Everything seemed to point to rejection for tenure. Now it occurred to Rebecca that she was living with the same sort of tension that Sanford Clapp inflicted on his students. "Sanford's revenge," she said to herself as she reached her apartment. "Lucky me."

The Saint, who had prepared lunch in advance of Rebecca's arrival, could tell that she was more upset than usual as she kissed him hello and sat down at the kitchen table without speaking. It was not easy for him to live with Rebecca under these circumstances. He had his own decisions to make. In addition to his schoolwork, he was in the midst of interviews with potential employers, many of whom were located out of the city and therefore required overnight visits. These trips played havoc with his schedule, which also included his work-study job in the law school library and his two extracurricular activities—teaching remedial reading at an elementary school two blocks from McKinley and, somewhat incongruously, target practice with the McKinley University rifle team. His father, a passionate hunter, had given Daniel his first gun at the age of five. Although as a boy he hated to kill, he loved to shoot, and in riflery he found both a discipline and a release from tension that continued to serve him well. He was a fairly good marksman and he competed regularly with the McKinley University team.

In addition to choosing a job and a city, the Saint also had to make his mind up about Rebecca. He thought he loved her, but the gap in age between them was a concern to him. Their relationship thus far had suited both his needs and hers. They had companionship in the form of another person who understood intimately the other's professional environment. The question of marriage had not yet arisen. Few at McKinley were aware of the arrangement. For delicacy's sake, Rebecca chose not to mention her live-in boyfriend to her colleagues. Katrina Walfish, the Saint's closest friend at McKinley, was the only student who knew of the liaison. The Saint did not accompany Rebecca to those few faculty social occasions that she chose to attend. He continued to pay rent on a tiny studio in a depressing walk-up in a marginal neighborhood about a mile from campus, for those times when he or Rebecca needed to be alone. He had moved most of his personal effects to Rebecca's place ten months earlier, during Christmas vacation of his first year at McKinley. Until recently, the Saint spent an average of six nights in seven at Rebecca's, even when she was out of town. "You only love me for my apartment," Rebecca frequently teased him. "It's true," the Saint would respond. "I just have to put up with *you* so I can stay here." Lately, though, with Rebecca's mood unpredictable, he thought it best—for the good of the relationship, and for his own mental health—to find reasons for sleeping elsewhere a few nights a week. Rebecca, so far, had not detected a pattern to his absences.

"You can't imagine what five years in Nigeria does to your concept of the American supermarket," the Saint said, in between bites of tuna salad, trying to break the tension in the air.

"Is that so?" said Rebecca, not paying attention.

The Saint tried again. "There's more food in that Shop'N'Go on the corner than in any fifty square miles of Western Nigeria. And we just take it for granted that there will always be food on the shelves. I remember one spring when the rains kept up for a month longer than usual. The paths were all flooded. The hunters couldn't get out to the forest. The government had to drop food in by helicopter."

"Mm-hmm," said Rebecca.

"You haven't even started your sandwich," said the Saint, trying not to lose his patience. "I'm sorry it's tuna fish, but I just didn't have time to make anything more interesting."

"Saint, it's not the tuna. I'm just a little overwrought, I guess."

"The tenure thing?" As if I had to ask, he thought.

Rebecca nodded.

"I'm sorry. Here I am talking about Nigeria when I should have been asking about you."

"Don't be so hard on yourself," said Rebecca, taking his hand. "You can't always know what I'm thinking."

You'd be surprised, he thought. "Are you really down?"

"I am," Rebecca admitted. "I'm dead certain to get turned down. I was just thinking about it on the way home. Yesterday, at the Committee of Ten meeting, I looked at each one of those guys and I thought there's no way they'd ever let me join the club."

"You really believe that?" the Saint asked, studying her.

Rebecca shrugged. "What am I supposed to think? Whenever I pass Frobisher in the hall, he doesn't even look at me. He just looks guilty and pretends he doesn't see me. He and the Dean are very close. I figure he must know something."

"Rebecca, the Virgin Murray doesn't exactly have a reputation for ease around women. And when did he ever say hello to you in the hallway?"

"I guess you're right," Rebecca said.

"Then what are you worried about?"

"It's the way they *all* look at me. Sanford, and Bob Stanger, and even Aaron Mountain. I feel like they know something I don't."

"Come on," said the Saint. "Last week it was Blotchett. You said he barely spoke to you at the blood drive. Today it's Frobisher. You've got to take this whole thing a little easier. Worrying about it isn't going to change anything."

He grinned. "And just because you're paranoid doesn't mean they're not out to get you," he said.

"Very funny," said Rebecca, trying to sound angry. She set to her tuna fish.

"I'm sorry. I was just trying to cheer you up. It doesn't

make any sense to me. You've got an excellent record as a teacher. Dean Strong even came out and said so at that alumni dinner last year when you spoke. Your *Law Review* articles have been cited three different times in Supreme Court decisions. And you've got that contract for the book on tender offers that you'll start this spring. You've got everything going for you."

"Except for one thing, Saint."

"What's that? That you're a woman?"

"No, although that probably doesn't help. The problem is that they think I'm a radical."

"Aren't you? At least compared to those other guys?"

"Well, a little bit, I guess. In some ways, anyone who's ever been to law school feels the same way I do. It's just that when people graduate, their feelings, their anger— Well, it all just fades. People try to put the whole experience out of their mind, like a bad dream. I can't blame them. And between studying for the bar exam and starting their new jobs, they don't exactly have time to think about reforming legal education. They'd rather not have to think about it. And I'm practically the only one on the McKinley faculty who wants to change things. And the last thing they want to do here is give tenure to someone who wants to shake things up."

"Why *are* you so interested in shaking things up?" the Saint asked. "If you weren't a reformer, they'd *have* to give you tenure. They'd even *want* to, just so they could say there's a woman on the faculty. It's as though you've deliberately chosen a path that's almost guaranteed to fail."

Rebecca did not answer immediately. She took a bite of her sandwich. "I never thought of it that way," she said. "I just get so angry whenever I think about what goes on here. It's like taking the brightest college graduates and sending them back to high school. I'm surprised we don't have homeroom and shop class. And I always wanted—from the time I was a law student—to change things. I just can't go through life being passive. Why did you go to Nigeria? It's the same thing."

The Saint nodded. "It may be the same thing," he said, "but we're talking about you right now. Look. You want to make it as a law professor—you want tenure here. At least you *say* you want tenure here. But then you take all your ideas for changing things—all the things you know would be most upsetting to Murray, and Sanford Clapp, and the rest of them. You take all your ideas and you put them in your tenure essay —you're almost begging them to turn you down."

Rebecca looked away. She acknowledged to herself that the Saint had a point. "You really think so?"

"I'm not trying to give you a hard time," said the Saint, reaching across the table and stroking Rebecca's hair, "especially since you've been so, I don't know, so nervous about the whole thing. I've just been wondering about this ever since I read the first draft of that tenure essay. It seems like you went out of your way to provoke the other professors."

Rebecca went to make coffee. "And you think I did it because I secretly want to fail?" she asked, her back to him.

"Do you have a better explanation?"

"Maybe," she said, taking the milk out of the refrigerator.

"Well, what is it?" the Saint asked, turning toward her.

Rebecca set two mugs of coffee on the table. She spoke softly and seriously. "I want them to take me on my own terms. I don't want to pretend to be the mild-mannered lady law professor who gets tenure and then shows her true colors. I want them to give tenure to the real Rebecca Shepard, the one who wrote that essay."

You're crazy, thought the Saint. "You've got guts," he said diplomatically. "But I really question your timing. You write an essay on law school reform you know they'll hate, and then you insist that we do the Professor of the Year thing the week before they make up their minds about you. I kept telling you, Let's wait till next year—it could blow up in our faces—but you just kept insisting. Maybe you really want them to turn you down."

Rebecca sipped her coffee. "They'll never know I was involved," she said. "Unless you rat on me. On the other hand, Jackson Ward figured out that I was involved."

"How'd he do that?" asked the Saint. "By the way, we've only being going together for a whole year already, and you still don't know I like my coffee black."

"What? Oh, I'm sorry." Rebecca put a hand to her forehead. "I know. I do know. I just forgot."

"It's no big deal," said the Saint. "Really. How did Jackson know that you were behind the letter?"

"Beats me," said Rebecca. "He said he recognized my handiwork. If he could, maybe everyone else could, too. Maybe even Sanford."

"Doubtful. Jackson knows you much better than the other professors. You went out with him for almost a year."

"I suppose," she said.

Suddenly the Saint gave a start. "I just had an idea," he said. "Is there still time to switch your tenure essay? Maybe you could use a draft of the article you showed me last week."

"What, the one on insider trading?" Rebecca asked. "It's a good idea, but that article is a long way from being publishable. And they've already set my legal education article in type. There's no way to pull it. And besides, I *want* them to read it."

The Saint stirred his coffee and licked the spoon. "It sounds like you'd rather shake them up than get tenure."

Rebecca frowned. "Maybe," she said. "Anyway, it's coming out on Monday."

"Your birthday," said the Saint.

"Some birthday," Rebecca said. "My article will come out, and the Dean and the others will laugh at it and use it as proof that I shouldn't get tenure."

"Don't be so sure. This is good coffee, by the way."

"It's from Honduras. I bought it at that little store on the corner. Anyway, how can you say 'Don't be so sure'? First they'll say I should have stayed within my field. Securities. Then they'll say I should never have gone into Securities Law in the beginning, because it's a 'man's field.' Some of them still believe it!" Her voice filled with indignation. "Those guys—Stanger, Frobisher, Clapp—they're still in the Dark Ages! Last week Stanger called me 'honey' and asked me to bring him a cup of coffee. He must think he's still running Blanchard's. And I've been here longer than he has!"

Rebecca was fast losing her composure. "I'm going to be thirty-two on Monday," she said. "I'm not a kid any more." She fought back tears. "Part of me feels that I shouldn't have to be doing this. Competing in a man's world. Setting myself up for rejection this way. Part of me feels I should be married, with two kids and a backyard, and have somebody taking care of me. But whenever I feel that way I just panic. I don't know how I'm *supposed* to feel. Look at where all my independence has gotten me. I'm about to be thirty-two and I'm about to be fired."

The Saint leaned across the table and kissed her lips. "It's all right," he whispered. "It'll be all right."

"No, it won't be all right," she said, pulling away. "And I'm wasting *your* time. You shouldn't be sleeping with a professor. You should have a woman your own age."

"What are you talking about?" asked the Saint, a little too quickly. "I don't want a woman my own age. I only want you."

"I don't even know why you put up with me," she said sadly. "I'm unhappy all the time, and I'm putting on weight, and—"

"Cut it out!" said the Saint. "Look. You're just upset about the tenure thing. I shouldn't have said those things about your article. I'm sorry. But this whole discussion has nothing to do with us. We're fine together. I don't want anybody but you. Do you understand?"

"Are you sure?" Rebecca asked, looking hopefully at the Saint.

"Of course I'm sure. And I wouldn't be surprised if they even gave you tenure."

"Really?" she asked, sniffling.

"Yes, really. Here. Let me help you dry your eyes." He wiped them gently with a table napkin.

"Thanks," she said. "It's just that when I think about the tenure committee they appointed for me, the whole thing seems hopeless. Sanford Clapp, who's totally amoral, and Frobisher, who does anything Dean Strong wants, and 'D.O.A.' Culpepper, who's a sweet guy, but I think he's going senile. He probably doesn't even realize I'm on the faculty. He must think I'm somebody's secretary. Dean Strong couldn't have picked three people less likely to recommend tenure than these three guys. See what I mean?"

"I don't know," said the Saint. "Dean Strong is not such a bad guy. He's ambitious as anything, but he's basically fair-minded. And the decision isn't up to the tenure committee. It's up to him."

"Still," said Rebecca, "if he wanted to find a great excuse for not giving me tenure, he's got it with that committee. They'll recommend unanimously to turn me down, and that'll be that."

"Just have a little faith, that's all I'm saying. Let's talk about tonight, because I've got a class at one o'clock, and it's already ten of."

"Okay. You're flying to D.C. tonight, aren't you?"

"That's right. I—I can't be here tonight. I've got to be there first thing in the morning."

"I understand," said Rebecca, even though she wondered why he couldn't stay with her and take an early flight the next morning.

"I'm planning on taking the eight o'clock shuttle," he said. "I've got two half-day interviews tomorrow, one after the other. I'm really not looking forward to it."

"It's not a lot of fun," Rebecca agreed. She pushed the hair out of her eyes. "How about an early dinner tonight? We could meet here at five, or we could go out, if you want..." Her voice trailed off. She looked so forlorn that the Saint asked himself how he could ever be angry with her.

"Let's meet here," he said. "And... I wouldn't mind some very quick—you know—time in the sack. I missed you last night."

"Saint!" Rebecca exclaimed, and then her tone softened. "I missed you, too. I'll meet you at five right here."

"I better get going," said the Saint, taking a last sip of his coffee. "See you then."

She smiled bravely. "See you then."

TEN

"Randolph Patton to see you, sir."

"Thank you, Carmen. Send him in."

Murray Frobisher sat behind his desk, in a desk chair so large that it almost dwarfed him, awaiting the arrival of his prospective new client. The "Virgin Murray" possessed as little interest in sex as was humanly possible. As an adolescent he did not purchase even a single copy of *Playboy* magazine. Today, alone among his friends and male colleagues on the McKinley faculty, he had not installed a video tape recorder in his home for the purposes of renting and viewing the occasional lurid cassette. Frobisher was aware of the existence of child pornography, although he could not imagine who would consume it or, for that matter, who would produce it. Frobisher was also aware that possession of child pornography with intent to distribute same was a serious offense in the eyes of the law. Getting this guy off will take everything I've got, he thought, his juices flowing in anticipation of the coming litigation. I just hope he can afford me.

The door opened and in walked a young boy, approximately four feet six inches tall, dressed in a blue pinstripe suit, white button-down shirt, and red repp tie, struggling under the weight of two heavy briefcases. Frobisher rose from his chair and peered at his young visitor. Must be one of the actors, he thought.

"And whose little boy are you?" asked Frobisher, never at ease around children.

"I'm Randolph Patton. You're Frobisher, right?"

Frobisher blinked a couple of times. "You're Randolph Patton? I was expecting someone—"

"Older. Everybody does. Mind if I sit down? These brief-cases are killing me."

"No, no, please," said Frobisher, indicating a chair across from his desk. "Sit right down. Can I get you some coffee? Are you old enough to drink coffee?"

"Don't get cute," said Randolph, seating himself and looking around. "I take extra sugar."

Frobisher kept his eye on Patton as he buzzed Carmen and ordered coffee.

The walls of Frobisher's office were hung with dozens of certificates, diplomas, awards, congratulatory letters, and honorary degrees, all testifying to the worthiness of Murray Frobisher as advocate and scholar. Bronze gavels, silver plaques, paperweights, and other trophies covered much of his large desk and an equally large table, strewn with papers, against the far wall. More awards obscured the books and papers that filled the floor-to-ceiling bookshelves to the right of the desk. Even the back of the door was a triumph of the ego. Murray had nailed up a sixteen-by-twenty-inch framed photograph of himself on the steps of the Supreme Court, surrounded and almost swallowed alive by an encircling band of journalists and sound men.

Randolph Patton took it all in. "Nice office," he said admiringly. "You get around a lot for an older guy."

"Thank you," said Frobisher. "Look, somebody's pulling my chain, right? You're not really Randolph Patton, are you?"

"In the flesh," said Randolph. "No pun intended."

Frobisher shook his head. "I'm sorry to— I just thought that a child pornographer would be a man in his fifties, with a shiny brown suit on, maybe missing a couple of teeth. I didn't expect a thirteen-year-old."

Carmen came in with the coffee. She was smiling broadly. "He's so cute, Professor," she said.

Frobisher glared at her as she left.

"I'm not thirteen. I'm fourteen *and a half*," Randolph corrected. "And I'm not a child pornographer. I mean, I don't do pornography of children. That's against the law. I'm a child who happens to produce pornographic videocassettes. There's a big difference."

"Of course," said Frobisher, nodding vigorously. "Forgive me."

"I need a lawyer," said Randolph. "Look, do you want the case or don't you?"

"You haven't even explained to me . . ." Frobisher was at a loss for words.

"How a kid who's just fourteen and a half could make porn flicks. Fair enough. It's like this." Randolph paused to sip his coffee. "When I was ten I got into computers. My parents gave me a personal computer for Christmas. Actually, they gave it to both me and my kid sister. She was nine then. She was learning how to program at school, and she taught me a lot of stuff. And I saw that the way her teacher was showing them how to program was really slow. So I designed this software program for teaching kids how to learn to use computers. I also designed a word processing/spreadsheet program. It's called PattonWorks. My dad was with Hewlett-Packard, and he brought the software designs in to his boss. His boss liked them. But when he heard that an eleven-year-old kid had written the programs, he said he wasn't interested. So my dad and I went into business for ourselves.

"We copyrighted the programs, and set up a research and development partnership and then a corporation to produce and market the software. One of my uncles does venture capital, and he really got turned on by our product. He invested about a hundred thousand dollars in seed money in exchange for pretty substantial equity participation. I tried to tell my dad that we were giving away the store, but there was no choice —we needed the capital. We got some mezzanine financing from the Chase Manhattan Bank— Am I going too fast for you, Murray? Okay if I call you Murray?"

Frobisher could barely speak. "Not at all—go ahead."

"Well, to make a long story short, the software hit the market three years ago and got excellent reviews in the computer magazines, and sales went crazy. Buy enough ads and they'll say anything, but that's another story. We went public at sixteen bucks a share, and the stock was trading over-the-counter at twenty-two times earnings. Any analyst who knows anything about high tech will tell you that's an incredible P-E ratio. About a year ago we got bought out by IBM. We made a fortune. Dad retired. Right about then my voice started to change, and I discovered sex.

"I've never actually *had* sex myself," Randolph admitted. "Dad says I'm too young. But last year I saw grownups have sex on some videocassettes my dad hides from my mom in the den. Computers are neat, but sex is neater. The videocassettes were pretty good, but every time two people, or three people, or four people, started having sex, someone would come in waving a gun or shouting something, and so the people having sex would have to stop. I thought that was pretty dumb, because if people want to watch a story that has a plot, they can just watch regular TV.

"I figured that grownups would pay a lot for videocassettes of people having sex who didn't have to stop for *anything*. I got a lot of business experience from running the software company, and I had all that cash just sitting there, so I opened up my own production company. We've already shot six videocassettes, and we've got another six scheduled for production. Here. Take a look."

Randolph opened one of the briefcases, revealing its contents: a pile of videocassettes, all emblazoned with a Patton Pictures logo and carrying titles like *Bedridden*, *Backstage at the Rock Concert*, and *In, In, In*. Frobisher remained speechless.

"Do you want to see one?" asked Randolph. "I've got a mini-VCR in the other briefcase."

"N-no, that's all right," said Frobisher, putting up both hands. "I'm sure they're really well made."

"You bet they are. I hired the best people in the business—directors, lighting people, cameramen, and porn stars. Ever heard of Jerry Spanbock? Best cinematographer in the industry. Works for *me*. We've even got Olivia Jones under contract to do four cassettes in the next six months." Patton blushed. "She's real good-looking. She lets me sit on her lap."

He grew serious again. "So I've got the business up and running, and by next month I want to have my cassettes in two thousand video outlets coast to coast. Gas stations, convenience stores, everywhere but the public library. But I've got some legal problems, and that's why I'm coming to you."

"Your homeroom teacher objects to your videocassettes, and he's making you stay after school to clean the blackboards," said Frobisher.

"Look, wise guy, if you're going to make cracks about my age I can go somewhere else for a lawyer, okay?"

"I'm sorry," said Frobisher. "Do you want to tell me about your legal problems?"

"That's what I was coming to." Randolph sighed. "The vice squad of the city police department is trying to close me down. There's no anti-pornography law in this state, so they charged me with pandering."

"Pandering?" repeated Frobisher. His interest was aroused. "That's the statute forbidding procurement of prostitutes. That's how they arrest pimps, not porn filmmakers."

"Well, they're following a pretty new interpretation now," said Randolph. "They're saying that since I'm paying these grownups to have sex with each other, I'm doing exactly what pimps do. I think it's totally unfair. What I'm doing is art. There may not be any plots in my videocassettes, but it's really challenging to capture sexual abandonment on videotape. They never arrested Picasso, did they?"

Frobisher was warming to the subject. This could finally take me back to the Supreme Court, he thought. His last trip there, on behalf of the American Civil Liberties Union, was almost two years ago. While he had argued many interesting and complex cases in the federal courts, nothing had come along with Supreme Court potential—until now.

"Randolph," he said excitedly, "they're violating your First Amendment rights! Do you understand that?"

"No," said Randolph. "Is it important?"

"Important?" cried Frobisher. "It's the whole ball of wax! Your civil liberties are being trampled upon! Today it's Olivia Jones in *Backstage at the Rock Concert* and tomorrow it'll be *Gone With the Wind*! You've got an excellent case on your side, young man. You could strike a blow for the independence of filmmakers everywhere! Your name could be on a Supreme Court case! Generations of law students will study with fascination the decision in *People* versus *Patton*, Murray Frobisher, attorney for the defense. You'll be famous, do you understand?"

Randolph winced. "That's sort of what I'm trying to avoid," he said. "I want to beat this pandering charge, but I want to do it quietly. Since I'm a juvenile, my name isn't part of the court records, and I want to keep it that way."

"Why is that?" Frobisher asked. He could not imagine why someone would turn down free publicity.

"If my parents knew what I was doing, they'd kill me."

"Where do they think you are after school?"

"Consulting for IBM."

"I see." Frobisher licked his lips. "Well, young man, I'm delighted to take you on as a client, and I'll do my best to keep your name out of the papers. There's just one thing, though, and that's my fee. You are aware, of course, that my track record of Supreme Court victories and A.C.L.U. work has enabled me to charge two hundred to three hundred—"

"Well, there's sort of a problem with that," said Randolph. "My distributor won't touch my cassettes until the legal action is over, because he doesn't want any publicity for selling tapes made by somebody who's just fourteen and a half. I'm in deep to the film company that leases me the studio, and I've got to pay salaries weekly or the union will shut me down. I've got a real cash-flow problem right now."

Frobisher frowned. Another deadbeat, he thought. A young deadbeat this time.

"I can't pay your regular fees, Mr. Frobisher, but I was hoping that we might be able to work something out."

"Like what?" Frobisher shuffled papers on his desk to indicate that the consultation was over.

Randolph played his trump card. "I was thinking of offering you a five percent equity participation in Patton Pictures."

Frobisher looked up quickly.

Randolph knew he had him hooked. "Once I get this pandering charge off my back, I'm going big time," he said. "I see fifty new cassettes a year, I see my own distribution network—cuts out the middleman. I see going public with the stock. I see big bucks."

So did Frobisher. "Five percent," Frobisher said, and he sucked in his breath. "I just don't know."

"Ten percent. My final offer," said Randolph.

"Done deal," said Frobisher, lurching over the desk to shake Randolph's hand. "Send me all the papers you've got relating to the pandering charge and I'll have you off the hook in no time."

"Super, Murray. Just super. Here. Keep a couple of tapes. You can show them to your friends." Randolph removed three videocassettes from his briefcase and put them on Frobisher's desk.

"You really don't have to—" Frobisher began, staring at the videocassettes.

"No, I insist," said Randolph. "One last thing. If you call me at home, and either my mom or my dad picks up, just tell them you're with IBM, okay? So long now."

Frobisher watched his young client repack his briefcase and he showed him to the door. I've always wanted to be in the movie industry, he thought as he settled into the chair behind his desk.

ELEVEN

Thomas Oliver Andrew Culpepper always walked to work, no matter the season, no matter the weather. He first developed the habit as a young government attorney in Washington, D.C., nearly half a century ago, saving ten cents a day in carfare in those final throes of the Great Depression. He continued the practice upon his arrival at McKinley Law School in the mid-1940s and abandoned it only during the period when he and his wife Anne lived in the suburbs raising their two children. Culpepper liked to walk for the exercise, for the ability to observe the city at close range, and for the chance encounters with McKinley students up as early as he. On most mornings, Culpepper arrived at the law school before eight. The morning after his appointment to Rebecca Shepard's tenure committee was no exception. He had read none of her academic publications, although he was very much aware of her presence at McKinley. He spent the entire morning in the library, having set himself the task of familiarizing himself with all of her scholarship before sitting in judgment of her.

His initial reaction was that she wrote well, that her research was solid, and that her arguments were well constructed. Culpepper found entirely sensible her criticisms of the Securities Act of 1933 and the Securities Exchange Act of 1934, the underpinnings of federal regulation of financial markets. Her understanding of the subject surprised and pleased Culpepper, who had arrived in Washington only a few years after the passage of the two acts and who had thought he knew their strengths and weaknesses as well as anyone.

Another early riser was Robert Stanger, who relished the peacefulness of the early morning and was frequently in his law school office, reading cases, drafting articles, or preparing for class, before seven. A fitness addict, he kept a small set of weights and a rowing machine behind his desk and he worked out daily while watching the morning financial news on a small color television he had installed on a bookshelf. In his first year at McKinley, he found himself unprepared for the long stretches of unstructured time that make up a law professor's day. It was too great a shift from his sixteen-hour workdays at Blanchard's department stores. He wandered frequently to the McKinley gymnasium, where he would find himself a pickup basketball game—another aspect of his "think young, stay young" approach to life. Unfortunately, a few months into his first semester at the law school, an over-aggressive McKinley College sophomore, trying to block a "patented" Stanger reverse lay-up, knocked him to the parquet floor and reinjured an ankle that Stanger had first hurt as a college first baseman. Thus ended forever his basketball career, and thereafter he limited his athletics to non-contact sports, such as lifting weights and rowing.

Stanger then turned to writing to sop up his excess time. He put little effort into preparing for class, assuming as he did that his off-the-cuff remarks about law and business would be adequate. Since he demanded equally little in the way of preparation on his students' part, they never complained. Stanger, who had never written anything longer than the cover letter for Blanchard's annual reports, took to academic writing easily. He found that his analyses of corporate law developments were well received among his colleagues for both the accuracy of his observations and the felicity of his writing style. He wrote a prodigious number of *Law Review* articles and several books, one of which, a comparison of British and American corporate law, won awards on two continents. His writing led to invitations to speak at seminars on corporate law and programs like *Wall Street Week*. He specialized in writing and speaking about hostile takeovers, which he opposed.

Although Stanger was, in academic parlance, a rising star,

he was not entirely comfortable with his role as law professor. He frequently found himself wishing that he could do more for his students than explain appellate decisions in the casebook and tell them how Blanchard's moved into Southern California, Dallas, *and* Chicago, all in the same year. The question of tenure for Rebecca Shepard brought to the fore his uncertainties about the teaching component of his duties at McKinley. Although he had little contact with her, he heard through the grapevine that hers was an unorthodox approach to legal education. On the day after the appointment of her tenure committee, he found himself wondering more and more about Rebecca and her teaching methods, of which he knew little. As he entered the faculty dining room for lunch, he looked around, hoping that he might find her there. She was not there, of course, having just finished an early lunch at home with the Saint.

"I wonder what she does that's so different," he said to himself as he pushed his tray along the cafeteria line in the faculty dining room.

"Why, hello, Bob," said Tom Culpepper, behind him on line. "Talking to yourself again? The sign of a great scholar. Or of creeping senility."

"Hello, yourself, young man," said Stanger, pleased at the sight of his colleague. "Could an upstart like me join an important fellow like you for lunch?"

"I'd be absolutely delighted," said Culpepper in his most courtly manner. "You honor me with your presence."

Stanger smiled. "Cut it out, Tom. You're embarrassing me. By the way, did you catch the football game last night? Those Redskins of yours looked pretty good."

"I only caught the first quarter," said Culpepper. "Those Monday night games come on a little late for us senior citizens."

"Busy these days?" asked Stanger.

"A little more so than usual. I've been boning up on Securities Regulation, a field I used to think I knew all about. I'm reading the collected works of Rebecca Shepard."

"No kidding," said Stanger. "I was just thinking about her. You're on her tenure committee, aren't you?"

"Indeed I am," said Culpepper. "But if you ask my opinion, the committee's just window dressing. Ed Strong does whatever he wants. Still, you've got to give it your all if he asks you to take part. Now, Bob, I'm no psychologist, but you look a tad troubled to me. Anything you might care to discuss with good old Tom?"

Stanger pursed his lips. He looked both ways before he spoke, fearful of being overheard. "There is something on my mind, actually," he admitted.

Culpepper chuckled. "Just think of me as your father-confessor, young man. What's eating you? What manner of vexation of spirit?"

"The whole thing, Tom," he said. As they spoke, they slid their trays down the buffet and chose their lunches—a turkey sandwich for Culpepper and cottage cheese and fruit salad for Stanger.

"I've been teaching law for three years," Stanger continued, "and I still don't understand what I'm doing."

"That's nothing," said Culpepper. "I don't understand what *I'm* doing, and I've been at it for forty years."

Stanger smiled. "In that case, I feel better already." He grew serious again as he poured coffee for himself and for Culpepper. "I just wonder what the point is."

They paid for their meals, found a table, and sat down. Culpepper studied his colleague. Stanger nudged Culpepper and pointed to an attractive woman student sitting down to lunch with Tony Sloop, whose arm was in a sling. "Too bad I'm a married man." Stanger chuckled.

"Too bad I'm an ancient goat," replied Culpepper. "Now, what kind of problems are you having with law school? Too many pretty coeds turning your head? Whiplash? Is that it?"

Stanger laughed. "Come on, Tom," he said.

"Let me try another approach, then," said Culpepper. "Aren't we equipping bright young minds to rise to the challenge of law and society?"

"You've been reading too many of Ed Strong's speeches," said Stanger, digging into his cottage cheese. "Although there *is* something noble to what we're doing. Or there ought to be, at least."

"How are we falling short of nobility?" asked Culpepper. "At what point does the crown slip from our heads?"

Stanger sipped his coffee. "I'm not sure. This morning there was a long article in the *Wall Street Journal* about truth-in-advertising laws. If they ever applied those laws to law school, we'd all be in jail."

Culpepper raised his eyebrows but did not speak.

"I looked at our catalog," Stanger continued. "We tell our applicants that law school will develop their thinking and bring them in touch with the great issues of the day, you know, be some sort of intellectual enterprise."

"Don't we do all those things?" Culpepper asked.

"No," Stanger said simply. "I don't think we do any of them. And it bothers me."

Culpepper nodded. He set to his sandwich. "I happen to agree with you, Bob," he said, between mouthfuls. "We really don't."

Stanger looked up quickly from his cottage cheese. "Are you serious, Tom? I always thought you were gung ho about the whole thing."

"When you get as old as I am, people stop asking for your opinions. How's your background in legal history, Bob?"

"Pretty weak," Stanger admitted.

"I could tell you to go to the library and read Judge Frank's *Courts on Trial*. But let me sum things up for you in a couple of sentences. In the bad old days, until about a century ago, law students simply memorized treatises. That's all they did. No cases, no theories, just law. Two witnesses to a will. Marriages of young people under sixteen are voidable without the consent of the parent. That sort of thing. That's assuming they even went to law school in the first place. Many people never did—they just apprenticed themselves to practicing attorneys. The idea of going to law school wasn't widely accepted during the nineteenth century.

"Then came the revolution. People became taken with the idea that law was like the music of the spheres—some sort of supernal force that existed since the beginning of time. And judges could hear this music better than anyone else. They were somehow more attuned to it. And they figured that the best way for law students to hear that music was to read decisions written by judges. So the Dean at Harvard, old Christopher Columbus Langdell himself, put together a casebook—a book full of cases, just like the name implies, and he set all the Harvard students to reading those cases."

"And that's how it started?" Stanger asked.

"Indeed," said Culpepper. "Thus was born what we call the 'case method.' Today virtually every law school in the country uses it. Well, I've always thought the idea was patently absurd. Law isn't only what gets written in appellate decisions. Law is what happens between lawyers, in law offices, in the courtrooms, even over the telephone. But Langdell was a bookish sort, and to his mind, if it wasn't written down in a judge's decision, it wasn't worth studying. So there you are. And now that Langdell had something brand-new to study, he thought it might be handy to have a brand-new way to go about studying it. He found one. In truth, he found himself a rather ancient technique."

"The Socratic method?" Stanger asked.

"Precisely," said Culpepper. "Old Socrates used to teach the youth of Athens not by cramming facts down their throats but by asking them questions and letting the students discover what they already had inside themselves. Law professors do the same thing today, or at least we claim we do."

"That's just my point, Tom," said Stanger. "The Socratic method might work with a group of six or eight students, but once you use it in a lecture class of a hundred or more, the way we do here—"

"Or at any law school," Culpepper added.

"Or at any law school," Stanger repeated, nodding. "It just turns into an excuse for bullying students. It turns the classroom into a power trip."

"For just that reason," said Culpepper, "I never use the Socratic method. I've never used it."

"What *do* you do?"

"Lecture. Reminisce. Talk about the *process* of passing and interpreting laws, about how Washington works. That sort of thing."

"You know," said Stanger, "that's what I try to do. Sure, I try to hit on the important cases, because the students would probably feel cheated if I didn't. But I put most of my efforts into explaining how the business world works, how things really get done."

"Sounds useful to me." Culpepper smiled. "I wish I had had a fellow like you for a Corporations professor when I was a young man. I might have gone places."

"Thanks for the compliment," said Stanger. "But I think you've done all right for yourself."

"Well, perhaps," Culpepper said modestly.

"To get back to the subject, though," said Stanger, "I've always felt that I was going against the grain here."

Culpepper nodded. "You are. Or should I say, *we* are."

"I'm no pioneer," said Stanger. "I just don't think the Socratic thing is an efficient way to teach law. I don't know what they believed a hundred years ago, but it just doesn't work today. And then there's the matter of the suicides."

Culpepper had been acknowledging greetings from Sanford Clapp, two tables away, but Stanger's words caused him to turn quickly. "What suicides, Bob?"

Stanger looked surprised. "How could you not have heard about them? Last year, one of the first-year women walked out of Sanford's Contracts examination and shot and killed herself; and one of the men O.D.'d on pills during the first week of classes this semester."

" 'O.D.'d?' " repeated Culpepper, unfamiliar with the term.

"Overdosed," Stanger explained.

"That's absolutely shocking," said Culpepper, shaking his head slowly. "I know that some of our students have experienced emotional problems here at McKinley—that's par for the course at any law school. Not to be harsh, but the study of law is quite difficult, and it's not for everyone. And I suppose if you took any group of six hundred young people—especially young people today—you'll run into a certain percentage who find life difficult. But *suicide*? No, that just can't be. I'm sorry."

"Weren't you at the Committee of Ten meeting last month?" Stanger asked. "We must have spent two hours talking about it."

"I suppose I missed that one," said Culpepper. "Honestly, I had no idea, Bob. What are people saying? Are they blaming the law school?"

"Not the whole law school," Stanger said quietly. "Just Sanford Clapp."

"But why Sanford?" asked Culpepper, looking over at him. "What's he done?"

"Both victims were his students, and they both told friends beforehand that Clapp was harassing them in class, asking questions they couldn't possibly have answered, and then humiliating them when they admitted as much."

"I find it hard to believe," said Culpepper, visibly disturbed. "Sanford never struck me as a cruel man."

"The record speaks for itself," said Stanger. "He can play hardball when he wants to. That's what some of my students tell me."

Culpepper finished his lunch and touched his napkin to his lips. "I'd best be getting back to the library," he said. "What you've told me is quite upsetting. I hope we've seen the last of it. Suicides. My word. At any rate, I've got a busy afternoon. Ed's asked me to serve on Rebecca's tenure committee. I've never read anything she's published, and I was going to get started on it today."

Stanger glanced at his colleague, but he decided that there was no need to point out that Culpepper had already mentioned reading Rebecca's articles.

"Word on the street says she's a real radical, a reformer type," said Stanger. "She wants to shake things up."

"Not unlike yourself, Bob," said Culpepper, rising to his feet.

"I see your point, Tom," said Stanger, looking thoughtfully at the older professor. "I see your point."

TWELVE

Katrina Walfish had earned her place in McKinley history with her brief appearance in the annual law school student musical the previous spring. The production, which Rebecca had directed, satirized various aspects of life at McKinley. Enough students come to law school with a talent for acting, singing, stage design, and writing new lyrics to popular songs to give the show a fairly polished air. Some students are so gifted, in fact, that they leave their classmates wondering why they ever took up law. The first unusual thing one notices about the production is the size of the chorus. All students, regardless of ability to carry a tune or follow basic dance steps, may join the chorus, which ranges in size from sixty to one hundred and ten people each year. The sure-footed, those with training or aptitude for the theater, and those students who have the misfortune of closely resembling their professors, are cast in larger roles.

The show typically follows the lives of a handful of McKinley students from admission through graduation. There are four performances. All sell out within hours. McKinley professors are allotted two tickets to each performance; most attend several times. Those professors not singled out for abuse generally feel cheated and left out of the fun. The show usually lasts for close to three hours, though, time enough to skewer almost every McKinley professor. Three hours never seemed long to the show's writers, or to the audience. There was general agreement among the students that the faculty collectively generated enough ill will each year to provide material for a new version of Wagner's *Ring*.

The second unusual thing about the production is that, once one looks past the surface level of jokes about inadequate student housing, churlish professors, and *Law Review* members' haughtiness, there is really nothing funny going on. The portrait of McKinley students that emerges from the endless round of skits, songs, and blackouts is one of young people unhappy with the course of education and the career that they have chosen. As one watches law school musicals, it is hard to avoid the conclusion that if anyone had explained to the actors exactly what law school entailed, half of them would never have enrolled. Last year's production, for example, was called *Doctor Stronglove* and depicted Dean Strong as a demented scientist in charge of a psychiatric institution that systematically removed from young men and women all traces of idealism and public service. According to the program notes, Doctor Stronglove's laboratory was cleverly disguised as a nationally renowned law school.

The first scene of *Doctor Stronglove* was a chorus number. The writers changed the title of the Beatles' song "We All Live in a Yellow Submarine" to "We All Live on Twinkies and Caffeine." The lyrics described how the students, who thought they were going to study law, instead found themselves subjected to various forms of mind control, including sleep deprivation, regimentation, and mass hypnosis. As the song ended they marched through a cleverly designed partition in the center of the darkened stage. They entered the partition wearing blue jeans, college T-shirts, sneakers, and other emblems of youth, freedom, and fun. The students—actually, other chorus members entering the partition from behind, out of sight of the audience—emerged four abreast in identical blue pinstriped suits, white button-down shirts, and red ties. Their expressions were somber, their eyes blank. At the side of the stage, Dean Stronglove rubbed his hands in glee over the rapid transformation.

The plot of *Doctor Stronglove* centered on the one student who entered his third year at the Stronglove Clinic still refusing to practice corporate law. He was interested only in doing child advocacy work, much to the horror of the staff psychiatrists, who could not figure out where they had gone wrong with him. Students playing Aaron Mountain and Murray Frobisher sang "I'm Gonna Wash That Thought Right Out of His Brain" and "You've Got Us Under Your Skin." The recalcitrant student turned down inducements to "go corporate" including twenty-five thousand dollars in cash, memberships at the most exclusive discos and private clubs in the city, a BMW, and two weeks in Acapulco with Vanna White. Doctor Stronglove decided that this was a case for the dreaded German psychiatric specialist, Doctor Clanford Slapp, currently Visiting Lecturer in Torture and Student Abuse at the University of Siberia Law School. A third-year student who bore a remarkable resemblance to McKinley's Contracts professor, right down to Clapp's trademark nose, sang, to the tune of "I've Got a Little List," from Gilbert and Sullivan's *Mikado,* a number called "I've Got a Little Chart." He proceeded to depict on a specially constructed blackboard covering half the stage "the world's most complicated contracts case," which Doctor Slapp claimed could bring any law student to his knees. So dense and complex was Doctor Slapp's creation that the student's mind finally snapped. He accepted an offer from a New York firm to practice employee benefits law, perhaps the dullest specialty imaginable, for a starting salary of eighty thousand dollars a year.

As Doctor Stronglove helped the convert into his blue pinstripes, the new Wall Street lawyer sang the show's finale. He announced first that he was dedicating the song to the psychiatrists of the Stronglove Clinic, and especially to Doctor Slapp, "who made me into the spineless jellyfish that you see before you." The song was to the tune of "My Way," and the first and last stanzas went like this:

> And now, the end is near
> And I approach my last semester.
> Three years are gone—one thing I fear—
> They've turned my brain to polyester. . . .

> Did I sell out? I have no doubt.
> Now I'll go climb the corporate stairway.

My mind is numb, I feel so dumb—
I did it their way.

The song, which brought down the house, was followed by an equally successful encore: the entire cast and chorus singing Madonna's "Material Girl." None of the words were changed. It received a standing ovation.

Katrina Walfish's role in all of this came late in the first act. She played, ironically enough, Nurse Rebecca Jeopardy, and she appeared in a white lab coat, a stethoscope around her neck, and a clipboard in her hand. Although she was Doctor Stronglove's chief nurse, she did a brisk business in smuggling patients out of the clinic and into deprogramming centers sponsored by the Legal Aid Society. When Doctor Stronglove asked her how the patients were progressing, though, she answered with pride that the Stronglove Clinic was a success. Every graduate from the previous spring was practicing corporate law in Manhattan. She performed a song in which she read from her clipboard, giving one sentence from the students' application essays and then announcing what firm they had joined. The song was called "How Do You Think You'll Help the Poor from Behind Your Desk at Cravath, Swaine and Moore?" Lyrics included lines like: "What'll you do for welfare mothers when you're making a living at Coudert Brothers?" and "That our prisons and jails are in a jumble/Is news to the folks at Finley, Kumble."

Katrina, who wrote the song, insisted on rehearsing it alone with the four-piece combo that accompanied her. No one else knew the contents of the lyrics, not even Rebecca Shepard. At the first performance, when Katrina completed the song, she and the student portraying Doctor Stronglove stood waiting for applause. It never came. Most of the students in the audience were convinced that Katrina had sneaked into the admissions office files and had stolen *their own* application essays. The humor was simply too close to home for the law students watching the performance, many of whom harbored some sense of guilt over entering law school with the idea of saving society from itself and leaving law school to join corporate America. After considerable debate, Katrina's number was dropped from the three remaining performances. It was simply too depressing.

In addition to her short-lived performance as Nurse Jeopardy, Katrina made another bit of McKinley history by introducing to the law school a welcome innovation she borrowed from students at Northwestern Law School in Chicago. She called it the McKinley Bar Review, and it was sponsored by the Women's Law Caucus. Every Thursday night during the school year, from fifty to eighty McKinley students would venture from the campus and "review" a different bar. Katrina, who did all the advance work herself, negotiated reduced prices, private rooms, and the hiring of disk jockeys for the entertainment of the McKinley students. Occasionally, some faculty members, most notably Tony Sloop, Rebecca Shepard, Bob Stanger, and Ronald Blotchett, attended Bar Review. Tony Sloop counted many friends among the McKinley student body and was said to be dating a student from his Civil Procedure class. For Stanger, Bar Review was another aspect of his "think young, stay young" program, and it afforded him the opportunity to try out his brand-new blue jeans. He usually left before eleven-thirty. Blotchett used Bar Review as a chance to hit on those attractive McKinley students who had not chosen to apply for clerkships, especially the first-years.

Katrina Walfish prided herself on being at the center of whatever was happening at the law school, academically or otherwise. She knew so many students, professors, and staff people that little happened at McKinley without her knowledge. Katrina understood that the timely use of knowledge was power in an institution like McKinley. By one o'clock on the day after the appointment of Rebecca Shepard's tenure committee, Katrina knew exactly which professors had been chosen. She was also aware that Sanford Clapp would never tolerate a student attempting to influence his decision. Katrina did not know Tom Culpepper well enough to try to lean on him. This left Murray Frobisher.

Katrina was naive about few things in life. The previous year, Katrina had attended Frobisher's Criminal Law class, but only sporadically. The experience led her to believe that she could not change Murray's thinking about Rebecca, but she hoped that she could at least understand it better. "Know your enemy" had long been her philosophy. That Rebecca Shepard might not have perceived it as being in her best interest to have Katrina Walfish agitating on her behalf never crossed Katrina's mind. Rebecca's struggle is my struggle, Katrina believed. Not trying to help was unthinkable. Now, at one-fifteen on the second day of October, still heady with her triumph over Ronald Blotchett earlier in the day, she approached Murray Frobisher's office door, hesitated, walked halfway down the corridor, stopped, turned around, walked back, and knocked twice.

"Sanford?" Frobisher's voice called. "Is that you?"

Katrina opened the door. Frobisher, seated behind his desk, tie loosened and collar unbuttoned, looked perplexed. "Where's Sanford?" he asked. "He and I are supposed to meet with Culpepper about Rebecca Shepard. You're Sanford's new secretary, aren't you?"

"My name is Katrina Walfish," she said, controlling herself. "I go to law school here. I was in your Criminal Law class last semester."

Frobisher looked her over. "You didn't show up too often, did you?" he asked.

"About as often as you did," she said, taking a seat and crossing her legs. "Nice tapes," she added, looking at the Patton Pictures cassettes.

He gave a little laugh. "You weren't supposed to see those," he said. Frobisher seemed pleased by her visit. Normally he chased students from his office with a "Not now, I'm in a hurry. Can you come back in an hour?" Of course, they never did.

"Oh, yeah, last semester," said Frobisher, remembering. "I was doing that big cocaine racketeering trial. I guess I wasn't around much. That was one of the classes I taught by videotape."

"That's why I never came," said Katrina. "If I want to watch TV I can stay home and watch *Donahue*. At least that way I can learn something. I always wanted to ask you how you could represent those people. Your clients were drug smugglers, extortionists, murderers—"

"How could I *not* represent them?" Frobisher interrupted.

He glanced at a framed letter from a former client who had stolen two million dollars from the City of New York. The letter, written on state prison stationery, read as follows: "Three to five for what I did is a miracle. I can never thank you enough."

"First," Frobisher explained, "they pay in advance, and in cash. Second, you get them anything less than death by lethal injection and they think you're the greatest lawyer since Perry Mason. And third," he said, fixing his eyes on Katrina, *"any* jerk can get an *innocent* man off. What do *you* want?"

"I want to know why you're so opposed to Rebecca Shepard getting tenure." Katrina, like Murray, did not mince words.

"What did she do, hire lobbyists?" Frobisher asked. "How come you're talking to me about it? Go ask the Dean."

"My spies on the faculty tell me you're leading the charge against Rebecca. I just want to know why."

"Since when do students have spies on the faculty?" Frobisher asked.

"Never mind," said Katrina, putting both hands on his desk. "Look, Professor Frobisher, I'm not just speaking for myself. I'm speaking for the entire Women's Law Caucus. We represent half the student body. Rebecca Shepard is one of the finest teachers on the faculty. She's got every credential a law professor could possibly have. How can you justify turning her down?"

Frobisher put up his hands. "Look, on paper I agree with you. But—"

"But what?" Katrina interrupted.

"But there are certain, you know, *intangibles*."

"Intangibles? Like what? Breasts? Ovaries?"

"Please," said Frobisher, looking pained. "Let's not get technical. It has nothing to do with her being a woman, if that's what you're implying."

"I'm not implying," said Katrina. "I'm *accusing*. There's a difference."

Frobisher made a sour face. "I don't owe students explanations of what I do as a member of the faculty, okay?" Suddenly his expression changed. "On the other hand, you happen to have one hell of a nerve coming in here and trying to push me around, and I like that."

"Oh," said Katrina, not knowing how to react.

Frobisher shrugged. "What can I say?" he continued. "Rebecca's a perfectly nice woman. I happen to like her as a person. Just the other day I was thinking about inviting her to lunch."

"It's about time," said Katrina. "She's only been here four years."

"Okay, so maybe I haven't extended myself—"

"Extended yourself? You don't even say hello to her in the hallways."

"Aw, that's no big deal," said Frobisher. "There are a lot of people I like I never say hello to. Anyway, how would you know about something like that? Does she tell you people everything? Look, you're an intelligent person, anyone can see that. What did I give you in Criminal Law?"

"An A."

"There, you see?" said Frobisher, leaning back and putting his hands behind his head. "You're very bright, but you don't understand the dynamics of a law faculty."

"Sure I do," said Katrina. "It's like the dynamics of a street gang. No new members who aren't exactly like yourselves, and anyone who gets in your way you cut to pieces."

"You're not being fair," said Frobisher. "All right, maybe we're not the nicest bunch of people. What matters is that we have a certain degree of cohesiveness that allows the law school to move forward. It's a delicate balance, as Dean Strong always says. And giving Rebecca tenure would knock over our little applecart, okay?"

Katrina bit her lip. She had expected that the discussion would go badly. She did not anticipate that it would be over practically before it started.

"Come on, cheer up," said Frobisher. "I know how crazy you girls are about Rebecca. It's not her gender that I'm opposed to. It's her ideas. She wants to turn the place upside down. If she were a man I would still be opposed to her."

"I don't know," said Katrina. "I thought if I came and talked to you, maybe you'd listen to reason."

Frobisher laughed. "I listen to threats. I listen to blackmail. But I never listen to reason."

Katrina, dejected, stood to leave. "I want to hate your guts so much," she said. "But I can't."

"Why is that?" Frobisher asked. "My good looks? My animal charm?"

"Don't be silly," said Katrina. She walked toward the door. Her tone betrayed resignation. "It's because if I were in your position, I'd probably be doing the same thing. If I see Sanford, I'll tell him you're looking for him."

"Thank you," said Frobisher, surprised. He watched her leave. "I like her," he said to himself.

THIRTEEN

Rebecca Shepard managed to create a sense of intimacy with her students while revealing virtually nothing about herself. In conversation and in class she volunteered little about her past or private life. Students who visited Rebecca in her office often unburdened themselves of all manner of personal problems, including conflicts with classmates, roommates, other professors, lovers, parents, and landlords. She listened with patience and sympathy. When asked, she gave advice. Students came away feeling that they had made a close and abiding friend. While Rebecca's concern was genuine, so was her need to keep some distance—her empathy extended only so far. Those few students sensitive to the emotional coolness that underlay her concern resented it. They wanted *all* of her, but this simply was not possible. No one can be intimate with sixty to eighty new faces a year.

We often reveal details about ourselves on the basis of an unspoken bargain—we expect that the listener will respond in equally intimate terms, and we feel cheated when they do not. A few of the students who told Rebecca exactly why their relationships were breaking down, or why they could not get along with their parents, were disappointed when Rebecca did not respond with details about herself. Such students, though, were a minority. Most visitors to her were grateful for the time and help she gave. Since they did not seek to learn about Rebecca's life, they assumed, not entirely correctly, that the intimacy between Rebecca and themselves flowed both ways. They would have been surprised to learn how little they really knew her.

Rebecca's silence about herself was partly a function of her upbringing. In her parents' home such things were rarely discussed. Rebecca's father was a leading English appellate judge and legal scholar. He lectured frequently in Britain and abroad. While still a child, Rebecca often accompanied her father to his speaking engagements or to court. She would stand in the back, a little girl with long, braided hair and a contemplative expression, absorbing her father's speaking style, if not the content of his words. She decided early that one day she would be the one on the podium, or the bench. Students who took the time to look up Rebecca's father in the law school library card catalog would find more than twenty books to his credit in jurisprudence and law and psychiatry, his primary fields of interest. Rebecca's parents attended Oxford in the early 1950s. Rebecca's mother was American. She came to Oxford to study the poetry of John Milton. On a whim she joined the Oxford Debates Union, where she was extremely successful, and where she met Rebecca's father. At Oxford, Rebecca's mother began a lifelong active association with the Conservative Party. Policy and fund-raising meetings often took place in Rebecca's parents' home, under the young Rebecca's watchful eye.

Rebecca was the older of two children (her brother, whom she saw once or twice a year, was a moderately successful abstract artist in London). She grew up in a world of adults and high expectations. These expectations, although never stated explicitly, revolved around the idea of her taking up the law. Her early exposure to her father's public speaking made the study of law a certainty, although it surprised and disappointed her parents that she attended both college and law school in the States. The move made perfect sense, from Rebecca's point of view. It allowed her a bit of breathing room between herself and the worlds of English law and politics, where everyone who mattered had known her since she was a child and therefore had found it difficult to think of her as anything else. At the same time, it gave her the chance to carry on the family tradition while breaking new ground. Rebecca's maternal grandfather had practiced law in Boston for fifty years, and an ancestor on her father's side was said to have been a legal adviser to Cromwell. Her parents were proud of Rebecca's achievements—first in her law class, editor of the *Law Review,* associate at Holyoke and Knout, and a member of the McKinley faculty. Their approval was more tacit than expressed, though. Worse still, from Rebecca's point of view, they expected her to receive tenure as a matter of course. She had never attempted to explain the McKinley faculty politics to them, although they certainly would have understood.

Other members of the McKinley faculty were far less reticent about themselves. Many took considerable amounts of class time to talk about their private lives, their achievements, how they spent the weekend, or how little they thought of certain, or all, of their colleagues. Murray Frobisher once devoted an entire hour to describing in vivid detail a subway accident that morning from which he had escaped uninjured and with four new clients. A favorite discussion topic among a few of the more entrepreneurially minded professors was their outside consulting or trial work. Sanford Clapp was among the worst offenders in this regard. Whenever he canceled a Monday class—it happened three or four times a semester—his students knew that he would spend the first twenty or thirty minutes on Tuesday on a detailed analysis of his latest trip to some distant city where he lectured on Contracts, humbly accepted an award, or most frequently, offered advice, at very high hourly rates, to business people or practicing attorneys. (Why successful business people turn to individuals with virtually no experience outside the classroom was a mystery the solution of which was of no interest to Sanford.)

Clapp would inform his students of his first-class airplane tickets, luxurious accommodations, and fine meals. He would describe in wickedly unflattering terms the important people who sought his counsel, and he would repeat the jokes and stories they told over Jack Daniel's and cigars. He happened to be an excellent raconteur, and many students recorded his stories in the margins of their notebooks for later retelling to family and friends. It was hard, though, for most students to listen to Clapp's adventures without feeling some measure of envy. The lives of first-year law students are bounded by the classroom, the library, the dormitory, and the cafeteria. If they have any friends in the city where they have chosen (or where they have been accepted) to study law, they rarely have the time to see them. Law students, to the chagrin of their friends and loved ones, seldom can make plans in advance, because of the size and unpredictability of their work load. Just as policemen fraternize mainly with other policemen, because people outside the fraternity cannot fully understand the attendant stresses and schedules, so law students tend to see no one other than fellow law students. When they meet people, at parties, for example, who do things other than study law, those others seem as exotic as men from Mars.

There was something unsettling, therefore, in hearing Clapp, or any other professor, recount tales of travel, honor, pleasure, and financial reward when the students themselves went nowhere but to the library most nights, possessed little that distinguished themselves from their two hundred classmates, lived with little time for escape from the twin grinds of briefing cases and attending tedious lectures, and, rather than earning money for their pains, plunged further and further into debt. Law students could not fail to be impressed, however, that the man who stood before them and with whom they developed a false sense of intimacy—simply because of their repeated contact with him—was so much in demand as guest expert. Implicit in all this was the promise that doing well in Clapp's class was the first step to glory, respect, first-class (or at least business-class) air travel, and high income. In a perverse sort of way, Clapp's tales of his extracurricular activities spurred students to work even harder. Had he known, he would have been delighted, and he would have told the students even more.

Rebecca, who also spoke and consulted frequently in her field of Securities Law, neither shuffled her class schedule to accommodate her clientele, nor did she discuss such matters in class. She did not share the view, popular among the McKinley faculty, that students would be interested in whatever a professor had to say. A few of the more egregious examples: One tax professor at McKinley, recently retired, spent three class hours every semester examining in painful detail an elaborate, but long-dead, provision of the Internal Revenue Code relating to the amortization of coal, because he once spent two years as counsel to a mining company. Ronald Blotchett, who taught the upper-level course on the federal court system until he dumped it onto Tony Sloop, devoted a full two weeks every term to his own lengthy, obtuse, and outdated article on the concept of diversity jurisdiction in the federal courts that the *Harvard Law Review* had published six years earlier, presumably in a fit of weakness.

Aaron Mountain, who never got over his defeat in Moot Court as a law student, read from yellowing notes for his students his entire twenty-minute argument. Then, in virtually the same words every year, he would vent his anger at the panel of three judges, two of whom were long dead, and all of whom, inexplicably, had failed to see things his way. Bob Stanger turned an average of one out of five Corporations classes into denunciations of the raiders who displaced him atop the Blanchard's department store chain. In short, most McKinley professors used their class time to lick old wounds, relive old triumphs, and do everything except teach. Rebecca was aware of this practice, both from her own days as a law student and from reports of McKinley students, whom she advised to do what she used to do—sit in the back, keep a novel on one's lap, and when the lecture strayed from the subject matter, read.

Rebecca Shepard rarely veered from her subject matter, because she found it so interesting. She was pleased with the combination of courses she taught. Torts and Securities Regulation complemented each other well, she believed. As a law student, Rebecca enjoyed her course in Torts more than any other first-year class, and she made it clear when she came to McKinley that her heart was in teaching that subject. Torts is essentially the study of how the legal system intervenes after people suffer accidents or indignities or after they or their property are otherwise damaged. Some examples: An intruder in a barn finds himself shot in the knees by a spring-gun that fires automatically when the door is opened. A three-year-old climbs into an automobile and pulls the emergency brake. The car rolls into traffic and causes an accident. Two hunters fire shotguns in the direction of a third hunter, wounding him in

the shoulder—but no one can tell which hunter fired the er-
rant shot. A woman treated with the drug DES during her
pregnancy develops cancer twenty years later traceable to the
drug. A respected Chicago attorney finds his name and reputation smeared in a radical newspaper. All these are cases from
a typical first-year Torts class.

The questions these cases raise are endless. Do individuals
have the right to protect their property by causing serious in-
jury, or death, to trespassers? Does society make parents fi-
nancially responsible for the actions of their young children,
or is it simply bad luck for the victims of a car crash that the
three-year-old set in motion? How does a court determine lia-
bility when the victim cannot tell which of several people
caused the harm? How much time passes before a drug company is no longer liable for the side effects of a drug? What if
the disease, like cancer, or asbestosis, takes twenty years to
reveal itself? Rebecca loved to teach Torts because of the nature of the questions the cases posed. The study of Torts, she
told her students, embraces law, psychology, medicine, the
media, and above all, chance. No sane person seeks to cause,
or be the victim of, a tort. These things simply happen to
people, and Torts was all about individuals and society coping
with random misfortune.

Securities Regulation, at first glance, seems completely
unlike Torts. Securities Law centers on large corporations and
high finance. The field is young, compared to Torts, the roots
of which trace back to the Bible. Federal regulation of financial markets began only in the 1930s. Securities Law casebooks suggest that the field is concerned primarily with the
free flow of information. Rebecca believed, though, that to
emphasize the disclosure rules or even the entire federal regu-
latory system was to miss the point. She believed that Securities Law, like Torts, was really about people. Growing up in
London, Rebecca never heard her parents—or any other
adults—mention money, except in the context of Conservative Party affairs. Business and finance were not proper topics
for the better sort of people. In America, no such restraints
applied. Rebecca, frankly, found the business world a compel-
ling subject for study.

If finance is the practice of taking large, if usually prudent, risks, then the study of finance is the study of individuals with enough courage to take such risks. Rebecca believed that these people were a remarkable breed, and she tried hard to make them come alive for her students. She invited many big names to her Securities classes—traders, arbitrageurs, analysts, and top executives. In her seminars on Insider Trading and Wall Street Today, Rebecca offered profiles on the people her students would encounter in their law practices as clients and as opponents. In addition to teaching the mechanics of compliance with securities laws, she taught her students to appreciate the human side of finance and not to fear it. She took pains to tell her class that Securities Law, although one of the most profitable and prestigious areas of practice, was, for attorneys in their first few years out of law school, duller than anything they could imagine. Securities lawyers, she told her students, were prisoners of paper. Dozens and sometimes hundreds of documents were necessary to provide proof that a given transaction had been conducted properly. While the business people took the risks and reaped the rewards, the lawyers had the unending task of cleaning up after their clients—filling out and filing away page after painstakingly proofread page. Rebecca told her students that unless they mastered the business and corporate finance aspects of securities transactions, they would be condemned forever to producing paper that, in the words of one commentator, simply "transfers wealth from one old bald, fat man to another old bald, fat man." The best of Rebecca's students took her warning seriously and cross-registered at the McKinley Business School in all manner of finance and accounting classes. After graduation, they did quite well for themselves.

As a law student, Rebecca wondered why Securities professors placed so much importance on the practical aspects of Securities Law, while Torts professors entirely ignored the practical side of their specialty. She wondered why Torts students never learned how to file lawsuits on behalf of injured clients, select juries, or try cases. Rebecca found an answer in a study of the Chicago bar, and she presented the study's findings to her classes each semester. According to the study, there were two distinct "hemispheres" of lawyers. Top-ranked, nationally known law schools, like Harvard, Yale, and

McKinley, fed the ranks of the so-called upper hemisphere of lawyers, who worked in large firms, represented important corporations and wealthy individuals and families, and handled matters ranging from antitrust and Securities Law to complex litigation and tax planning. These lawyers were well paid, and they ran all of the important committees of the local bar association.

The so-called lower hemisphere was home to lawyers who attended less prestigious or "local" law schools. They practiced alone or in small firms. As a rule, they made less money than their upper-hemisphere counterparts. They represented small companies and middle-class and poor individuals. They handled lawsuits over auto accidents, medical malpractice cases, divorces, and workman's compensation claims. Some of their cases might blossom forth into the sort of court decisions that McKinley students one day might study with wonder and amusement. The lower-hemisphere lawyers chaired no committees of the local bar association.

Rebecca concluded that graduates of prestigious law schools learned nothing about the practical side of Torts because such cases, they somehow came to believe, were beneath them. The money involved rarely would cover their high hourly rates; the problems, they believed, were too simple to be interesting. Rebecca sensed that admission to one hemisphere or the other had less to do with merit than with the socioeconomic status of the parents of the student. She also believed that the quality of education at the prestigious law schools varied little from that of the local law schools. Rebecca wanted nothing more than to find a way to end the dual-hemisphere world of lawyers. She knew it would be an impossible task, and, after all, she had already set out to redesign legal education. Rebecca was of the opinion that one revolution at a time was enough for any woman.

FOURTEEN

Later that afternoon, Robert Stanger stuck his head through the doorway of Aaron Mountain's office. "Coming to the Professor of the Year reception?" he asked.

"Is it four-thirty already?" Mountain asked, not even looking up from an old copy of the *McKinley Law Review* on his lap.

"On the nose."

"Look, Bob, this isn't the corporate world. We don't have to be there at precisely the time the reception begins."

Stanger entered and sat down opposite Aaron Mountain, who seemed unusually morose. Stanger thought that Mountain's depression was related to losing the Professor of the Year to Rebecca Shepard and Tom Culpepper.

"Cheer up, Aaron, I'm sure you'll win next time."

"Win what?"

"Professor of the Year. You know, that award."

"I wasn't even thinking of that," said Aaron Mountain.

"Why do you look so glum, then?"

"It's the *Law Review*," he said, tossing his copy into the trash. "I find it absolutely idiotic that all but a handful of the most prestigious law publications in the country are run by students. They couldn't tell horseshit from the Hope Diamond."

"That's strong talk, Aaron," said Stanger, who, after a career as a partner in a top law firm and president of Blanchard's department stores, also felt it odd that a group of third-year law school students should have total control over what he, and what all other law professors, were allowed to publish. Mountain was voicing a frustration shared by professors at nearly every law school. With the exception of half a dozen or so journals, mostly at the University of Chicago, students edited every important law publication in the country, a situation that obtains in law and in no other discipline.

Law reviews are monthly or quarterly journals produced by students. They contain long, scholarly articles about legal topics written by professors, and short pieces, called case notes, about important recent decisions, written by the students themselves. Judges frequently cite law review articles as justifications for ground-breaking decisions. Law professors judge one another in part on the quality and quantity of law review articles they publish. Students admitted to law reviews pay a high cost in tedium for the glory of belonging. A law review member must commit endless hours every week to the checking of references and case citations in professors' articles, answering the telephone, or performing other kinds of equally mindless clerical work. Law review members neither complain about the dullness of their tasks nor entertain any notion of reducing the burden for next year's staff. "If I had to go through this, so will you" is the message. This message is repeated endlessly in a thousand guises in both the study and practice of law.

"Did the *McKinley Law Review* turn down an article you wrote?" asked Stanger.

"Yes, the *McKinley Law Review* turned down an article I wrote," Mountain said, mimicking his guest's gravelly voice. "And so did the *Harvard Law Review,* and the *Yale Law Journal,* and Stanford, and Berkeley, and eight other law reviews. And do you know *why* they turned it down?"

"Why is that, Aaron?" Stanger asked, sorry now that he had not gone directly from his office to the reception.

"Because it was *too subtle.* The law review editors could not understand it. My ideas were over their heads."

Stanger knew the whispers about Mountain—that he was offered tenure only because they needed to give tenure to someone that year, and the only alternative was Dara Sample, and that Mountain's enthusiasm for the quality of his own legal writing, to put it gently, was misplaced.

"Your article was too subtle for the staffs of a dozen top law reviews?" Stanger repeated, trying to understand. "The best law students in the country?"

"Idiots," said Mountain. "All of them. What burns me up most is the McKinley students saying no. There ought to be some sort of home-court advantage for tenured faculty who write articles for the law review of their school. And what does the *McKinley Law Review* publish instead of my piece?"

"Tell me, Aaron," said Stanger, making a mental note to stop being friendly to Mountain.

"Some horseshit by Rebecca Shepard. I nearly bust a gut in the Committee of Ten meeting when I heard that. She doesn't even have tenure, and the *McKinley Law Review* editors gave her article priority over mine."

"My spies on the *Law Review* tell me that the Shepard piece is pretty good," said Stanger gently.

"My spies tell me the same thing, but that's not the point," said Mountain. "It's the principle of the thing. Why should the *Law Review* publish her article over mine, just because it's better?"

Stanger did not know how to respond. Then he remembered the reception. "Shouldn't we be heading toward the Thorne Lounge, Aaron? You may not feel like congratulating Rebecca, but Tom Culpepper will be terribly hurt if we all don't show up."

"I suppose you're right, Bob," he said, standing up slowly. "Let's go to the party. I'll deal with those *Law Review* idiots in the morning."

The party was in full swing by the time Stanger and Mountain arrived, although it might be more accurate to say that two separate celebrations were gathering steam in the room named for the late Dean of the law school. Tom Culpepper, standing under a portrait of Dean Thorne and enjoying a sherry, was accepting congratulations from the men of the McKinley faculty and from a number of his current and former students who had taken an hour or two from their law practices to honor their old mentor. Across the floor, the members of the Women's Caucus crowded around Rebecca

Shepard, overjoyed that one of their own had scaled the heights.

The Professor of the Year award was an innovation of Dean Strong's. He thought that a sense of competition might improve the caliber of teaching at McKinley. Instead, the balloting each year created massive embarrassment for the full-time McKinley faculty, because the students invariably gave the award to adjunct professors—those who worked full-time as a lawyer or judge and who came to McKinley twice or three times a week to offer courses in their specialties. Karen Conner, Adjunct Professor of Wills and lately the object of Ronald Blotchett's attentions, had won last year. The year before it went to Jonathan Cook, a civil rights lawyer, who taught his specialty three mornings a week. Speculation over the possible retirement of Tom Culpepper was largely responsible for his sharing in the award this time around. Rebecca's strong standing with the Women's Law Caucus helped her to a tie with Culpepper.

Katrina Walfish was grinning broadly as she stood at her professor's side; Rebecca's victory is my victory, she thought. Katrina had led the Women's Law Caucus drive to have Rebecca chosen as Professor of the Year the week before her tenure decision. If the Caucus had hoped to embarrass the McKinley faculty into giving Rebecca tenure, they would have had only to overhear the male faculty members surrounding Culpepper to learn that they had a long way to go.

"This is going to make it even harder to reject Rebecca," said Sanford Clapp to Murray Frobisher.

"Don't worry," said Frobisher. "We'll find a way. We don't give tenure on the basis of popularity contests."

"My spies on the *Law Review* tell me that Shepard's piece is pretty good," Clapp said.

"That's what my spies told me," said Stanger. "And that's what Mountain's spies told him."

"Who are your spies?" Frobisher asked Stanger. "I wonder if we have the same spies."

"Look at the way the women students crowd around her," said Clapp. "You'd think she was giving something away."

"I hear she *is* giving it away," said Mountain, "and to a student."

"No," said Clapp, his eyes narrowing. "Who's she sleeping with?"

"I hear it's Daniel Conway. The one the students call the Saint."

Although Rebecca stood at some distance from the cabal of law professors, she caught the mention of her boyfriend's nickname. Suddenly she remembered that she was to have met him at her place at five o'clock, and now it was nearing six. The Professor of the Year reception was still going strong, and the jubilant members of the Women's Law Caucus continued to surround her, making an early exit discourteous and, as a practical matter, impossible.

"I'll be right back," she said, and she ran down the corridor to the pay telephone near the law school's front door. Rebecca fumbled for the correct change and called her home. Her heart sank as the Saint failed to answer. He must have left early for the airport, she thought. He must think I stood him up.

A dejected Rebecca returned to the party, uninterested now in the conversation of the women students. To Rebecca's horror, Katrina announced that the Women's Law Caucus was sponsoring a potluck dinner for Rebecca immediately after the reception. Rebecca wanted only to find a hole in the floor of the Thorne Lounge and crawl in. When she and the Saint had scheduled their assignation for five o'clock, she had completely forgotten about the Professor of the Year reception. I hope Saint won't hate me for this, she thought.

Rebecca finally regained her composure and invited Katrina to step with her out of earshot of the other students.

"Katrina," Rebecca lied, "I'm extremely grateful for your putting together the potluck supper, but I've got dinner plans of my own this evening and I really can't stay."

Katrina felt betrayed. "But we were counting on you! We feel as though you owe it to us to be there. We're your number-one constituency."

"That may be true, but don't you think you could have checked with me first? Doesn't it ever occur to you that I have a life of my own?" Why am I coming down so hard on Katrina, Rebecca asked herself.

"Rebecca, I'm sorry but I just thought you'd want to celebrate with us." The idea that Rebecca might not want to attend the dinner made no sense to Katrina.

Rebecca finally lost her temper. "This isn't the first time this has happened! You and the other students just assume I've got nothing better to do than spend all my time with you! My time is so limited as it is and I don't like to be told that I'm expected to be someplace. Do you understand?" Why am I doing this? Rebecca asked herself. I've got a right to be upset, but Katrina and the women students are practically my only allies here.

Katrina was crushed. "Does this mean you're not coming to the supper?"

"That's right." Rebecca stood there, arms folded, hating herself for standing up to Katrina.

"But Rebecca, you're our faculty adviser, and how do you think it's going to look for me when I have to go tell the women that you won't even come to our dinner?" Katrina was near tears.

Here I go again, thought Rebecca.

"Wait a minute, Katrina," she said, sighing. "Of course I'll come to the dinner. I'm just upset about something else. It's got nothing to do with you." She closed her eyes and brushed back her hair. "I'm sorry I spoke the way I did."

"I really can't figure you out sometimes," said Katrina, looking quizzically at her complicated mentor. "Well, as long as you're coming to the dinner I guess it doesn't matter."

"Shall we go back to the party?" asked Rebecca.

"Let's."

All through the remainder of the reception and the potluck dinner that followed, Rebecca could think only of the Saint. When the dinner ended around nine-thirty she rushed home, hoping to find a note. It was waiting for her propped up against the telephone. "I suppose something urgent must have come up at the law school. Oh, well. Am taking a cold shower instead. Wish me luck at the interviews. I love you. Saint."

Thank goodness he understands, thought Rebecca, who

undressed and prepared for bed. On the night table were the page proofs of her *Law Review* article. Once under the covers, she picked them up and read through them again. When she finished she put out the light, but despite her fatigue, sleep eluded her. "I can't wait until this tenure business is over with," she said aloud. "I wish the Saint were here." At length she drifted off.

WEDNESDAY, OCTOBER 3

FIFTEEN

Dean Edward Strong rarely spent a lunch hour alone. Midday, he found, was the best time to keep in touch with his various law school constituencies. If the athletic Dean was not out running with students by the river or playing racquetball with Robert Stanger or Sanford Clapp, he would be enjoying lunch with University trustees, potential donors, influential partners from the downtown firms, or, on occasion, a senator or even a cabinet member. The Dean's influence extended far beyond the confines of the law school. His twice-weekly column about law, "Strong Opinions," appeared in over two hundred newspapers across the country. He also taped in his office a weekly three-minute spot about law for the nationwide morning show, *Wake Up, America*. Whenever the Supreme Court handed down an important decision, it was to McKinley's Dean that the media turned for an interpretation. In short, Dean Strong was one of those handful of law professors whose names the media had made into virtual household words.

While many of Dean Strong's luncheon partners thought they were currying favor with the rising young academic, the truth was actually the other way round. Most law professors viewed a deanship as the end of the road, a prestigious conclusion to a successful career in the law. Dean Strong, appointed while only thirty-four, viewed his position as a stepping-stone to greater things. To reach his goal, the Dean knew, he would need all the well-placed friends he could find. Most law professors and judges viewed elevation to the Supreme Court as a matter of chance. Dean Edward Strong viewed it purely as a matter of time.

The Dean had star quality. He knew it, and so did all those who came in contact with him. His angular six-foot frame, thoughtful brown eyes, full head of dark hair, and endless supply of stories from his days as a Supreme Court clerk, assistant Attorney General, and legal adviser to the American Embassy in Paris all reinforced a sense of inevitability about a Senator Strong, a Mr. Justice Strong, and perhaps even (dare he think it?) President Strong.

Students were fascinated with the private and public lives of the unmarried Dean whose youthful appearance and love of midday exercise made them feel that he was one of their own. They whispered about his cars (two BMW sedans), his duplex (he signed the lease a month before the building went co-op), and his nights on the town, the details of which frequently found their way onto the gossip pages.

Dean Strong taught Evidence to a sea of McKinley students every year despite the demands of his deanship, his newspaper columns, his television appearances, and, of course, his heavy lunch schedule. The Dean had won his academic reputation six years ago with his treatise on Evidence, but, to his regret, he no longer found the time to keep up with recent developments in the field. His lectures, therefore, blended together slightly out-of-date material from unrevised notes along with stories about himself and other famous people in Washington and Paris. The students never minded, though. They merely watched him with admiration, or envy, or both, and wondered how they might hitch their wagons to his rapidly rising star.

Today there would be no racquetball, no running, no lunch with a senator. Dean Strong had cleared his calendar so that he could devote himself to solving his Rebecca Shepard dilemma. If he recommended to the trustees that she receive tenure, he might face an insurrection among the faculty. If she was denied tenure, the law school would incur negative publicity for violating the terms of the court-ordered consent agreement. Either result meant potentially disastrous consequences for the ambitious Dean's career.

His secretary had been buzzing for almost a full minute. Dean Strong had not heard.

"Ms. Kennecutt, I thought I told you I didn't want to be disturbed."

"Professor Frobisher to see you, sir. He says it's urgent."

Murray's no alarmist, the Dean said to himself. I wonder what he wants. "Send him in," he told his secretary.

Frobisher entered, all the color drained from his face. "Bad news, chief," he said, dropping into a chair. "Another suicide."

"No!" The Dean bolted upright. "A student?"

"Yeah. Someone named Susan Garrett. That's number three in six months."

"Do the newspapers know?" Instant damaging publicity, thought the Dean. That's the last thing I need.

"Yeah," said Frobisher. "I heard about it on the radio on the midday report. It's not good, Ed. They talked about how this is the third McKinley first-year student to commit suicide since last spring."

"Could it have been an accident, like pills, or alcohol?"

Frobisher shook his head. "She hanged herself in the dormitory. There's no doubt. It's a suicide."

Strong looked at Frobisher and called his secretary. "Ms. Kennecutt, would you please get out a memo immediately to all faculty members announcing an emergency faculty meeting at four P.M., and that absolutely no one on the faculty or staff is to say anything to the media. All requests for information are to be passed on to me. And if any reporters call, I'm in a meeting and cannot be disturbed. Also, classes are canceled tomorrow and Friday, and there will be a memorial service at nine-thirty tomorrow morning. Could you get that out to everyone—students and faculty. And call the University Health Service and get me Susan Garrett's health records.

"Have you got all that? Thank you. And please, absolutely no disturbances. Unless it's that call from New Haven I've been expecting. Thank you, Ms. Kennecutt."

The Dean and Frobisher sat silently, unable to fathom the wave of suicides. The buzzer sounded—it was the Dean's secretary again.

"Ms. Kennecutt, I thought I told you no calls." The Dean listened intently. "Put him on," he said.

"It's Daniel Conway, calling from Washington," said Dean Strong. "He was Garrett's student adviser. He heard about her suicide over the radio and says he might know something about it. I'll put him on the speakerphone so you can hear."

"Dean Strong?" The Saint's voice crackled through the speaker on the desk.

"Yes, Daniel?"

"I just heard about the suicide on the radio. Susan was one of my advisees. I'm sure this is a bad time to call, but I couldn't wait. It's Clapp. He did it. I mean, she hanged herself, but he pushed her over the brink."

The Dean and Frobisher stared at each other.

"Do you know what you're saying, Daniel?" the Dean asked, not taking his eyes off Frobisher.

"Yes, sir, without question. Susan had been having an extremely difficult adjustment to law school. She was a little bit unstable when she arrived. I called her folks to find out about her, and they said that she'd had a nervous breakdown in high school, but that since then she'd been okay. A little sensitive but okay. Her dad was really set on her going to law school. She was keeping up with all of her classes, but she wasn't getting the hang of Contracts. She had Professor Clapp. And he kept on picking on her in class.

"She says he just humiliated her three different times in front of the whole class. She finally went to Rebecca—Professor Shepard—for some tutoring, but even that wasn't helping. Each of the three students who committed suicide was in Clapp's class, and each one told me that he was *humiliating* them in the classroom before they . . . before they—" The Saint's voice broke with emotion. "He's destroying those kids. You've got to stop him."

"Saint, it's Murray Frobisher. Are you sure about all of this?"

"Absolutely sure. I'd swear to it."

"Thank you, Daniel." It was the Dean. His voice had taken on a mechanical quality. "I very much appreciate your honesty and your speed in telling us this. You can be sure that I'll handle it in the proper manner. I'll speak to you when you get back from Washington. Goodbye now."

The Dean disconnected, and Frobisher stood up to leave. "I've got to get back to my office," he said. "Another new client coming in."

The Dean forced a smile. "Above or below the age of sixteen?"

"Above, I think. He's a walk-in. I don't even know his name. I'll see you later. Good luck." Frobisher left the office.

Dean Strong called his secretary. "Ms. Kennecutt, could you please get Rebecca Shepard on the telephone? And please ask Sanford Clapp to come to my office. Immediately."

SIXTEEN

Murray Frobisher returned to his office, shaken not only by the latest suicide but also by Daniel Conway's contention that Sanford Clapp might have played an indirect role in her death and in the deaths of the other two students. It disturbed Frobisher that a student would accuse a professor of causing a student to take her life. At the same time, though, Frobisher admired Conway's courage in speaking up quickly and risking Sanford's wrath. Although Frobisher never discussed it with anyone, there was no love lost between himself and Sanford Clapp. Their mutual discomfort was not merely that of two men who had spent too many years serving at the same institution. Such hidden animosities often exist below the surface in academic faculties, and burn unchecked for years, like fires in coal mines. Frobisher's negative feelings toward Clapp reflected the fact that Frobisher appreciated Dean Strong's leadership at McKinley as much as Clapp resented it.

Frobisher had a sweet deal at the law school, thanks to Dean Strong, and he knew it. A different dean might not have permitted Frobisher to carry a full load of criminal clients while neglecting his teaching and scholarship. Dean Strong permitted Frobisher's use of McKinley as a base of operations for several reasons. First, Frobisher was a "name"—a well-known criminal lawyer and a man well connected with judges, lawyers, and the civil rights and non-profit groups he represented. Frobisher's presence, Dean Strong believed, was "good" for McKinley. Second, the Dean appreciated Murray's insight into the personalities of the McKinley professors with whom Murray had been teaching long before Strong arrived at the law school. Finally, Frobisher shared Dean Strong's vision of a McKinley Law School second to none.

Murray worked almost as hard as the Dean did at making that vision a reality. He had an excellent eye for people, and he could spot talented law professors as easily as he could select juries. For example, he had urged Dean Strong to hire Tony Sloop, on the theory that Tony one day might develop into an expert on Art and the Law, an emerging field, and thus reflect further glory onto McKinley. Frobisher, single-handedly, was in the final stages of negotiating with a managing partner of a leading investment bank the endowment of a new professorship in Law and Banking. Murray was holding out for a contribution of one and a half million dollars to the law school, and he expected to get every penny. Murray, after all, had gotten a criminal charge against the twenty-year-old son of the managing partner in question reduced from "possession of cocaine with intent to distribute" to "driving while intoxicated." A million and a half, Murray reasoned, was a small price to pay to keep that sort of story off the front page of the *New York Post*.

While Clapp professed loyalty to McKinley—in his way, he really did love the law school—Frobisher believed that Sanford, at bottom, was all talk and no action. Worse, Clapp had the habit of harassing the Dean in Committee of Ten meetings and criticizing him in public. Murray knew that Sanford wanted the deanship for himself, and Murray knew that if that day ever came he would have to find himself a new law school. When Frobisher spoke at colleges, as he frequently did, to encourage applications to McKinley, he often found himself having to deny that Sanford Clapp was a difficult man to study under. "No, no, no, you heard wrong," Murray would tell his audience, who invariably started the question-and-answer phase of his appearance with a comment about Clapp. "Sanford's a pussycat," Frobisher would say, the words sticking in his throat. It was one thing, Frobisher concluded, as he rounded the corner between the Dean's office and his own, for Clapp to harass and intimidate. It was another thing altogether for him to drive students over the brink. The suicide wave could easily end up depressing the number of applications, Murray feared, and that would be bad for McKinley. Clapp, he decided, needed to be taught a lesson of some sort.

Waiting impatiently at Murray's office door was Jackson Ward. Murray was in no mood for Jackson. What the hell does he want? Murray asked himself. He must want to talk about Rebecca. He pointed to a large manila envelope atop the pile of papers that Jackson held under one arm.

"Let me guess," said Frobisher, as rudely as he could manage. "You're taking up a collection for Rebecca's going-away present. Sorry, I gave at the office."

"I just need a minute, Murray," said Jackson, accustomed to Murray's combative style.

"A minute's all you'll get," said Frobisher, unlocking the door and motioning Jackson to follow him. "I've got a client coming. Your timing couldn't be worse. What's up?"

Jackson Ward was never comfortable around Murray Frobisher. Jackson admired his dedication to his work but thought his extensive self-promotion unbecoming for a law professor. Moreover, last year Ward had criticized Frobisher in a Committee of Ten meeting for his practice of teaching his Criminal Law class by videotape. Jackson knew that Murray had never forgiven him. He took a seat opposite Murray's desk.

Murray did not even face his visitor. Instead he chose to forage among court papers on a table behind Jackson's back. Jackson ignored the affront and went right to the point. "What's it going to take to get you to give up your opposition to Rebecca's getting tenure?"

Murray stopped foraging. "My weight in gold," he said. "And I weigh two hundred sixteen pounds."

"Seriously, Murray," said Jackson, who knew nothing of the latest suicide.

"I am serious. Look, Jackson, is that what brought you in here? First it's that Walfish girl, and now it's you. Look. You might as well go back to your little ethical ivory tower. I'm sick of Rebecca and I'm getting sick of you."

Jackson controlled his temper. "That's not exactly the sort of collegial response I might have expected from you."

"Look, buddy, I've got a client coming in here in five minutes, I can't find the papers related to his case, the law school is going to hell in a handbasket, and I really don't have time to worry about Rebecca right now. But I can state my position on her getting tenure in terms even you can understand. *Over my dead body.* Was I clear enough? And I think I'm speaking for a majority of the other professors here. I'm certainly speaking for Sanford Clapp. And we're a majority of Rebecca's tenure committee, so that's it. Case closed, okay? Anything else on your mind?"

"Not really," said Jackson. "No harm in asking. I don't think that Rebecca's been properly appreciated around here, and I'd hate to see her. . ."

Ward's voice trailed off as he noticed Randolph Patton's videocassettes on Murray's desk. He picked them up to examine them and saw that they had been resting on a court document entitled *Dara Sample* v. *Trustees of McKinley Law School, Record Sealed by Order of Court.* Ward, holding his breath and reading quickly, noted the date of the document—it was five years old—and also noted that Murray defended McKinley. He put the videotapes down to one side of the court paper.

"You'd hate to see her thrown out of here even though everybody else is sick and tired of her," said Frobisher, completing Jackson's sentence for him. "And I'm sorry I'm such a rotten host, but I've really got to end this conversation. I've just gotten some very distressing news, and my new client will be here any minute. Where the hell are those papers? I'm going to kill Carmen. Nobody could practice law in this pigsty."

Jackson's pulse quickened as he read the cover of the document. He turned to see whether Murray's back was still turned. It was. Jackson slipped the consent decree into the manila envelope.

"I just wanted to see how you feel," he said nervously.

"You saw," said Murray. "Aha! Here it is! *U.S.* versus *Rooney,* that's the ticket. I wonder what *this* clown got arrested for." He finally turned to face Jackson. "No further questions?" he asked.

"None, Murray," said Jackson, a little too quickly. "I'll see you later."

Jackson Ward, deep in thought, departed Frobisher's office, the consent decree safe among copies of his ethics syllabus. He barely noticed Murray's new client brushing past him in the hallway. Murray watched Jackson walk down the hall.

"I honestly like the guy," Murray said to himself, "but he just doesn't know when to quit." And then he looked at the newcomer.

"I know you," he said slowly and emphatically by way of greeting, and he invited the stranger to enter and sit down. "I've seen your face before, haven't I?" he asked. Frobisher had forgotten completely about Susan Garrett and the Saint's accusations.

The man gave a quick smile, taking great pleasure in being recognized.

"Don't tell me who you are," said Frobisher, settling happily into his large desk chair. "I love things like this."

Frobisher examined him closely. He looked to be around thirty. He wore a blue-and-green houndstooth checked jacket that clashed with the green of his pants. His smile revealed a missing incisor on the upper right side. For all his oddness of appearance, there was something familiar about him. Frobisher studied him and finally slammed his hand down on his desk. "Aha! I've got it!" he exclaimed. "You're the guy who tried to kill the President last week! I saw you on the news!"

The stranger grinned and shook his head. "You're close," he said.

"I could have sworn you're the guy, what's his name, Frank Rooney. Loony Rooney. You've got the same name as him. He shot at the President and just missed, and they were holding him for observation in a mental hospital. Well, you look just like him. I hope you're not insulted."

"I *am* Frank Rooney," said the stranger. He pointed to the stack of videotapes on Murray's desk. "I see we share similar tastes in cinema," he added.

"Give me those," said Frobisher, grabbing the cassettes and shoving them into a desk drawer. He glared at his guest.

"You just told me you weren't Rooney, and now you tell me you are. Look, did you shoot the President or didn't you?"

Rooney gave a sly grin. "I didn't shoot the President," he told Frobisher. "I shot *at* the President. There's a very big difference."

"One that you might care to explain? And if you really are Loony Rooney, how'd you get out of the mental hospital?"

"The judge sent me from the hospital back to regular jail, and then my family bailed me out."

"Didn't they set bail at half a million bucks?" Frobisher asked suspiciously.

"I told you, my family put up the money."

My kind of client, thought Frobisher. Maybe I ought to play ball with him for a minute or two.

"Would you mind explaining the difference between shooting the President and shooting *at* the President?"

"Sure," said Rooney. "If you want to kill the President, you shoot the President. If you only want to miss the President, you shoot *at* the President."

"I'm not sure that letting you out of the mental hospital was such a good idea," said Frobisher, leaning back in his chair and waiting for Rooney to explain matters.

"It's like this," Rooney said, crossing his legs. "I come from a pretty well-off family. My father made a lot of money selling a granite-based product. It's a material they use to surface highways with. It's like asphalt, but it's cheaper, and it lasts longer. My father took each of my two older brothers into the business, and he would have taken me into it also, but I couldn't see me spending the rest of my life"—he made a face—"selling dirt."

Murray rubbed his chin. "Makes sense," he said.

Rooney nodded. "So I thought, I have to find some way of making a decent living." He paused. "No, not a decent living," he corrected himself. "A *lot* of money. Just like my father and my older brothers. But everything I thought of just took too long. The idea of waiting a long time to make money didn't sound like a lot of fun. I want it *now*. I want to meet nice girls and buy them dinners with my own American Express card. I want to go on cruises. You know? Have fun in life. So then I had my big idea.

"You know how hijackers, or assassins, get their names in the headlines, and get big write-ups in *Newsweek* and *People*, and then they get psychoanalyzed in magazines like *Penthouse* and *Hustler*? And then they write their life stories, and they make a fortune? Well, I looked at those guys and I thought, Hey, why not me?"

Frobisher sat tensely behind his desk, not knowing whether to call his secretary or the police.

"You're thinking, this guy is really nuts," said Rooney. "But I'm not. Just listen. I think it's immoral that these people should be allowed to profit from their criminal behavior, and I think it's wrong that society should glamorize criminals. But we do. And my father always told me a shrewd businessman is one who capitalizes on sudden opportunity."

"How do these people always find their way to me?" Frobisher asked softly.

Rooney did not hear. He was too involved with his story. "So I thought, Say I take a shot at the President. Not to kill him, not even to hit him. But to miss—on purpose. A few feet over his head. I'm a pretty good shot, by the way. I've got a couple of uncles on the force. What'll happen? First, I'll be on the network news that night. That'll be fun. Then the papers. Then *Newsweek*, and *Time*, and a cover story in *People*. And then the book contract and maybe even a movie deal. What's the down side? I get arrested. I go to jail, there's a trial. But even jail's no big problem, because they'll put me in a special wing, and I'll get special food. Just like that guy Hinckley. But I get the best lawyer I can find—that's where you come in—and either I get off completely or I do eighteen months, write my book in prison or in the mental hospital, and come out a rich man. It's a no-lose proposition."

Frobisher had heard enough. "Do you want a lawyer or an agent?" he asked angrily.

"Both," said Rooney, unruffled, "and I want *you*. And I can afford you. My father's paying. He doesn't want to see me go to jail at all. Not even for eighteen months." He laughed. "It would be bad for his business."

Rooney fished a check out of his jacket pocket and placed it on Frobisher's desk. "This is my first payment toward your retainer, Professor Frobisher. Will you represent me?"

"You don't like your father, do you?" asked Frobisher, reaching forward to look at the check. He turned it over in his hands.

"You're a very perceptive man," said Rooney, nodding.

"This check is for fifty thousand dollars!" Frobisher exclaimed. And then, suspiciously: "Where'd you come up with the money?"

Rooney laughed. "It's my dad's. He understands from his own business that the best is very expensive, Professor Frobisher. And I know I can make it all back, and then some, with the advance on my book."

Frobisher did not know how to respond. He felt uncomfortable in the presence of a man whose disdain for the niceties of the legal system matched Murray's own. Murray believed that clients were supposed to believe in courts and judges—only lawyers were allowed to be cynical and take advantage of the system. Rooney was violating the code. Still, the trial would be in the public eye—Cable News Network might even cover it live—and fifty thousand dollars *was* fifty thousand dollars.

"I guess you've got yourself a lawyer," Frobisher said reluctantly. "I'll need everything you've got related to the case. I think I heard on the news that you've got a preliminary hearing coming up in a couple of weeks. I suppose you'd like me to be there."

"Of course, Professor Frobisher. And I brought everything with me." Rooney reached into his jacket pocket again and pulled out a batch of papers held together with a rubber band. He handed them to Frobisher, who removed the rubber band and flipped through them.

"Hey, these aren't court papers!" Murray exclaimed. "They're letters from publishers."

"Completely unsolicited." Rooney grinned. "They're capitalizing on sudden opportunity, just like my father says."

Frobisher read the letters. Each was from an executive at a well-known publishing house. Each letter expressed the hope that Mr. Rooney had not signed a contract with another publisher to tell his life story, each offered between two hundred and four hundred thousand dollars for the privilege of doing so, and each invited Mr. Rooney to lunch, once he was discharged from the mental institution.

Frobisher exploded. "They're robbing you blind! They're criminals! Your story could be a best seller. You could sell a million copies in hardcover and then another million in paperback! And that's before world rights, translation rights, serialization in *Time*, or the *New York Post*—you could be worth millions to a publisher, and they think they can buy you for a piddling two hundred K! Mr. Rooney, as your counsel I must advise you that these offers are far below what your unique story deserves. Why would somebody want to shoot the President? It's something the reading public is dying to know."

Frobisher's juices were flowing now. "And I love the part about your hating your father! You were firing at the President but you were really trying to kill Dad! It's so Freudian! By the way, do you know anyone from Beirut? They're really in lately with assassination plots. No? No matter."

Frobisher's eyes narrowed. "You said you needed an agent, right?"

"That's right," said Rooney.

"Well, I'm your man for that too. I know all about those publishers. I represent Ed Strong—he's the Dean here—with his publishers, and I know all their little tricks. You're a smart man, Rooney, you've come to the right place. Tell me, you haven't signed anything yet, have you?"

"No, I thought you'd do some negotiating for me."

"You're damned right I'll do some negotiating for you. Look, I can't promise you a million dollars but it's a definite possibility. America wants to know what's going on inside your brain, and they'll pay big bucks to find out."

"You're talking my language, Professor Frobisher."

"But Frank, may I call you Frank?"

"Sure."

"There's just one problem. Look at yourself. You're dressed like someone in the gravel business. Look at that jacket. Is that the jacket of a man who shoots the President?"

Rooney looked surprised and hurt. "I had no idea—"

"Look, you may know a lot about shooting Presidents, but you don't know anything about appearance. You've got to look the part. Go to a nice men's store and pick out some decent shirts and slacks. You don't have to dress like a fashion model, but if you look like a slob, the publishers won't take you seriously. And it's goodbye million dollars."

Rooney nodded quickly.

"And another thing. You've got to find a dentist, or an oral surgeon, or somebody, and you've got to get that tooth replaced. Don't take this personally, but you'll never get on *Donahue* with that missing tooth."

Rooney nodded again.

"Give me a few days to get a bidding war under way with the publishers. You know what—come back tomorrow around ten, and we can start thinking about a defense strategy. You're a personable guy. With you in the right suit and tie, I think a jury would buy whatever you told them. And try not to shoot anybody else for the time being, okay?"

"I can't make any promises." Rooney smiled, standing up to leave. "After all, a guy who shoots at the President is capable of anything."

Murray saw him out of the office. He went back to his desk and looked at the check for fifty thousand dollars. "I love the law," he said solemnly, and then he burst out laughing. A moment later he remembered Sanford Clapp and the latest suicide, and he grew serious again.

SEVENTEEN

As Murray Frobisher struck a deal with Frank Rooney, Jackson Ward sat in his own office, the manila envelope unopened on his desk. "I've been teaching Ethics for ten years," he said aloud, "and I never understood a damned thing about it until this minute." He realized now that despite his status as expert in the field, he had never experienced the critical moment in which one realizes that one's contemplated behavior may fall outside the bounds of propriety—or that it is unquestionably unethical. He had studied such moments, lectured about them, written about them, even testified in court as an expert witness. Now, for the first time, he faced that moment himself. As he contemplated the unopened envelope, he thought of his favorite ethics case, one that he had discussed countless times in classes and seminars.

The case involved a defendant accused of murdering two young women. The defendant not only admitted to his attorney that he had committed the crimes but he told the attorney where he had left the bodies. Together they went to an abandoned railroad siding a few miles out of town—and Jackson, in his lectures, always emphasized the lawyer's trepidation at visiting a murder scene alone with the confessed killer. As it happened, the defendant behaved himself, understanding that he was already in enough trouble. The attorney photographed the bodies and returned to his office.

When it became known that the lawyer literally knew

where the bodies were buried, the judge in the case ordered him to reveal their location to the court. He refused, and he refused a second time when the bereaved parents asked him where they could find the bodies, so as to give them a decent burial. Although the attorney was subjected to much criticism in the local press, Ward argued that he had done the right thing. The attorney-client privilege, protecting the rights of the defendant, outweighed the concerns of the immediate family, and also outweighed the importance of the prosecutor securing a guilty verdict for the defendant. Ward liked the case because it presented the attorney-client privilege issues in stark relief. Ward had written *Law Review* articles and books in which he argued that the privilege was one of the cornerstones of the protection of the individual in American society. If people accused by the state of crimes cannot trust their lawyers, Ward argued, whom can they trust?

Now he drummed his fingers on his desktop. Jackson, like most of the McKinley faculty, was unaware of Dara Sample's lawsuit over her denial of tenure. Only the Dean and Murray Frobisher knew of the litigation and its outcome. To read the consent decree would constitute, to Ward's mind, the sort of assault on the attorney-client privilege of which he had never dreamed himself capable. He sensed that Rebecca's future at McKinley was bound up with the contents of the document on his desk. Jackson found himself balancing his personal loyalty to Rebecca against his loyalty to McKinley as an institution and to the system of legal ethics he so vigorously championed.

He glanced again at the envelope, went out to the hallway, looked both ways down the corridor, locked his office door, and slid the consent decree out of the envelope.

"I could get disbarred for this," he murmured, and he began to read.

EIGHTEEN

"WHAT'S on your mind, Ed?" asked a smiling Sanford Clapp as he stood in the doorway of the Dean's office. "Ms. Kennecutt said it was urgent."

"Sit down, Sanford," said Dean Strong.

Clapp took a seat opposite the Dean. "Let me guess," he said. *"Wake Up, America* is giving you the boot, and they want me to take over."

The Dean was in no mood. "This is serious, Sanford."

"What's up?" Sanford noticed the Dean's tenseness and became concerned.

"Susan Garrett. One of your Contracts students."

"Oh, if *that's* all it is," said Clapp, leaning back in his chair. "Has she been complaining about me? I admit I've been tough on her, but no tougher than I am on a lot of students."

"You admit you've been tough on her?" asked Dean Strong, his expression taut.

"Well, yes, you might say that. Why? What's going on?" Sanford sensed that he had walked into a trap.

"Sanford, she committed suicide last night. She hanged herself in the dormitory."

Clapp looked ashen. He put a hand to his lips. "I never thought she'd do that. I was just having fun with her. You know, strictly Socratic method stuff. It couldn't have been *my* class, Ed. She must have had problems from before she got here."

The Dean nodded. "That's partly true, Sanford. She had a breakdown in high school, but her parents say that she's been all right since then. Her health records say the same thing. Sanford, is it possible that you might have been a bit too harsh on Susan Garrett in class?"

Clapp fixed his eyes on the Dean. "What are you suggesting, Ed?"

"Nothing. I'm not suggesting anything. I'm just asking you a question." The Dean's tone was as noncommittal as he could manage.

"I didn't do anything to Susan Garrett that I don't do to a hundred other students," said Clapp, his anger rising. "All I do is ask questions and show students where their answers are incorrect. The Socratic method, same as at any other law school. We've got to train our students to be tough and to stand up for themselves under fire in the courtroom—"

"You know and I know that ninety percent of our graduates go into corporate law and never even see the inside of a courtroom," interrupted Dean Strong. "But I didn't call you in here to debate the merits of the Socratic method. Sanford, this is the third suicide in your class since last spring."

Clapp did not have to be told. "Are you suggesting that I'm somehow responsible, Ed? Is that it?"

The Dean frowned and plunged ahead. "What I'm about to say need go no further than this room, Sanford, and I'm repeating to you what I've heard because I want you to hear it from me and not from the gossip mill. I have it on good authority that all three students who committed suicide did so after you were particularly brutal to them in class. Could there be any truth to that, Sanford?"

"You *are* accusing me," Clapp spluttered. "You're accusing me of killing those students. I didn't do it, Ed. If they can't take it, they shouldn't have come to law school in the first place."

"And your job is to flush them out?"

"No, damn it! Well, yes! Yes, it is! Law is hardball, it's not for the weak-kneed, Ed! You know that! People who can't take it don't belong here."

"Don't you think committing suicide is a fairly dramatic way to withdraw from law school?"

"Ed, I'm not responsible for what students do on their own time. And I'm not going to take any more of your crap, either. I didn't kill those students, they killed themselves, and I'll be damned if I accept blame from you or from anybody else!"

The Dean tried to remain calm in the face of Clapp's rage. "Sanford, I repeat. I'm not accusing you of killing anybody. I'm just asking you to be a bit more humane in the lecture hall. How do you think this is going to look? Do you realize what a black eye this is for McKinley?"

"A black eye for McKinley's Dean, you mean," said Sanford Clapp. "One more suicide and you'll never get on the Supreme Court, will you, Ed?"

The Dean controlled his anger. "That was uncalled for, Sanford."

"Well, how do you think I feel, summoned like a bad boy to the principal's office? Why aren't you yelling at the admissions director? He's the one who's responsible for them getting in here in the first place!"

"Look," said Dean Strong, "I didn't intend this to become a shouting match. I asked you to my office because I wanted you to hear this directly from me and because I wanted to hear your side. I'll ask you once again. Could you please just take it a little easier in the classroom?"

Clapp put a hand up to cut him off. "Hold it. A minute ago you said you had it on 'good authority' about me and my Contracts class. Where'd your 'good authority' come from?"

At that moment Rebecca Shepard burst in. "Ms. Kennecutt said you were trying to telephone me— Oh, hello, Sanford."

"Rebecca," said Dean Strong, "could you wait outside for just a moment? Sanford and I are finishing something up."

"Of course." Rebecca sensed the tension in the room. Her first thought was that Sanford had guessed her role in the Professor of the Year letter. Something told her that whatever was going on was far more serious. She quickly stepped out of the office.

Clapp turned on the Dean. "Is *that* your source? Is she the one who's been complaining about me?"

"Absolutely not, Sanford," said the Dean. "On my honor. I haven't spoken to Rebecca since this whole thing broke. I give you my word on that."

"Well, then, why did you have her come running in here? She didn't have Susan Garrett in any of her classes."

"I've been told that Rebecca had been tutoring her in Contracts. She spent two hours with Susan on Monday, the day before she, er, took her own life. That's why she's involved."

"I see," said Clapp, eyes narrowing. "How did you find out that Rebecca was doing that? Law school deans aren't normally aware of which professors are tutoring which students. Somebody must have told you. And I'll bet I know who it is! It's that Conway, the Saint! He's been sleeping with her since last year! He's the one who must have tipped you off about me. Am I right?"

The Dean was caught off guard. "Well, I—I'm not supposed to reveal—"

Clapp leaned in for the kill. "Yes or no, Ed?"

"Well, all right," Dean Strong admitted. "It was Conway. I won't lie to you. But I—"

"I *knew* it!" Clapp shouted, standing and turning away from the Dean. "That son of a bitch Conway! Accusing me of pushing students over the brink! Toward suicide! I want his ass! I want his ass out of the law school! He will never get a McKinley degree while I'm on this faculty, do you understand?" He spun around and faced Dean Strong. "Is this the way you stand up for your faculty, Ed? A student accuses a professor of—of murder, and you take the side of the student?"

"I'm not taking anyone's side, Sanford," said Dean Strong, rising to his feet. "I'm not necessarily accepting anyone's opinion. I brought you in here because I wanted to do you a favor. Everybody knows what an asshole you are in class—pardon my language, Sanford, but I'm just furious right now—and everybody knows all three suicides were your students, and how long do you think it'll take before people put two and two together? I'm trying to help you, Sanford, because I didn't want the accusation to come as a surprise to you. I wanted to hear your side of the story. I've got the welfare of the law school to think about."

And the welfare of your career too, you slime, thought Clapp.

"Well, all right," said Clapp, backing down somewhat.

"Maybe I might have been a bit too harsh on those students. Maybe I'll take it easier in the future. But I don't think you understand how *furious* I am over being accused by a student of causing a suicide. Of causing *three* suicides. This sort of thing can't go unchecked, Ed. I'm sorry. I got your memo about the faculty meeting at four o'clock. I'll be there, and I'm going to move for disciplinary charges to be brought against Daniel Conway. I repeat: I want him out of the law school, and that's my final word on the subject."

"Sanford, don't you think you're being a little harsh?"

"Harsh? I think I'm perfectly justified in this. Conway's lucky I'm not bringing him up on criminal charges as well. I won't be satisfied until you boot him out of this law school. The nerve of him, sleeping with a professor for a year and then accusing another professor of murder."

"But Sanford—"

"Don't 'But Sanford' me, Ed. I'll see you at four o'clock." He marched out of the room and walked past Rebecca Shepard without a word. She entered the Dean's office.

"Close the door, do you mind?" the Dean asked wearily. "Would you like a drink?"

"No, no, thank you," said Rebecca, alarmed.

"I take it you've heard about the suicide," said the Dean, massaging his temples.

"Yes, I have," said Rebecca. "I had been tutoring Susan for about two weeks."

"I'm sorry."

Rebecca nodded gravely. "So am I," she said. "It's a first for me."

"Unfortunately it's a third for McKinley," said the Dean. "And maybe a third for Sanford."

The Dean took two ice cubes from a small refrigerator behind his desk and poured himself a glass of Scotch from a bottle he kept in an important-looking red box labeled *Rules and Regulations of the Securities and Exchange Commission*.

"Clapp is furious at your boyfriend," said Dean Strong.

Rebecca gave a start. She was unaware that Dean Strong knew of her relationship with the Saint.

"Daniel? Why? What happened?"

"He called me from Washington and suggested that Clapp

might have pushed Susan Garrett, and the other two students, over the brink. He said he heard about Susan over the radio."

"I wouldn't be at all surprised," said Rebecca. "I couldn't believe the things Susan said that Clapp did to her in class."

"I suspected as much myself," said the Dean, sipping his drink. "Anyway, now he wants Conway thrown out of McKinley. He figured out that Conway told me that his classroom tactics were the last straw for Garrett and the other two. Clapp just said he was doing his job—teaching in accordance with the Socratic method." He gave Rebecca a rueful smile. "I was supposed to devote this afternoon to your tenure case."

Rebecca did not attempt to hide her surprise. "Does that mean I still have a chance? I thought that battle was lost a long time ago."

"Not at all. You'll understand if it moves to the back burner for now. I've got to find some way of placating Clapp, and of dealing with the fallout from the suicide."

"I don't want to add to your woes," said Rebecca, "but the students are talking about a strike. I just snuck out of a Women's Law Caucus meeting. That's why Ms. Kennecutt couldn't find me, and that's why I rushed into your meeting with Sanford. For which I apologize. Anyway, the women are furious."

"I don't doubt it," said the Dean. "I canceled classes for tomorrow and Friday. Maybe things will cool down by Monday. That's the day the *McKinley Law Review* comes out. I'm looking forward to reading your piece. I'm hearing good things about it."

"Thank you," said Rebecca, wondering who knew enough about the article to comment on it to the Dean. I guess there are no secrets at all in this place, she thought.

"Back to more pressing matters, though. You say that Susan had been complaining about Clapp's treatment of her in class?"

"That's right," said Rebecca, recalling Susan's nervousness. "She told me that Clapp had given her the Kingsfield routine from *Paper Chase*—told her she'd never be a lawyer, told her that she should never have come to McKinley, because she was taking the place of some more qualified student. He even called her an embarrassment to the law school, in front of a hundred other students."

"I didn't realize Clapp had gotten that far out of hand," said the Dean.

Rebecca nodded. "The final blow came Monday morning," she said. "She asked him a question in class—how she had the courage to put her hand up after all that Clapp had put her through is beyond me. She asked whether a particular rule of contract law governed in a majority of the states. A harmless question. Clapp must not have known the answer, because he went into a tirade about his not being a walking encyclopedia, if she was so interested why didn't she go look it up herself, why did she think we have a law library, and so on."

"She must have thought Sanford was gunning for her and her alone," said Dean Strong.

"If she'd stuck around a little longer she would have seen that he treats everyone that way," said Rebecca.

"That's just what he said. Rebecca, I've got to prepare for the Committee of Ten meeting. Thank you for coming over so quickly. I appreciate your candor very much. If you'll excuse me."

"Of course, Dean Strong. I'm glad to help out. This can't be easy for you."

He was grateful for her sympathy. "No. It's not. See you at four o'clock."

"See you then."

Dean Edward Strong watched the door close behind Rebecca Shepard. He asked himself whether Frobisher really would resign if he recommended her for tenure, as he picked up Susan Garrett's health records and began to read through them for a second time.

NINETEEN

The four top editors of the *McKinley Law Review* squirmed uneasily in their chairs in Aaron Mountain's office. It was a quarter past two. Aaron Mountain had been informing the editors for the last fifteen minutes that they could not tell horseshit from the Hope Diamond, that they were idiots, that he had no idea how they ever became *Law Review* editors, and that they would be lucky to find work as collection attorneys for the Household Finance Corporation by the time he was finished with them. Mountain always favored a direct approach when talking to students.

"I don't think your comments are entirely fair," ventured Timothy Clark, editor-in-chief.

"Fair? What the hell do you know about 'fair'? It never occurred to you to be fair to me," snapped Mountain.

Mountain was not simply blowing off steam. He felt genuinely aggrieved by what he considered the editors' failure to live up to an unspoken bargain. Although the editors might not have sensed it at this moment, Mountain put the same effort into currying favor with them that he once put into buttering up his colleagues when he was a candidate for tenure. He had grown so accustomed to the idea of not even trying to succeed on his own merits that currying favor with *someone* was an integral part of his character. Now that he had tenure, and therefore no longer needed his fellow professors, he merely agreed with them at every turn in Committee of Ten meetings. Instead, he devoted himself to the editors. They were, after all, the students most likely to join the elite world of lawyers who could make a difference in Mountain's hitherto-fore undistinguished legal career.

If the *Law Review* editors became kindly disposed toward Mountain, or, better still, if they became *indebted* to him, their innate sense of fairness might mean some sort of payoff for Mountain down the road. If the students became clerks to federal court judges, they might find occasion for citing Mountain's ponderous *Law Review* articles. If, as attorneys, they became involved in planning seminars in distant cities—especially Honolulu or Miami in winter months—they might invite good old Professor Mountain to take part. If they went to Washington, they might find helpful Professor Mountain's comments on a pending bill. If a few of them made it to the nominating committees that recommended candidates for elevation to the state or federal bench, perhaps they might consider making Professor Mountain Judge Mountain. In short, Aaron Mountain looked upon *Law Review* editors as a mother lode of future patronage.

Mountain was no slouch at favoring *Law Review* students. Nearly every *Law Review* member signed up for his classes, much the same way football players at large universities know exactly which courses to take. Mountain did not expect *Law Review* members to show up, or even to prepare for the final examination. There was no recorded case of a *Law Review* student receiving anything less than an A. In class, he kept a list of *Law Review* students handy and called on them almost exclusively. Non-*Law Review* students who ventured answers or comments found their ideas rejected so thoroughly and so harshly that they repented of ever raising their hands. When a *Law Review* student was unprepared to answer a given Mountain question—a situation that obtained more often than not, considering Mountain's grading policies—the student had only to give a slight shake of the head, or a tiny hand motion, and Mountain would look elsewhere. The practice was comparable to that of auctioneers who arranged signals in advance with discreet bidders. In Mountain's classes, subtlety was everything.

Mountain's benevolence extended outside the classroom.

He gave research assistant jobs only to *Law Review* students and justified the practice by explaining that only they understood the complexities of his field. That he never asked them to do any research, and that he signed their time sheets and permitted them to collect pay from the law school for twelve to fifteen hours a week of no work at all, was an added incentive for thinking kindly of Aaron Mountain in days to come. Mountain usually kept five or six members of the *Law Review* editorial board on his payroll. No other professor had more than one research assistant. Dean Strong objected, but never with conviction. Mountain caused the least amount of trouble of any of the tenured faculty, and the Dean saw no reason to deprive him of his sole questionable activity.

Mountain did not stop at dispensing sinecures. The WATS line in Mountain's office was at the disposal of the *Law Review* editors who needed to make long-distance personal telephone calls. He allowed the editors to charge meals in the faculty dining room to his expense account. "He does everything for us," one *Law Review* member marveled to a friend, "except pick us up, stroke our little heads, burp us, and tuck us in at night." The *Law Review* students, by and large, accepted Mountain's munificence as their due. After all, they reasoned, if law school wanted all students to think they were equal, why have a *Law Review* at all? Mountain's point of view was even simpler. He knew ingratitude when he saw it. After all, what had Rebecca Shepard ever given them?

"Professor Mountain," said Eric Tompkins, executive editor, "you still haven't told us what we did to upset you. All you've done is call us a bunch of names."

Aaron Mountain seemed ready to explode. "And I'll call you a lot more names before I'm finished. I don't think you understand how humiliated I feel."

"All we did was send your article back to you with some queries, Professor," said Andrea Van Ness, an articles editor.

"No, that's not all you did," he said, pointing at Van Ness. "You outright rejected my article, and you're printing Rebecca Shepard's in its place. Rebecca doesn't have tenure. I do."

"But Professor Mountain," Timothy Clark began, "we don't even *consider* whether a professor has tenure when we read a submitted article. We go strictly on the merits of the piece."

"Merits?" Mountain responded. "You wouldn't know a merit if it walked up and bit you."

"Professor Mountain," said Thomas Crandall, another articles editor, "I'm the one who rejected your article. I read it through three different times and I found it a confused mess. You misrepresented the positions of other professors, you quoted Supreme Court decisions out of context to make them say things exactly opposite from their holdings, your conclusions were not at all based on your premises, and your writing style was so pedantic and overblown that I had to practically slap myself to keep awake. That's why I turned it down."

The other three editors looked at Crandall in disbelief. They braced themselves for Mountain's next volley of abuse.

It never came. Crandall, almost alone among his fellow editors, had never accepted anything from Mountain—not a job, not a meal, not even the use of Mountain's WATS line. Crandall was one of the few *Law Review* members who had never taken a class with Aaron Mountain. For his part, Mountain was aware that Crandall was in no way beholden to him. This awareness caused him to modify his approach.

"Thank you, Mr. Crandall, for setting me straight about my article," Mountain said quietly, taken aback by the young man's forthrightness. "I'm sorry if I came on a bit strong just now."

A *bit* strong, thought all four editors.

"I just don't think it's fair," Mountain continued, "that an untenured professor should have her article printed while a tenured professor's article is turned down. I admit that what I wrote isn't the *Law Review* version of the Second Coming, but I don't think it's quite as bad as Mr. Crandall suggests. It's just that there ought to be a different standard for judging the writing of McKinley professors in the *McKinley Law Review*. That's how it is at other law schools."

"You mean a lower standard," interrupted Crandall, the bit still in his teeth. "You're saying that we should publish garbage as long as it's McKinley garbage."

The others held their breath but Mountain only smiled. "I'd hardly call my article garbage," he said.

I would, thought each of the editors.

"What I propose is this," Mountain said. "Rebecca will understand if her article comes out in a month's time instead of on Monday. I'd like you to pull her article out of the upcoming issue and print mine in its place."

The editors looked aghast.

"Conflict of Laws is an extremely complicated field," Mountain said. "It's possible that you didn't exactly understand my article. Mr. Crandall, the Supreme Court holdings on Conflicts are hard to grasp even if one has been teaching as long as I have. You've never had the benefit of my class, so the field must be especially difficult for you."

Crandall stared at Mountain in disbelief.

Mountain continued. "One is not born with a deep understanding of Conflict of Laws, and even after two years of law school one still might not understand every nuance of the field. *But I do*. And the article I wrote is an important piece of scholarship, and it simply must find its way into print, and quickly."

Eric Tompkins, executive editor, spoke up first. "Sir, the next issue just went to the printer's. There's no way we could pull out Professor Shepard's article at this stage. They're printing and binding the issue even as we speak. We'd have to throw out everything."

"Our subscribers would be furious over the delay," added Andrea Van Ness.

"I see," said Mountain, thinking it over. "Your next issue comes out in a month, doesn't it? Why don't you print my piece then?"

"That's not really possible," said Thomas Crandall. "I understand how you feel about your article, but it's just not *McKinley Law Review* material."

Aaron Mountain reddened. "And I say it *is*. I was hoping it wouldn't come to this, but you've left me no alternative. You know that Professor Blotchett asks me to comment on the clerkship applications of *Law Review* students, since I have so much *contact* with you. You did know that, didn't you?"

They nodded glumly.

"Now, all four of you have submitted applications for judicial clerkships for the coming year. But how am I to recommend any of you when you clearly cannot recognize solid legal scholarship? Don't you think that my recommending you for clerkships would be a disservice to McKinley?" He paused to let his words sink in.

"Are you threatening us?" asked Andrea Van Ness.

"'Threatening' is such an ugly word, don't you think?"

"Could we have some time to discuss this among ourselves?" asked Timothy Clark.

"Certainly," said Aaron Mountain.

"Excuse us for a moment."

The four stepped out of the office and took the elevator to the basement, where the law school maintained a dismal lunchroom for its students. The room offered little more than a few vending machines, a dollar bill changer, a microwave oven, some round tables and polyurethane chairs, walls painted a drab yellow, no windows, and insufficient fluorescent lighting. Most law students found in its unwelcoming ambience a metaphor for law school itself. The students bought some coffee and diet soda and took seats at one of the tables. Other students sat nearby, squinting at cases in the uneven light.

"Do you think he's serious?" asked Andrea Van Ness.

"I wouldn't put it past him," said Timothy Clark.

"But that article is awful! It'll embarrass the *Law Review*," said Thomas Crandall.

"Yeah, but I'm counting on that clerkship," said Eric Tompkins.

"You'd give in to him?" It was Timothy Clark.

"Why not? It's just one article over the course of a year," said Tompkins, looking at the floor. "And besides, well, after all he's done for us—"

"It's not right!" said Crandall. "He's abusing his authority! He's been trying to buy us off forever."

"What about the integrity of the *Law Review*?" asked Andrea Van Ness.

"Yeah, but what about our careers?" asked Tompkins.

After twenty more minutes of give and take, the four editors trooped back into Mountain's office.

I'm going to be sick, thought Crandall.

"We've thought it over," said Timothy Clark, editor-in-chief, "and based on our reconsideration of the, um, of the merits of your article, we'd be honored to print it in the November issue."

"I knew you'd see it my way." Aaron Mountain smiled, and the editors rather sheepishly left the office.

Idiots, thought Mountain, settling comfortably into his desk chair. Just idiots.

TWENTY

After a leisurely lunch at the Blue and White Cafe, Randolph Patton, software genius and fledgling pornography mogul, returned to the McKinley Law School building for a look around. The day before, he had informed his ninth grade teacher, who was in awe of the wealthy young entrepreneur, that he would be away all the next day—"on business." His teacher, as usual, failed to object. This left Randolph free to spend the early afternoon—until three-thirty, when he would be expected at home—exploring the home base of his new counsel and ten percent partner, Murray Frobisher. Randolph, two large briefcases in tow, went first to the mailroom near McKinley's front door. The McKinley faculty received their correspondence in large wooden mailboxes with their names painted on them in ornate script. Students received their mail in beat-up alphabetized file folders that offered neither privacy nor dignity.

"I've got to ditch these briefcases," Randolph said aloud. He knocked on the mailroom door. A clerk opened the top half of the door, looked down at the elegantly dressed Patton, and laughed.

"What do you want, kid?" he asked. "Aren't you a little young for law school?"

Patton ignored the affront. "My father is Judge Spanbock," Randolph said stiffly, borrowing the name of Patton Pictures' chief cinematographer. "He's here for the seminar on the Supreme Court. Would you mind keeping his briefcases for an hour or two?"

The clerk, himself a third-year law student applying for judicial clerkships, immediately changed his manner.

"Judge Spanbock!" the student exclaimed. He racked his memory but he could not think of a Judge Spanbock. He tried to finesse it. "Isn't he on the Second Circuit? Just appointed, right?"

"Yeah, that's right," said Randolph, playing along. "He's way up on the Second Circuit. Look, my dad's a pretty important guy, okay? And he asked me to put these bags down where they'll be safe."

"I'd be *honored*," the student gushed. "Just hand them over. I'll keep an eye on them all afternoon."

"That's just super. But don't let anyone open them. They've got all kinds of judicial papers in there, and it's pretty secret, all that stuff."

"I'll shoot anyone who comes near them," the student joked, lifting both cases and setting them in a corner of the mailroom. "Hey, these things are pretty heavy."

"No kidding," said Randolph, shaking out his arms, which were tired from carrying the briefcases all day. "He's a busy man, and he's got a lot of stuff to carry. Look, I'll be back for the bags around three o'clock."

The student wondered whether someone was pulling a fast one on him.

"It must be pretty cool to have a father who's a federal judge," he said, his tone suspicious.

"You get used to it," said Randolph, sensing that he ought to move on. "See you around three."

Randolph turned his back on the mailroom clerk and wandered off in the direction of the library. The clerk watched him disappear into the crowd of students emerging from various first-floor lecture halls. He waited until Randolph was out of sight and then he examined the contents of the briefcases. That evening, he would enter into a prolonged argument with several classmates in which he would insist that a Judge Spanbock of the Second Circuit was handling a top-secret obscenity case involving pornographic videotapes. His classmates would insist with equal fervor that there was no Judge Spanbock.

Randolph, meanwhile, gained entrance to the library by sneaking under the turnstile while the monitor's back was turned. Once inside, he wandered past table after table of law students so involved with their studies that they never looked up, or more accurately, looked down, to notice their young observer.

"These people work too hard," Randolph told himself.

At length he came upon a glassed-in room containing two computer terminals.

"That's more like it," he said, and he entered and seated himself before one of the machines. The terminals provided access to two computer data bases that permitted students to search for and retrieve legal decisions by typing in key words or phrases. If one were researching, say, racial discrimination in public housing, one could type those words into the machine and within moments the computer would produce the names of every relevant case. Students were not permitted to learn to use the computer until their second year of law school, for fear that they might not learn traditional methods of legal research. Once trained, though, students with half an hour to kill between classes often logged on to the computer and sought judicial references in court cases to vegetables, articles of clothing, or parts of the body. It passed the time.

Randolph had no interest in the data base relating to law. Instead, he turned the computer on, typed in some commands and passwords, and within moments was following the trading activity in the over-the-counter market of the common stock of his computer software company. To his dismay, the stock was down three-eighths of a point in moderate trading. Randolph gave the computer a few more commands and tapped into a computer-game network that he had helped to develop. With a few keystrokes he called to the screen a Flight Simulator program and was landing a Boeing 767 on the east-west runway at Mexico City International Airport.

"What do you think you're doing?"

Randolph, startled, turned around. His plane, unattended, crashed into a residential neighborhood six hundred yards short of the runway. Randolph looked at the smoking wreckage on the screen and winced.

"Young man, what do you think you're doing with the law computer?"

It was Miss Pander, the librarian, accompanied by a student who worked part-time shelving books. Miss Pander looked extremely displeased at the sight of a fourteen-year-old seated at one of her terminals. She did not like the computers themselves, which, she calculated, took up the space of about a thousand books.

"I was just . . ." Patton groped for words.

"It's all right, Miss Pander," said the student. "I'll take care of it."

"Those machines are expensive, and they're not for children," said Miss Pander.

"I'll take care of it," the student repeated. Miss Pander glared at Randolph, looked at the student as if to say, "You *better* take care of it," and left the room.

"My name is Peter Chesnut," he said. "Sorry about the accident. I guess Miss Pander kind of surprised you."

"Oh, that?" Randolph looked ruefully at the smoldering fuselage. "I guess I killed everyone on board, not to mention whatever got hit on the ground. That's flying for you."

Chesnut smiled. "Didn't I see you going into Professor Frobisher's office?" he asked. "Are you his son?"

"No, how could you possibly think that?" asked Randolph, shaking Chesnut's hand. "Name's Randolph Patton. I was seeing Murray on business."

Chesnut sat down at the terminal next to Randolph. He had brown eyes, curly dark hair, a pleasant manner, and was wearing a light blue McKinley Law School sweatshirt, blue jeans, and running shoes. "Patton?" he repeated. "You're not *the* Randolph Patton, are you? The computer kid? Aren't you the founder of General Software? I can't believe it!"

Randolph blushed. "Yeah, that's me," he said, delighted to be recognized. "How do you know so much about me? Did you read about my company somewhere?"

"Read about it?" Chesnut exclaimed. "I've been using your software for three years! You're a genius! It's the best word processing/spreadsheet package in the industry!"

"Well, I wouldn't call myself a genius. I think of da Vinci, Michelangelo, Henry Ford as geniuses." Randolph reverted to the stock answer that he usually gave reporters. And then, with surprise: "You really use my software?"

"Oh, yes!" Chesnut was an earnest, clean-cut young man who spoke quickly when excited, as now. "PattonWorks is awesome!" he exclaimed.

"Really?" said Randolph. "This is super! A real-live customer! I don't think I've ever met anyone who actually *uses* the program."

"I can't believe that," said Chesnut, "because it's terrific. Basically, I was a double major in college, economics and film. I did all of my economics course work senior year on your software. And I've done all of my outlines and briefs here at McKinley on the word processing part."

"Economics and film, huh?" asked Randolph, becoming interested.

Chesnut nodded quickly. "I guess it sounds pretty dull to you, huh, Mr. Patton?"

It sounded anything but dull to Randolph. While interviewing candidates—engineers, business people—to run his software company, his favorite device for putting the potential hires at their ease and gaining a sense of their ability to think and speak clearly was to ask them about their college or graduate thesis. He decided that it was time to put the same question to Chesnut.

"Call me Randolph. Tell me, did you do a thesis in college?"

Chesnut laughed. "How do you know about theses? You're only fourteen!"

"And a half," Randolph insisted. "Look. I've been hiring Ph.D.'s and M.B.A.'s by the busload, okay? I happen to know what a thesis is."

"Excuse me," said Chesnut, taken aback. "I hope I didn't insult you. Yes, I did a thesis."

Randolph tried to sound casual. "Was it in econ, or film—or both?"

"Both," said Chesnut. "I was a joint major."

"Really?" said Randolph, not hiding his interest. "What was your thesis about?"

"Oh, you wouldn't be interested," Chesnut said, shaking his head.

"Try me," said Patton, folding his arms across his chest.

"Well, basically," Chesnut began, "it was a study of cash flow techniques for certain small film production companies. You know, how they can manage their costs. New independent production companies have a lot of really unique problems. I mean, they've got very high start-up costs, union rules, equipment is expensive, and unless they amortize things correctly and work out good distribution deals, they could be dead in the water. But why am I telling *you* this? It would only be interesting to someone trying to get started in the industry."

Randolph's eyes narrowed. "How do you know so much about the film industry?"

Chesnut shrugged. "I don't know," he said. "I guess I just love the movies."

"Well, I guess that makes two of us. By the way, whatja get on your thesis? What grade, I mean?"

"Magna," Chesnut said modestly. "I might have gotten summa, but my father got sick the week before it was due, and I wasn't able to do the last chapter. Also, my specific interest in film is a little outside the mainstream. My professors weren't about to— Well, never mind. But tell me about you! What are you seeing Professor Frobisher about? Is someone suing your software company?"

"Huh?" said Randolph. "Murray? No, I was seeing him about something else. A new venture. Tell me, Peter—your name was Peter, wasn't it? You're interested in working in film?"

Chesnut nodded.

"Doing what?" Randolph asked.

"That's what I'm not sure of," said Chesnut, frowning. "I can't act, and I can't write very well. I'm good with numbers, though. Half of my thesis was spreadsheets. I don't really like numbers, but I'm good with them. That's why I studied Economics, I guess."

Randolph considered all of this. "So why did you go to law school?" he asked.

"I don't know exactly," Chesnut admitted. "I thought I'd become an entertainment lawyer."

"Is that so?" Randolph asked. "Are you taking a `lot of courses in entertainment law? Is there such a thing? Can you really major in entertainment law?"

Randolph, who knew a lot, did not know that there were attorneys who specialized in entertainment law. He found himself wondering whether Murray, whose reputation as a generalist was second to none, was the right choice to represent Patton Pictures.

"It's a specialty, all right," said Chesnut, "but you can't major in anything in law school. You just take courses. McKinley doesn't offer any courses in entertainment law, but I've taken a lot of classes in labor law, and I've been cross-registering in corporate finance and accounting courses at McKinley Business School. But I don't want to waste your time this way. I'm sure you're a very busy, um, person."

"No, no," said Randolph, "I'm not busy at all. We could be on to something important here, you and I. Tell me, when do you graduate?"

"December, thank goodness," said Chesnut. "Only two more months. I took a semester off last year. I hate this place. I think studying law is the most boring thing in the world."

"You do, huh?" said Randolph. You just passed the first test, he thought. Randolph looked through the glass walls of the computer room and saw students hunched over their casebooks, perfectly motionless. Anyone who can't stand this stuff is probably my kind of guy.

Randolph leaned back in his chair. "Do you have a job yet?"

"Well, I've got a few offers from firms."

Randolph sucked in his breath.

Chesnut continued. "My grades were pretty good, and I was on *Law Review,* so it's been pretty easy for me to get offers from the top firms. But I haven't accepted any yet."

"Why not?" Randolph asked, studying him.

"Well, basically, none of them will guarantee that I can do entertainment law. If I end up having to do corporate or litigation I might just shoot myself. Okay, the money's great, but it would be like condemning myself to a lifetime of—of that," and he pointed to the students briefing cases. "If I never read another case as long as I live, I won't complain, and I mean it."

Randolph tried to appear as casual as possible. "Have you given any thought to working for a film production company instead of a law firm?"

"Come on!" said Chesnut. "I'd love to! But who'd hire me? I've got no experience, I've got no contacts. It's all 'who you know' in that business."

"You know me," said Randolph, and he removed his wallet from his back pocket and fished out a business card. He handed it to Chesnut, who examined it.

"Patton Pictures?" Chesnut read aloud, not knowing how to react.

"My new venture," said Randolph, not without a measure of pride.

"You're kidding!"

"Do I look like I'm kidding? This is serious stuff, okay? It's capitalized with the proceeds from the software business. I had to park the cash somewhere, and this is it. Look here, Peter. If everything you've told me about yourself is true, then I'd like you to come to work for me the day after you graduate."

Chesnut looked suspicious. Law school, after all, is a place for the risk-averse. Some business school students might take a chance and accept a job with a start-up computer or biotechnology company at a low salary, secure in the knowledge that if the company succeeds, their stock options will be worth a fortune. The same frame of mind that leads many people to study law, though, also leads them to look no further for employment than to those large firms that come to the law school looking for students to hire. (This is a variation of what people in sales call a "forced choice close," in which customers are offered several models of a given product or several delivery dates to choose from, in order to distract them from the question of whether to buy at all.) Most McKinley students put more effort into finding adequate housing than into looking for a job. After all, there are far more vacancies in the top law firms each year than there are decent, affordable apartments within a short commute of McKinley. Peter Chesnut may not have wanted to work for a large firm, but he was not about to work for a fourteen-year-old. Randolph sensed his uncertainty.

"Okay," said Randolph, "you're not sure. You don't think I'm on the level. Let's get serious, Peter. How many ninth-graders do you know who own their own *office building*? I do. Patton Towers. Twenty-two stories. General Software has the top five floors, and we rent the rest out to law firms, account-ants, all kinds of professionals. We've got a bar-restaurant on the main floor, we've got a health club, a pool, parking for five hundred cars in the basement—and Patton Towers is the new home of Patton Pictures. It's for real. It's going to be big, and I mean real big. I'm offering you a piece of the action. Look, who are you kidding. You don't want to be a lawyer. It's written all over your face."

Randolph could tell that Chesnut's resistance was weaken-ing. He poured it on. "I tell you what—take a week off. Take two weeks. I'll send you to the Caribbean—get you rested up—and then you'll start fresh, let's see, you'll need a title. Comptroller. You'll be comptroller, Patton Pictures. I need someone who can bring some discipline to the operation, keep our costs down. What you did in your thesis is exactly the kind of intelligence I want to bring into the organization. You'll report directly to me, you'll have your own staff. You'll hire them. I'll give you total control. Who's going to give you an offer like that? Warner Brothers?"

Chesnut's expression suggested that he could not believe what was happening.

"Now," Randolph continued, looking at the floor, "I can't compete with the salaries the big law firms are paying, but I can offer you an equity position, stock options, benefits— I see. You're still not sure. I'm a good boss. Ask my engineers. Look, you don't have to tell me now. I don't expect an answer right away. Take a few days to think it over. Talk to your girlfriend. Or your wife. You married?"

Chesnut was utterly dumbounded. He looked from Ran-dolph Patton to the card and back to Randolph Patton. The young film producer looked intently at the law student, eye-brows raised, studying Chesnut's expression for a clue to his reaction.

"There's just one thing I've got to tell you," said Randolph, looking uneasy. "I guess I can't put this off forever."

"Like what?" Chesnut's throat was dry.

Randolph frowned. He feared that if he told Chesnut what Patton Pictures produced, Chesnut would never accept a job. Randolph thought about it for a moment and then decided on the direct approach.

"We make pornographic videocassettes," he said, his tone matter-of-fact, as if he were discussing baseball cards or model airplanes. "No plot. Straight sex. Ninety minutes' worth. We show everything. We've got Gloria Jones, we're negotiating with Johnny Toole's agent. I'm no Ingrid Bergman."

"Ingmar," Chesnut corrected, shaking his head slowly.

"Yeah, Ingmar," said Randolph. "Whatever."

"Patton makes porn," Chesnut said slowly. "Mr. Patton, I guess it's time for me to tell *you* the truth."

"What are you talking about?" Randolph asked, concerned.

"The real reason my thesis got magna instead of summa was that my adviser couldn't recommend summa for a study of—a study of the porn film industry!"

Now it was Randolph's turn to be shocked. "You're kidding me!" he said.

"Do I look like I'm kidding?" Chesnut asked. "Porn has the highest profit margin of any branch of the industry. You don't need writers, you don't need fancy sets, you don't need stars. Although if you can put Gloria Jones and Johnny Toole in the same film, you'll have the biggest thing since Fred Astaire and Ginger Rogers. Look, my thesis was about cash flow. And nobody's got cash flow like guys who make porn. And it doesn't have to be trashy or exploitative. I think erotica can be art."

Randolph was making little gurgling noises.

"Basically," Chesnut continued, "I never really saw myself going into pornography. But you don't always get your first choice in life, I guess. It's kind of ironic, me writing a thesis about porn and then running into you. Wow."

"Yeah, wow," said Randolph, regaining his composure. "Look, I'm pretty surprised by your attitude. Most people are turned off when I tell them what I do for a living. This is great, though. I come here looking for a lawyer and I get a lawyer and a comptroller in one shot. Hey. Do you remember the last line of *Casablanca*?"

"Sure! 'Louie, this could be the beginning...'" Chesnut began.

Randolph finished the sentence: "'... of a beautiful friendship.' Look. Go down to the mailroom, and you'll find two briefcases. Check out what's inside of them, and meet me at the Blue and White Cafe in fifteen minutes, and we can talk some more about our future together. I've got to call my parents and tell them I'll be late for dinner. Peter, I think we're on the same wavelength. Oh. When you get to the mailroom, and if they give you a hard time about the briefcases, just tell 'em Judge Spanbock sent you."

Peter Chesnut nodded. "Blue and White Cafe in fifteen minutes. I'll just tell Miss Pander I'll finish the shelving tonight. See you there, Mr. Patton."

Randolph, at the door, turned back and flashed a warm smile. "Everybody at the studio calls me Randolph."

TWENTY-ONE

"I should begin by thanking each of you for fitting this emergency meeting into your busy schedules," said Dean Edward Strong to the assembled Committee of Ten of the McKinley Law School.

"Before we discuss the serious matters before us—the Susan Garrett suicide, the program for tomorrow morning's memorial service, the threatened student strike—I have one announcement of a more pleasant nature to make. In the midst of all the catastrophes befalling our law school, something very special happened about an hour ago. Delivered to my office, at last, was the long-overdue portrait of the late Dean Sprowl, my immediate predecessor here at McKinley."

Ronald Blotchett, who had been leafing through a paperback on his lap entitled *Power Dreaming*, looked pained at the mention of the man whose son ran off with his wife. Dean Strong did not notice.

"Dean Sprowl was much beloved by the students and his fellow faculty members, so once this current crisis dies down we might have a brief ceremony to celebrate the hanging of his portrait here in the Thorne Lounge.

"Now that that's been said, let's move on to more pressing matters—"

"Where's it going to hang, Ed?" It was T. O. A. Culpepper.

I knew I couldn't get out of this that easily, thought the Dean.

"I thought it would look nice hanging right here, next to the portrait of Dean Thorne, who was, of course, Dean Sprowl's predecessor. Now, if we might turn our attention—"

"I don't think that's such a good idea," said Culpepper, looking concerned.

"Why's that, Tom?" asked the Dean. Please don't let this happen, the Dean said to himself.

"I'm not sure if you remember this—it might have been slightly before your time," Culpepper began. "But Dean Thorne and Dean Sprowl never saw eye to eye on anything. Dean Sprowl had a very different image of McKinley, and of legal education, from that of Dean Thorne. I think that on a symbolic level hanging the two portraits side by side is not such a good idea. If Dean Sprowl's widow ever came to the law school and saw her late husband's portrait hanging next to that of Dean Thorne, why, she'd be terribly upset."

"Tom's right," said Aaron Mountain. "They hated each other's guts. Hanging those portraits together would be like oil and water."

"Oil and water?" Stanger repeated. "You mean like oil and vinegar."

I knew this would happen, thought Dean Strong. Grown men.

"Shouldn't Sprowl have his own lounge?" asked Murray Frobisher. "It's only fair. If Dean Thorne got one, so should Dean Sprowl."

Herbert Sprowl had been something of a mentor to Frobisher.

"Do we have the space in the building for another lounge?" asked Stanger.

"How often does Dean Sprowl's widow come to visit, anyway?" asked Sanford Clapp, putting aside his war against the Saint in order to take part in a promising discussion. "And who cares what she thinks?"

The comment offended Culpepper. "Look here, Sanford," he said, "Louisa Sprowl is a gracious woman who has given a lot of herself to the law school. I think we should take her feelings into consideration as we choose a place to hang her late husband's portrait."

"She'll probably come to the ceremony," said Aaron Mountain. "We don't have to offend her needlessly."

This was too much for Ronald Blotchett. "If she comes, I'm staying home," said Blotchett. "I don't want anything to do with any of them."

"For crying out loud," said Clapp, "Louisa Sprowl didn't run off with your wife, her son did. You can't hold that against her."

"I hardly think that she'll be offended by her husband's portrait hanging next to that of his predecessor," said Edward Strong, his patience waning. "After all, they were both deans."

"I still think Sprowl should get his own lounge," said Frobisher. "Why should he have to hang in somebody else's lounge?"

"What kind of precedent would that set, Murray?" It was Stanger. "Does that mean that we'd have to give every dean his own lounge? No offense, Ed, but where would we find the space?"

"If we set aside a separate room to be the Sprowl Lounge," Aaron Mountain reasoned, "wouldn't we have to hold half of our meetings there?"

"I think Louisa Sprowl would be deeply moved," said Tom Culpepper, "by the dedication of a Sprowl Lounge. I think it's a lovely gesture."

"I don't like the sound of Sprowl Lounge," said Clapp. "It's very unpleasant to the ear. What if we gave him a classroom instead, Sprowl Hall?"

"That's a good idea," said Frobisher. "Then we can hang his portrait in his own classroom."

"Which room should we give him?" asked Mountain.

"If you make a Sprowl Hall, so help me, I'll quit and go to Harvard," Blotchett threatened.

"Good thinking, Ron," heckled Clapp. "Boston's a college town. Lots of nice healthy nineteen-year-olds for your clerking couch."

"That's enough, Sanford," said Dean Strong. "Now, gentlemen, er, members of the McKinley faculty, may I remind you that every portrait of every past dean and professor of law at McKinley hangs here in the Thorne Lounge and all I suggested was—"

"We know what you suggested," Clapp interrupted. "We just don't think it's such a hot idea, all right?"

"What about hanging it next to the window, over there?" suggested Culpepper.

"Where exactly?" asked Murray Frobisher.

"Right there, next to the portrait of Professor Martland," Culpepper said.

"It'll never work," said Frobisher. "They were both professors of antitrust law and their philosophies were completely opposed. Paul Martland was a free market man and Sprowl was an interventionist."

"Does it really matter?" asked the Dean.

"*They* thought so," said Frobisher. "They hated each other's guts. They used to glower at each other during faculty meetings."

"Did Martland really favor completely free markets?" It was Stanger again. "As I read his articles, I got a sense that he saw a place for some limited government intervention."

"Yeah, but nothing like Sprowl," said Frobisher. "Sprowl would holler conspiracy if two executives from competing companies so much as nodded at each other in the men's room at O'Hare. Sprowl was a terrific guy but he went a little overboard on his ideas about antitrust."

"Gentlemen, please—"

"Take it easy, Ed," said Clapp. "We're just trying to form a consensus."

"*About where to hang a painting?*" The Dean was incredulous. "All right. If you can't make up your minds quickly, then the portrait of Dean Sprowl is going to hang in my office, and that's the end of it."

A chorus of "But, Ed!" and "That's not fair!"

"I'm sorry," said the Dean, "but if you can't agree nicely among yourselves, then none of you can decide where the painting goes. I feel like a kindergarten teacher. Now, if we could please get back to the more important questions—"

"Dean Strong, if I may say a few words." It was Tom Culpepper.

"Of course, Tom. Go ahead."

"Thank you. I think each of us is in full accord with your handling of the Susan Garrett tragedy. In all my years at the law school I never knew of a single suicide by a student, and I've been told that in the last six months alone there have been three. I'm sure we're all quite saddened by this turn of events. But under the circumstances, I think the decisions you have made are clearly in the best interests of McKinley—the memorial service tomorrow morning, the cancellation of classes through the weekend. Some students, I understand, have been talking about a strike. I think your decision to cancel classes will give everyone a chance to cool off."

"Thank you, Tom," said the Dean. "I genuinely appreciate your thoughts. Normally I don't like to act so unilaterally, especially with such an important matter as this. But I thought that we could discuss it here. Comments? Debate?"

Silence.

The Dean looked at Clapp. "You could have talked until midnight about where to hang the portrait but not a word about Susan Garrett, or canceling classes?"

More silence, broken finally by Murray Frobisher. "Whatever you do is fine, Ed," Frobisher said blandly.

"I can't figure you people out," said Dean Strong.

"Who's going to speak at the memorial service?" asked Aaron Mountain.

"Who normally speaks at memorial services?" asked Stanger. "Is there a precedent?"

All eyes turned toward Culpepper.

"In 1945," he began, "at the conclusion of the Second World War, we had a memorial service for those McKinley men who fell in battle, and Dean Thorne spoke. In 1952, at the conclusion of the hostilities in Korea, we had a memorial service for those McKinley men who fell in battle, and Dean Thorne spoke. In 1975—"

"I think Sanford Clapp should say a few words," said Tony Sloop. "After all, Garrett *was* one of his students."

"Tony, no!" said Rebecca Shepard.

"What's your game, Tony?" asked a surprised Dean Strong.

"No game at all, Ed," Sloop said, feigning innocence. "I

just thought that since Sanford had been Susan's Contracts professor he probably knew her best of all of us, and so he'd be best qualified to say a few words in her memory."

"I really don't think I'm the best person to—" stammered Clapp.

"I think it's an excellent idea," said Murray Frobisher. Atta boy, Tony, he thought. I knew you'd come through for me one day.

"Hear, hear," said Aaron Mountain.

The Dean saw the alarm in Clapp's face. "I think that Sanford has suffered terribly today upon learning of the death of another of his students. He should not be asked to speak in public when—"

"Ed, I couldn't disagree with you more," said Frobisher. "Sanford is the perfect person to speak tomorrow at the memorial service. It'll be a healing gesture toward the students. They'll see that we really care. In fact, I move that we vote on it right now."

"Seconded," said Aaron Mountain.

"Any objections?" asked the Dean hopefully. "No? Well, all right. All in favor of Sanford speaking at the memorial service for Susan Garrett say aye."

A chorus of ayes.

"All those opposed, say nay."

Three nays: the Dean, an ashen Sanford Clapp, and Rebecca Shepard.

The Dean frowned. "Motion carries."

Sanford Clapp looked gratefully at Rebecca and mouthed, "Thank you."

"I don't think any of you realizes what a bad idea this is," said Dean Strong. "All right. Memorial service tomorrow at ten. Sanford and I will offer some remarks, as will—let me find my notes—Katrina Walfish of the Women's Law Caucus. Classes canceled until Monday to allow things to cool down. If there's no further business, I move—"

"Not so fast, Ed," said Sanford Clapp. "You know damned well there's 'further business.'"

The Dean closed his eyes and sighed.

"Members of the faculty," Clapp began, and he rose to his feet. "I need your support in a terribly crucial matter. One of our students has been caught in a serious violation of the McKinley Honor Code, and we as a faculty must act and act quickly."

Rebecca held her breath.

"One of our students has accused a professor of *murder*. This is the most flagrant violation of the respect due the faculty that I have ever seen. I want that student brought up on disciplinary charges. I want a full-dress hearing before the Judicial Board. I want a conviction, and I want his ass out of this law school. I am the professor who has been so accused, and the student in question is Daniel Conway."

The entire faculty responded at once.

"How could you?" asked Rebecca.

"Murder? That's a serious charge," said Frobisher.

"He actually accused you, Sanford?" asked Mountain.

"This is related to the suicide, I trust," said Tom Culpepper.

"What's the precedent?" Stanger asked. "How have we dealt with similar accusations in the past?"

"Well," said Culpepper, "in 1956—"

"Tom, please. I don't want to hear about 1956." The Dean's voice cut through the babble. "Sanford, he didn't accuse you of murder, and you know it."

"Well, he practically did. He stained the honor of the McKinley faculty, and I'll make myself as plain as possible. I want his ass out of this law school!"

Rebecca was horrified, even though this was not the first time she had seen Sanford Clapp take aim at a McKinley student at a faculty meeting.

"Isn't Daniel Conway the one they call the Saint?" asked Jackson Ward.

"That's right," said Frobisher.

"Didn't Conway get a degree from the Harvard Divinity School?" Ward asked.

"That's right," said Frobisher.

"Didn't Conway work as a missionary in West Africa for five years before he came to McKinley?"

"That's true, too," said Frobisher.

"Sanford, do you really expect me to believe," said Ward, "that a graduate of a divinity school who gave five years of his life to his church would falsely accuse a professor of murder? Come off it. I think you're just jealous of him because—"

Please, Jackson, don't do it, thought Rebecca.

"—because he and Rebecca are in love and you've had the hots for her ever since she arrived here!"

Pandemonium broke out. Rebecca buried her face in her hands.

Sanford Clapp's face went purple. "Jackson, I'm a happily married man! How dare you—"

"Oh, cut it out, Clapp. The only person in this room who doesn't know how you feel about Rebecca is Rebecca herself."

Rebecca, in fact, was aware of Sanford's attentions, and although she would never have admitted it to anyone, she was ever so slightly attracted to him.

"I don't have to take this from you," blustered Clapp.

"Well, a lot of people have had to take a lot from you," said Ward. "Including three students, one of whom was named Susan Garrett!"

"Gentlemen, please!" implored the Dean.

"You!" shouted Clapp to Jackson Ward. "You're no better than Conway! You're accusing me, too! All right! All right! This is a faculty meeting, and Jackson is free to say anything he wants about me. And it's not a crime in this state to find a woman attractive, even if she's not your wife. But we can't have students accusing professors of killing other students! It just won't wash! And let me remind you that an offense against the dignity of one McKinley professor is an offense against all of us." Clapp sat down.

"Hear, hear," said Aaron Mountain, breaking the silence.

"I hate to admit it," said Stanger, "but there really is something to what Sanford is saying. I've met Conway, and I think he's a great guy, but we've really got to close ranks on this one."

"Still," said Culpepper, "'throwing his ass on the street,' or however you put it, Sanford, does sound unduly harsh, don't you think?"

"What about a year's suspension?" asked Aaron Mountain.

"That sounds more appropriate," said Culpepper.

"Do you know what you're saying?" said Rebecca, unable

to keep silent any longer. "A year's suspension because a student merely related an opinion to the Dean? It's like something out of Orwell!"

"I'm sure we all know how you feel about Conway." Clapp leered.

"Please," said the Dean, "let's keep away from personal attacks. I personally am opposed to bringing any sort of charges against Daniel Conway. My own investigation into the matter suggests"—and he looked squarely at Clapp—"that Daniel was entirely justified in his suspicions. Nonetheless . . ." Clapp was turning purple again. "Nonetheless, the power to bring disciplinary charges resides in the faculty, not in the Dean. In other words, it's up to you all to decide how to handle it. Unless there are any further comments, and I believe we've heard from everyone, let's bring the matter to a vote. 'Resolved that the McKinley faculty bring disciplinary charges against Daniel Conway'"—the words were plainly distasteful to the Dean—"'for, er, offending the dignity of the McKinley faculty.' All in favor?"

Again, a chorus of ayes.

"All opposed?"

Four nays—the Dean, Jackson Ward, Tony Sloop, and Rebecca Shepard.

"Motion, I'm sorry to say, carries, six to four. Meeting adjourned. See you all at the memorial service, tomorrow morning at ten."

Rebecca glared at Sanford Clapp, whose eyes were shining with righteous indignation. I hope you're satisfied, you vindictive son of a bitch, she thought. I just hope you're satisfied.

TWENTY-TWO

The Saint's taxi finally pulled up outside Rebecca Shepard's building. It was after 10 P.M. Thundershowers in Washington had delayed his departure. The plane sat on the runway until the storm abated. Rebecca's agitation turned to relief when she finally heard his key in the lock. She ran to the door, unlocked it, and buried her face in his chest before he could even drop his battered suitcase.

"I missed you so much," she said, holding him close. "It's been an awful day."

"I missed you, too," he said. He let his suitcase fall and he wrapped his arms around her and kissed her lips.

"Come inside," said Rebecca. "I just made some coffee."

"Perfect," said the Saint. "I could use something warm."

They went into the kitchen, where the Saint took off his overcoat and his suit jacket and sat down at the table.

"I'm absolutely exhausted," he said. "Two half-day interviews would be bad enough, but flying in bad weather is just the worst."

"How'd they go?" Rebecca asked, pouring coffee.

"Couldn't have gone better," said the Saint. "I think I got both jobs."

"Saint, that's wonderful! Are you sure?" She set two mugs of coffee on the table and sat down.

"Almost certain," he said, a hint of pride in his voice.

"That's great," Rebecca said, but her mind was elsewhere.

"Why did you call Dean Strong? Do you know what you've done to yourself?"

"You mean about Susan?" the Saint asked. "How could I not have called?"

Rebecca took his hand. "Clapp figured out that you're the one who blamed him for Susan Garrett and for the other two suicides. He had the faculty bring you up on disciplinary charges. He wants to get you thrown out of McKinley."

"You're kidding! When was this?"

"At the Committee of Ten meeting this afternoon. Dean Strong called it to discuss Susan Garrett. There's going to be a memorial service tomorrow morning. Sanford is going to speak. It was Tony Sloop's idea. I guess he was trying to give Sanford a taste of his own medicine. Saint, I think Sanford's serious! He's going to get you suspended for a year, if not dismissed."

"Hold it, wait a minute," said the Saint, putting up both hands. "Let me get this straight. Clapp brought me up on disciplinary charges because of what I told Dean Strong? All I did was make a comment! Can he do that?"

"It was some comment. Think about it—you practically accused him of murder. Tenured faculty can do whatever they want, Saint, because they all stand up for each other. It's their unwritten law."

"But that's not fair!"

"Saint, this isn't Nigeria, and they don't settle things by having council meetings until dawn. If Clapp wants you out of McKinley, then you might just be out of McKinley."

"And he has the nerve to speak tomorrow in Susan's memory?" He sipped his coffee. "That man has no shame."

"I told you," said Rebecca. "It wasn't his idea. It was Tony's, and Frobisher backed him up. The rest just went along. They thought it would be a healing gesture toward the students."

"A healing gesture? Everybody knows what a—what an animal Clapp is in class. Him speaking will be like waving a red flag at a bull. The students will erupt!"

"Clapp knew it, too," said Rebecca. "You should have seen the look in his eyes when Tony made the suggestion. Abject panic."

"It's nice to think of Clapp on the receiving end for once," said the Saint.

"Mm-hmm. The Women's Law Caucus met all afternoon. They're very angry, and I can't say I blame them." She smiled. "I didn't exactly try to calm them down, though."

The Saint laughed. "I'll bet you didn't," he said.

"They passed a resolution calling for an end to 'brutality and banality in the classroom' and they're going to picket the law school building for the rest of the week."

"I sense the guiding hand of Katrina Walfish," said the Saint, and he smiled.

"You guessed it. She was in rare form. The women will never know it wasn't Clapp's idea to speak. When he steps up to the podium tomorrow you'll see bedlam."

"I'm not so sure I'd like to be there," said the Saint. "I'd like to be as far away from the law school as is humanly possible."

"Saint, are you serious? What a great idea! That could be wonderful! We could leave first thing in the morning and be away until Monday!"

"Where would we go?" he asked, taken with the idea.

"*Anywhere*, I know a beautiful little country inn. It's about a three-hour drive from here, but it's worth it. The weather may not be great, but at least we can walk in the woods and just be alone, and get away from all of this."

The Saint looked at her appreciatively. "Rebecca, that's the best idea you've had since you fell in love with me. You're still in love with me, aren't you?"

"Of course I love you, Saint. Come here and kiss me."

He did so. "We really can't miss the memorial service," he said, stroking her hair. "It wouldn't be right. But we could put our bags in the car before the service and take off once it ends."

"That's what we'll do," said Rebecca, kissing his eyebrows and detaching herself. "You must be half starved. I hope you don't mind more tuna salad. I didn't have time to shop. Tell me about the interviews."

"Oh, Rebecca," said the Saint, "what a day. I spent the morning at Holyoke and Knout—"

"Holyoke and Knout? That's my old firm! I didn't know

you were interviewing with them! Anyway, what do you want with Holyoke? They're big-time corporate. I thought you were going to graduate and save the world."

The Saint shrugged. "I didn't really want a job there. I guess I wanted to see what it was like, because you worked there."

"I'm flattered," said Rebecca. "And where were you this afternoon?"

"At the Environmental Law Foundation. Great bunch of people."

"It's another world compared to Holyoke, though. Tell me everything."

"Well," said the Saint, stretching his legs. "They put me up—Holyoke and Knout, I mean—in this fancy Washington hotel. I had an incredible view of the Capitol, the Washington Monument—everything. The hotel was filled with unbelievably well-dressed men and women. They were getting back from some sort of gala at the Kennedy Center. Well. I got in pretty late so I took a Jacuzzi—a Jacuzzi! In my own room! And then I found that someone from the firm—the recruitment coordinator—had left me a bottle of champagne on the night table by the bed. I brought it back with me. We can open it at the inn, if you want. That was all last night.

"Then this morning I woke up early, and I took a long walk around the city, and I saw all the important buildings—from the outside, because it was too early to go in anywhere—and when I got back to my room there was a message from the firm. The limousine would be picking me up at a quarter to ten. A limousine! I spent five years in Nigeria and never even saw an automobile most days! I felt more like a rock star than a law student."

"I never got any of that treatment when I was going for my interview," said Rebecca. "I drove all night with another woman law student and we stayed at a motel outside Baltimore."

"I think I would have been happier with the motel," said the Saint. "I sat in the limo thinking, Who's paying for all this? For the hotel? For my Jacuzzi? The champagne? The answer is pretty simple—the client and the American taxpayer."

Rebecca rolled her eyes, as if to say, "Here we go again." The Saint did not notice.

"Because the clients are oil companies, foreign governments, auto makers. And the firm can write it all off as a business expense. I sat there wondering if the clients knew where their money was going."

He noticed her expression and stopped. "What's wrong?" he asked.

She laughed. "You can spare me your 'I Hate Corporate America' routine," she said, her expression playful. "I've heard it a thousand times."

He gave an embarrassed grin. "I forgot who I was talking to," he said. "Hey, how come you worked there, Rebecca? Where was *your* social conscience back then?"

The question surprised her. "Don't give me any grief over my Holyoke and Knout days," she began. "They were—and are—one of the best corporate firms in D.C., and I wanted the best training I could get. Do you think it's possible for a woman—all right, for *anyone*—to get a job at a top law school like McKinley without the proper credentials? Look, it's easy for you to sit in the limo and have your liberal sensibilities offended. I didn't have that luxury. Holyoke and Knout was a line I needed on my resume, and there were no two ways about it. Of course, now that I'm about to get fired from McKinley, it doesn't really seem so important."

"Don't say that," said the Saint. "I keep telling you. They don't decide anything until next Friday."

"That's not exactly right," said Rebecca. "They don't *announce* anything until next Friday. But I think they made their decision a long time ago. Although today Dean Strong said that he was looking forward to reading my tenure essay. So maybe there's still hope."

"You see?" said the Saint through a mouthful of tuna. "That's the spirit. Anyway, I get to the firm and in three hours I have six interviews, and then I have to go out to lunch with two more lawyers. They asked me the same questions so many times that I felt like a suspect in a police station. I kept hearing myself saying the same things over and over—'I want to practice with a large Washington firm,' 'I want the best training'—and I finally lost my self-control in the last interview before lunch."

"Who was that with?" asked Rebecca, making the tea.

"I think his name was Tom Burdette."

"No, not that old fart! He used to chase me around the firm library and then make me promise not to tell his wife. What happened with Burdette?"

"He asked me one classic interview question after another, and he climaxed with 'What would you be doing if you weren't in law school?'"

"What did you tell him?" asked Rebecca.

"I told him the truth—that I'd be back in the acupuncture clinic in West Africa. He nearly fell out of his chair. 'Acupuncture? Isn't that where the Red Chinese go around sticking needles in people?' I don't think your pal Burdette is too interested in natural healing."

Rebecca doubled over laughing. "Burdette's a partner, Saint! What makes you think Holyoke is ever going to hire you now?"

"Well, I had lunch with two third-year associates, both born-again Christians. And they told me that Stanford Knout, one of the name partners, had seen my resume. It turns out that Knout did the same sort of missionary work in West Africa that I did, minus the acupuncture, I suppose. Anyway, he let everybody know that under no circumstances was I to be turned down for a job."

"I never knew that about Knout," said Rebecca. "You learned more in one day than I did in two years. Would you actually go to work for them?"

"I can't see it," said the Saint, sipping his coffee. "I wouldn't be very happy there. Even though they donate their services to a lot of good causes. They showed me the client list. Civil rights groups, environmental groups, and a lot of religious organizations. Must be Knout's doing."

"It's nice to hear that they're not utterly without conscience," said Rebecca, kneeing the Saint under the table, "after the way they waste their clients' hard-earned money on Jacuzzis and limousines—"

"Oh, cut it out." The Saint grinned.

"On people who don't even appreciate them!"

"Very funny," said the Saint. "But I haven't even told you about the Environmental Law Foundation. Goodbye, wood paneling; goodbye, thick carpets; goodbye, oil paintings on the partners' walls."

"Goodbye, limo; goodbye, champagne," added Rebecca.

"You bet. I took the subway to their offices and then had to walk up four flights. But it was worth it. That's where I heard about Susan. It was on the radio as I came in. Anyway, I ran into one of my buddies from West Africa—he's been working there about a year now. No formal interviews. None of the pomp and circumstance of a Holyoke and Knout. Just two dozen or so mostly young, really dedicated attorneys, representing environmental groups in court and coordinating lobbying efforts in Congress. They weren't even wearing ties. It got me excited about being a lawyer for the first time since I came to McKinley. I wanted to work there. I felt that my efforts really could make a difference. I must sound so Sixties, but I was really moved by what was happening in that office. I like the tuna salad, Rebecca."

"You should. You made it. But your idealism is nothing to be ashamed of, especially when I feel so burned out."

"Can I ask you a personal question?" asked the Saint.

"Of course!"

"You won't be offended?"

"Saint!"

"Rebecca, I know you had the same feeling for saving the world that I do. You told me how you wanted to devote your life's work to ending discrimination. If you felt so strongly about equal rights, why did you go into Securities Law?"

Rebecca waited before she answered. "You're right," she said. "That *is* a personal question. I thought you were going to ask me about how I lost my virginity, or something minor like that. Now, I know this may sound crazy, but by teaching Securities Regulation I *am* striking a blow for women's rights. Do you know how many women law professors teach Securities in this country? A handful. A small handful. Do you know how many women law professors have ever gotten tenure in Securities Law? None. Zero. Until the last few weeks, I actually had the nerve to think I might break the string. I know. You're about to say, 'But nothing's been decided yet.'

Let's quit fooling ourselves. I won't get tenure. Not at McKinley, not anywhere.

"It doesn't seem possible, but law—practice and teaching —really is one of the last bastions of discrimination in this country. It's only been changing in the last few years, now that more women go to law school, but look at the facts. On most law faculties, men outnumber women four or five to one. There have been only a few women deans in the *history* of law school. Okay, so now there are some women law professors, but what do they teach? Mostly it's Employment Discrimination, Family Law, and Trusts and Estates. These aren't exactly bread-and-butter kinds of courses. They're fringe courses, and everybody knows it.

"Okay, the big firms are hiring more women. But until a few years ago, do you know what department the women were always sent to? Trusts and Estates. Why? Because the clients are all dead. The law firm wouldn't have to embarrass itself, and make a client uncomfortable, by sending a woman. To do what they believe is a man's job.

"After all," Rebecca continued, "a lot of clients are up front about wanting men to handle their cases. Is a lawyer really that much better because his plumbing is on the outside and because he can talk about sports and how cute the secretaries are? I don't think so. The male lawyers say that women are unable to compromise, that they don't appreciate the nuances of negotiating. I went into Securities Law because I wanted to destroy that stereotype, and teach women that they could do anything the men do—negotiate, make deals, write up documents for the Securities and Exchange Commission— everything. And yet still remain women.

"I wanted them to be able to say, there goes Rebecca Shepard. She's a success in Securities Law—a 'man's field'—but on her own terms. She's not a backslapper, she doesn't have her head buried in the sports page, she's not pretending to be a man. She's a woman, and a Securities professor, and she doesn't have to compromise at either to succeed at both.

"That's why I went into Securities Law, Saint. But what kills me is that despite how hard I've worked, teaching and writing and counseling and tutoring students—despite everything I've done, I've failed at everything. No tenure, no job after next May, no home, no husband. I don't mean to offend you—I love you very much—but I just feel as though I . . . I corrupted you. You were a missionary, and then you were sleeping with me. This should never have even started. And you need someone closer to your own age—"

"Please, Rebecca," the Saint interrupted. "You break my heart when you give me that 'someone my own age' line. As for our sleeping together, that was a decision that I felt comfortable with at the time, and I still do. But I feel so helpless when you talk about not having someone to support you. You're such a successful person that I can't even understand how you can feel that way. And the kind of law I want to do barely pays anything at all. They told me what the starting salary was at the Environmental Law Foundation. It's about fourteen times the average per capita income in my village in Nigeria, but at least in Nigeria you can sleep on the ground and live off nuts and berries and what the hunters bring home. I could never support you on that salary. Heck, I could barely pay back my student loans.

"You know why I went to Holyoke and Knout today? Because of the money."

Rebecca looked up quickly.

"I thought, if I can get a job with them, or with someone like them, I can support you the way you'd like to be taken care of. Or at least the way you always talk about wanting to be taken care of."

She took his hand. "Oh, Saint, I never meant to hurt your feelings, or make you think about doing something you'd hate. I'm really touched that you'd even think about sacrificing your ideals for my sake, but I'd never let you do that. And I'm sorry about that 'no husband' talk, about the 'someone your own age' thing. I don't know what comes over me, and I hate myself for feeling that way. I just feel as though I've ruined my own life, and I don't want to see someone with as much to offer as you throwing your life away on someone like me."

"I can't believe what I'm hearing," the Saint exclaimed. "Throwing my life away? *I* believe in Rebecca Shepard, even if you don't. I read your tenure essay. I think it's going to revolutionize the teaching of law. Rebecca, you've just got to have some faith!"

Rebecca smiled bravely. She leaned forward and kissed him. "I don't have any right to complain about anything. I've got you."

"Now you're making sense," he said. "Hey. We'll do the dishes in the morning."

"What are you talking about?" asked Rebecca.

"You know darned well what I'm talking about. Come on. Finish your coffee."

"Forget the coffee," said Rebecca. "You know, I felt really cheated last night."

"Oh, yeah. Where were you?" asked the Saint as they went down the hall to Rebecca's bedroom. "You get a better offer?"

"Oh, I felt awful about it. When we made plans for last night, I'd completely forgotten about the reception for Professor of the Year. It dragged on and on, and by the time I could get to a telephone, you'd left for the airport."

They entered the bedroom and the Saint undid the first two buttons on her shirt. "Forget about it," he said. "I figured something came up. I knew you wouldn't just blow me off."

"And pass up a chance to see you in your boxer shorts? Not on your life."

"That's just how I feel about you," the Saint said. "Hey. I brought us a present."

"What's that?" Rebecca asked as she undressed and slid under the covers. The Saint removed his trousers and shirt, and joined her in bed. He reached up, turned off the lamp, and plugged in a night light. He leaned across the bed to the night table where he had left his shirt and took a small package from a pocket.

"I bought some incense from a Hare Krishna when my flight got delayed. I thought we could light it and spend tonight celebrating his First Amendment right to harass people in airports."

"You always were a sucker for freedom of religion cases," said Rebecca, smiling. The Saint lit the incense and he kissed Rebecca.

"I'm so glad you're back," she said.

"Me, too," he said, caressing her hair. "Hey, that incense smells awful."

"I should have warned you," said Rebecca. As they held each other in the glow of the night light, they turned for a moment to watch the stick of incense burn. "At least it looks better than it smells," said Rebecca. "You romantic thing, you."

Meanwhile, three blocks away, in the women's dormitory of the McKinley Law School, another small red dot of light glowed into the evening. The glow belonged to the cigarette of Marlene Feight, electronics expert and second-year law student, who had fallen asleep smoking in bed. Her fingers relaxed their grip on the half-smoked cigarette, which slowly turned her sheets and blankets into a smoldering conflagration. The smoke detector in her room rang loudly. Marlene opened her eyes, saw the flames, bolted upright, and yelled, "Fire!" She leaped out of bed and ran down the corridor. Alarms went off everywhere. The fire spread quickly through the door Marlene left open, but not quickly enough to trap any of the women inside.

"Fire! Get out! The dorm's on fire!" Pandemonium ensued. The smoke detectors triggered an alarm at the firehouse four blocks away, and fire trucks, firemen, hoses, and equipment came spilling onto the scene. In the small park across the street from the dormitory shivered one hundred and twenty women students wrapped in blankets, overcoats, or the clothes they were wearing when the fire broke out. Some clutched their casebooks and class notes, the possessions they believed they could least afford to lose. In tears and in horror they watched the fire fighters flood their rooms to put out the blaze. Fortunately, their quick work saved everything but the area nearest to Marlene Feight's room.

If anybody recognizes me, I'm dead, thought Tony Sloop, recovered sufficiently from his fall from the performance art studio ceiling to pay a nighttime visit to a McKinley student who found the young professor as attractive as he found her. With her overcoat pulled over his shoulders, he slowly made his way to a clump of shrubbery in the back of the park where he thought he might hide.

If anybody recognizes me, I'm dead, thought Sanford Clapp, who had told his wife he would be working late, writing his speech for the following morning's memorial service, but who had in fact been spending the last forty-five minutes with a McKinley student, attempting to regain some of his lost youth. Clapp wore boxer shorts, a terrycloth robe, and fuzzy bedroom slippers—the only clothing he could find as he fled. At the back of the park he noticed some shrubbery and thought he might hide behind it, if he could only cross the crowded park without being noticed.

Slowly, and from two different starting points within the park, Tony Sloop and Sanford Clapp made their way to the little patch of shrubbery. By a stroke of ill fortune the two arrived at the same moment.

"Is that you, Sanford?" Sloop asked, nearly falling over laughing.

"Why, Tony!" Clapp exclaimed, furious at being discovered. "Imagine meeting you here, you preachy little snot! Making me speak at the memorial service! I'd like to wring your neck."

"Up yours, Sanford," said Sloop, unable to stop laughing.

"My office or yours, you little pecker?"

"Come on, let's not waste time," said Sloop, regaining control over himself. "My car is over there," and he pointed to a Fiat convertible thirty yards away. "If we can only get into it without being seen. I've got the keys right here. On the count of three—"

"I knew it!"

The men turned in the direction of the all-too-familiar voice.

"Hold it!" ordered Katrina Walfish. They froze, mouths open, Sloop in an overcoat, and Clapp in boxer shorts, terrycloth robe, and fluffy bedroom slippers, the flash from Katrina's camera capturing on their faces the same expression that headlights capture when a frightened rabbit darts onto a country road.

THURSDAY, OCTOBER 4

—

FRIDAY, OCTOBER 5

TWENTY-THREE

The next morning, Rebecca Shepard sat on the easy chair beside the desk in her office, going over her lecture notes for her next Torts class, which she would teach the following Monday—assuming that the strike was over by then. She and the Saint had planned to meet in her office at a quarter to ten, attend the memorial service for Susan Garrett, and then depart quickly. Rebecca wanted to prepare now for Monday's class so that her conscience would be at rest over the long weekend. The Saint had packed their bags in her car and was reading cases in his usual spot in the sub-basement of the law school library.

The subject of discussion in Rebecca's next Torts lecture would be a decision from the law courts of seventeenth-century England. The case involved two boys who tossed a lit firecracker into a crowded farmer's market, as a prank. One person after another seized the burning thing and threw it away from his or her market stall until it finally came to rest in a hayrick and burned the hay to the ground. The case, though old, was instructive: Could the original tossers of the firecracker be held responsible for the damage it caused at the end of its wanderings? In other words, was it foreseeable that *something* would catch on fire, and should the boys have to pay for the damage they caused? The case neatly illustrated the principle that the law for centuries has held people responsible for the foreseeable results of their actions—and, in certain circumstances, for the unforeseeable results as well.

Suddenly Rebecca's door flew open. Sanford Clapp, his face purple with rage, stormed in.

"You did it!" he snarled. He waved a clipboard at her.

Rebecca involuntarily covered her mouth with her hand. "Did what?" she murmured.

"The letter! The Professor of the Year letter! I even *bought you lunch!*"

Rebecca thought back to her subsidized salad and glass of wine, which had to have set Sanford back no more than two dollars and fifty cents. Despite her fear, she suppressed a laugh.

"I made a fool of myself in front of you," Clapp said angrily. "And in front of my wife! And in front of half the faculty! Even in front of my Contracts class! And now you're going to pay for it!"

He advanced menacingly and Rebecca thought for a brief moment that she might be in actual physical danger. "I don't know what you're talking about—" she began.

Clapp cut her off. "I know damned well it was you. It didn't take that much figuring out. I suspected you from the beginning, you know. You were acting so strangely when we had lunch, when you pretended you were sick all of a sudden."

I wasn't pretending, Rebecca thought.

"And then the way you were looking at me at the Committee of Ten meeting. I wasn't born yesterday, you know. I figured the students are too scared to pull a stunt like that, and then I did a little detective work. First I went down to the print shop, and I checked the log. And sure enough, one Daniel Conway had done a little photocopying on Friday, and he charged it to *your account*. And Charlie down there even remembered doing it for him. Charlie said that Conway gave him a one-page letter and told him to make thirty-five copies, and that Conway insisted on him doing it right away, and that he couldn't leave it around."

Rebecca's heart sank.

"And then I went to the mailroom," Clapp continued. "And in case you didn't know it, they keep a log of everyone who comes in to stuff the faculty mailboxes. You wouldn't run the risk yourself of getting caught. So you send your little Boy Scout, your little religion major. Sure enough. Nine-fifteen A.M., Monday, October first. Daniel Conway. *I took the log*," he said, brandishing the clipboard. "It's going to be Exhibit A at the Judicial Board hearing when I get Conway bounced out of this law school."

"But Sanford—"

Clapp cut her off again. "I'm not interested in your excuses," he said, and suddenly he smiled. "I really should be thanking you. You made a difficult job very easy for me. I didn't know on what grounds I could oppose your getting tenure. I didn't have anything at all against you, except for the fact that I'm opposed to everything you stand for. But you've just handed me the perfect excuse. We even voted at the Committee of Ten meeting last week to bounce whoever did the Professor of the Year letter. And now it turns out to be you! You and Conway! Wait until I tell the Dean. Goodbye, Rebecca. It's been a pleasure. A true pleasure." Sanford stalked out and slammed the door behind him.

Rebecca sat motionless in her easy chair, her lecture notes on her lap. She sighed. "This wasn't supposed to happen," she said to herself.

She thought of the Saint, and suddenly her expression grew grave. "Daniel!" she exclaimed. "How could he let me *do* it? Didn't he realize my career's on the line? Where was his common sense?"

Rebecca stood up and looked at her watch. Then she strode down the hall, ignoring greetings from Tony Sloop, whom she passed without noticing. She was in something close to a blind rage. She went to the elevator, pushed the "down" button, and tapped her foot impatiently until it arrived. When she stepped in, she did not even notice Aaron Mountain standing beside her, offering his usual sullen greeting. At the ground floor she marched to the library door, past the monitor (one of her Securities students, surprised and somewhat hurt when Rebecca failed to return her greeting), and down the corridor to the stairwell. Rebecca walked down two flights of stairs to the sub-basement where the Saint was known to study. She found him at a long table with five other law students, all of whom were briefing cases.

"Rebecca, what a surprise," the Saint began, smiling. "I never see you down here." Then he noticed her tight-lipped expression. "What's the matter? Is everything all right?" Instinctively he knew that an explosion was coming. He had never seen her this angry.

"Come over here," she said sharply. She directed him to follow her to a set of bookshelves not quite out of earshot of the five students, all of whom were absorbed in this unexpected but welcome domestic drama.

"What's wrong?" the Saint asked, fearful, as he followed her.

"Where the hell are your brains?" she hissed.

"What are you talking about?" the Saint asked, stung by her words.

"How could you have let me get involved with that stupid letter?"

"It was just a joke."

"Some joke, Daniel! You might have just cost me my career!"

"What happened? What's going on?"

"I'll tell you what's going on. Sanford figured out we did it. And he's going to use it against me. He's livid. He's going to make sure I don't get tenure."

The Saint was stunned. "Are you serious?" he asked.

"Don't I *look* serious? He went to the print shop and then he went to the mailroom. How could you have put my name down when you copied the letter?"

"What was I supposed to do?" the Saint asked. "Students can't get things copied unless it's for a professor."

"You could have gone across the street to that copying store. What would it have cost, two dollars? Sanford said he was going straight to Dean Strong. For crying out loud, how could you have done such a stupid thing? Where were your brains?"

"Rebecca, will you please get a grip on yourself? Only this morning you told me what a great idea the letter was. Calm down."

Rebecca's eyes narrowed. "I will not have a student talking

to me that way! Look, you know I've been overwrought about this whole tenure thing—you know I was relying on your judgment. And now you've cost me my career! I'm through with you! I want all of your crap out of my apartment by nine o'clock tonight! Okay? That's it! The whole thing was ridiculous, anyway, getting involved with a student. I don't even know where my brains were. I don't even want to look at you. And forget about the Grey Mountains. We're not going. No. I have to get out of this place. *You're* not going."

She turned and walked quickly away. He watched her disappear into the stairwell, and so did the five students at the table, who could not possibly have avoided hearing the conversation. As the Saint returned to the table to retrieve his notebook—he no longer had the heart to get any work done —five pairs of eyes looked up briefly from casebooks, studied him, and returned to the casebooks.

"She gets in these moods sometimes," he attempted to explain. "Aw, nuts," he said, and he gathered his materials and went off.

TWENTY-FOUR

Meanwhile, Sanford Clapp, a man of his word, took his clipboard straight to Dean Strong. The Dean received Clapp's accusation with thin-lipped silence. This took the edge off Clapp's pleasure. He had expected Dean Strong to express satisfaction at his cracking of the case and perhaps to offer congratulations and "a job well done, old man," for Clapp's defense, by means of ingenious detective work, of the honor of the McKinley faculty.

"Aren't you going to say anything at all, Ed?" Clapp asked, his disappointment evident.

"What *can* I say?" Dean Strong asked, his tone resigned, his notes for his speech at the memorial service before him on his desk. "I was afraid Rebecca was behind it. I was just hoping it wasn't so, or if she *was* involved, that it might not have come out until after the tenure decision."

Clapp did not understand. "But why, Ed? Why are you protecting *her* all of a sudden? This law school would be a hell of a lot better off without her, and you know it. And now I've just brought you a—a smoking gun! A perfect opportunity for getting rid of her! And you just sit there!"

Dean Strong said nothing.

"In fact," Sanford continued, "you're *obligated* to get rid of her now! We took a vote! At the Committee of Ten meeting last Monday—whoever was behind the letters would be dismissed. Don't you remember?"

"I remember the vote very well, Sanford," said the Dean with more than a trace of exasperation. "We voted that the *student* responsible would be dismissed. The punishment doesn't apply to faculty members."

"Oh, but Ed"—Sanford shook his head angrily—"why do you always have to be so *literal?* Look at the spirit of the thing!"

"Sanford," asked Dean Strong, his expression dour, "what's this I hear about you carrying on with a woman student *in her dormitory room?*"

Clapp was speechless.

"Is that your idea of improving student-faculty relations?"

Clapp reddened. "All right, so I got caught." He quickly regained the offense, though. "You know, Tony Sloop was there, too. But that doesn't change anything about—"

"No, I disagree," Dean Strong interrupted. "I think it changes a lot. I think you're arguing from a very weak moral position right now. Don't you?"

"Aw"—Sanford grimaced—"what the hell am I supposed to say? I got caught one time with my pants down."

"With your pants off."

"All right, all right," said Clapp, waving a hand. "Have it your way. But I still don't see what one thing has to do with another, that's all. There's no *rule* against, er, visiting students in the dormitory."

"You're right," said the Dean, controlling his temper. "There's nothing in the Faculty Handbook about visiting students at eleven at night in the women's dormitory. The trustees of McKinley University, as far as I know, have also failed to voice their opinion on the matter. Sanford, thank you for pointing that out to me. I wasn't aware of the gap in policy. Get out of my office, will you, Sanford? I've got no patience right now."

The light was gone from Sanford Clapp's eyes. Slowly, defeated, he stood to leave, but not without a parting shot. "I gave you a sword, Ed, and you dropped it," Clapp said, pointing a finger at the Dean. "And do you know what happens to the careers of deans who . . . who disregard the will of their faculty? *Nothing.* They go *nowhere.* And that could happen to you, Ed. Just wait and see. I'll see you at the memorial service."

Sanford Clapp left the Dean's office and slammed the door behind him. He stalked off in search of anyone he could tell about his great discovery and about Ed Strong's stiff-necked ingratitude. He found many such people—colleagues and even a few students. Word spread quickly around McKinley.

Edward Strong sat at his desk, covering his face in his hands. He reached for the intercom. "Ms. Kennecutt," he said, "would you please track down Rebecca Shepard and ask her to come here at once. Thank you."

Clapp's revelation was disturbing enough for the Dean. His departing words had found their mark as well. Ambitious people tend to recognize the same quality in others. Clapp certainly saw it in the Dean. As a loyal McKinley faculty member, he suspected Edward Strong of carpetbagging—of using the law school, which Clapp in fact loved deeply, as a stepping-stone to greater things. Sanford Clapp himself had made the short list of contenders for Dean of the law school when Herbert Sprowl, the previous Dean, stepped down. Clapp might have been offered the post, the story had it, but for his abrasive side, which was said to offend certain of the trustees. Clapp, therefore, examined every move of Dean Strong for signs of placing personal career interests over the needs of the law school. Dean Strong knew that Sanford would view his lack of enthusiasm over the evidence implicating Rebecca as such a case. Ironically enough, the Dean mused, Clapp's assessment of the situation would not be that far from the truth.

Ed Strong long ago had drawn up a list of goals for his Deanship. At a minimum, he wanted to mark his term of office with the appointment of some "star" professors enticed from other law schools, bring about a sizable increase in the law school's endowment, and make some improvements in the law school's physical plant to make the building less stark and unpleasant. (Students joked that the poured concrete covering the first two stories of the law school building during the last attempt at renovation made it the safest place in the city in the event of nuclear war.) Most important, Dean Strong sought to put an end to the talk that McKinley was coasting on a reputation for academic excellence that was no longer deserved.

So far, the Dean had not succeeded in any of these areas. With the exceptions of Jackson Ward and Robert Stanger, Dean Strong had failed to attract any big names to the McKinley faculty. The endowment was keeping pace with inflation, but only barely. Although architects' drawings for a less dismal students' lounge had been posted conspicuously for more than a year, the actual construction work was the victim of endless and inexplicable delay. Worst of all, that the law school was indeed coasting on former glory was something repeated everywhere but in the corridors of McKinley.

If Dean Strong's basic goals had yet to be achieved, his grandest thoughts had gone nowhere. The Dean was not the sort of person to be satisfied with one important position after another. A part of him wanted to be not merely excellent but legendary at whatever he did. As law clerk to the Chief Justice, for example, he set records unmatched since for hours worked, words produced, and drafts of decisions written. As counsel to the American Embassy in Paris, for his role in delicate trade negotiations between the United States, France, and Saudi Arabia, he had won praise not only from the Ambassador but from the President himself. (In addition, he made a variety of political, business, and cultural contacts that would serve him well if he ever entered politics.) As Dean of the law school, Edward Strong would not be satisfied to be considered a fairly good dean who served McKinley well. Rather, he merely wanted to preside over the next revolution in legal studies. He wanted his name to go down beside that of Dean Langdell, the Harvard Law School Dean who assured his place in legal history by introducing the case method and the Socratic method.

Dean Strong's problem was that he had no idea how to go about creating, or even supervising, a revolution in the study of law. For this reason, Rebecca Shepard was so important to him. For the same reason, he was so distressed by Sanford Clapp's news. Rebecca Shepard was Dean Strong's main chance for greatness as a dean. She was the first person he had met who brought what he believed to be fresh ideas to the teaching of law. He was not as interested in her role-playing exercises in class; many people attempted those sorts of things, with varying degrees of success. Dean Strong sensed, though, that Rebecca—with her abandonment of case-briefing and rote memorization, her emphases on how law and society evolve and on the actual day-to-day lives of lawyers, her open-door policy, her unfeigned affection and concern for her students, and her love for teaching—was altogether different from any law professor he had ever known.

The things she did made sense, really. Fewer than one percent of all disputes ever end up in court. Even fewer cases become the subject of appellate decisions, so there was no real reason to study appellate decisions almost exclusively, as happens in most law schools, including McKinley. Dean Strong analogized law school's infatuation with appellate decisions to an imaginary medical school where they trained every student, whether he was going to be a surgeon or a general practitioner, in only one area—open heart surgery. An important skill, to be sure, but not the only one that every doctor will ever need. As many patients need such surgery as clients need their cases argued at the Supreme Court, but this was what law school emphasized, to the exclusion of virtually everything else. Law firms, moreover, had been complaining with mounting intensity about the inability of law school graduates to perform any but the most basic tasks of legal research. The Dean believed that the time was ripe for some sort of overhaul.

But how to start it? Dean Strong feared that Rebecca's effect on her students was due to her own personal magic, and that her methods, in the hands of a Sanford Clapp or a Ronald Blotchett, would go nowhere. He wanted to find out, though. If Rebecca Shepard could show McKinley a better way to educate students, the Dean reasoned, and if Rebecca's methods were to be copied elsewhere, then no small amount of credit would naturally fall upon the shoulders of the Dean courageous enough to give her a free hand. The first step to permitting Rebecca to adopt her methods to other courses was to grant her tenure. Overcoming the opposition of Clapp, Frobisher, and the rest would have been enough of a test of the Dean's political skills. To turn over any measure of responsibility to someone who did not seem to respect McKinley as an institution—to someone who publicly mocked the rest of the faculty—this was difficult even for Dean Strong. But then there was the consent decree. If McKinley denied Rebecca tenure, where would they find another woman? Such was the Dean's dilemma.

Ms. Kennecutt was buzzing. Rebecca Shepard was waiting outside the Dean's office. Dean Strong stood up and began to pace. She opened the door quietly. Just as the Dean began to address her, he noticed that her eyes were red, presumably from crying. For a long moment neither spoke.

And then: "I let you down," Rebecca said quietly. Her voice was flat.

"Why did you do it?" the Dean asked. "And why *now*? Don't you realize what you've done? Do you know how hard you've made my job?"

Rebecca blinked uncomprehendingly. "*Your* job?" she asked.

"I've never told you this," said the Dean, his tone that of a defeated man. "But you're practically the only voice of sanity in this institution. You're the only one who . . . who avoids all the stupid little jealousies and nonsense that the rest of the faculty just wallows in. You're practically the only professor who commands real respect from the students. And from me. I was going to make sure that you got tenure."

Rebecca was stunned.

"And I was going to put you in charge of a curriculum review committee, a real one, with teeth. I wanted to make McKinley a laboratory, and I wanted to try your methods with other classes. We would have done things your way. And then you pull a stunt like this."

Rebecca shook her head slowly. "You're not serious, are you?" she said, her voice barely audible.

"Completely serious. Now I don't know what the hell I'm going to do."

Rebecca was near tears. "You could have told me, Ed."

"What are you talking about?" he asked. "Told you what?"

"You could have given me a sign. Some indication that you liked my work. *Anything*. In the four years I've been teaching here, I haven't gotten *one word* of encouragement from you, or from anyone else. It's like I've been working in a vacuum.

I've had offers to go elsewhere. I didn't have to stay here. I did because it was just criminal to have a law school like McKinley without a single tenured woman. And practically everything you've ever done or said was a signal to me that I wasn't going to make it. Even that tenure committee you picked. How can you tell me that you were going to give me tenure all along?"

"Now hold on, Rebecca," said the Dean. "That committee was just window dressing. I wanted the faculty to feel as though they had been consulted. If I put people like Jackson or Tony on it, they'd feel as though their objections hadn't been considered."

"Really?" Rebecca asked, wanting to believe him.

"I give you my word," said Dean Strong. He sighed. "I guess I owe you an apology. You're right about my not having given you a sign that you—that you were on the right track. It's just that this faculty is such a delicate balance, I didn't want it to look like I was favoring anyone at anyone else's expense."

Rebecca took out a handkerchief. "You might have thought of my feelings, Ed," she said. "That's all. If you appreciated what I was saying, you might have said so."

The Dean shook his head slowly and looked at his watch. "I've got to get to the memorial service," he said. "We'll continue this later, if you'd like."

Rebecca raised her eyebrows, as if to ask, "Is there any reason to?"

The Dean nodded.

"Let me think things through," he said. "I promise you I'll—I'll do what's right."

Rebecca stood up. "I'm sorry I let you down, Ed," she said. "If you'll excuse me," she said, and she left the office.

TWENTY-FIVE

DO GRADES GO UP AS STUDENTS GO DOWN? teased the banner headline over the photograph of the midnight pair of surprised academics, Tony Sloop and Sanford Clapp. The staff of the *McKinley Law School News,* the weekly student newspaper, had labored all night to produce a special issue covering the Garrett suicide, the threatened strike, the dormitory fire, and, on the top of the front page, Katrina Walfish's moment of triumph, nabbing two faculty members if not in flagrante delicto then at least shortly thereafter. A copy of the newspaper lay beside or on the lap of every McKinley student and professor at the packed memorial service. A thoroughly chastened Sanford Clapp was finishing his hastily written tribute to Susan Garrett.

"And so," said Clapp, his voice breaking, "the McKinley community bids farewell to one of its most promising members, a student whose memory shall inspire us all to make an even finer institution. Thank you very much."

Silence, broken by scattered booing. No one knew quite how to react.

"Thank you, Professor Clapp." It was the Dean. "I now call upon Katrina Walfish, chair of the McKinley Women's Law Caucus—"

"And head photographer for the *Law School News,*" shouted a woman student, to much laughter.

The Dean's face reddened. "—for some concluding remarks."

Katrina Walfish had not been to bed at all the previous night. When the fire broke out she had been in the dormitory on the telephone with her boyfriend Paul in Denver. She grabbed at the first valuable thing she saw, which happened to be her camera, which happened to be loaded. Now she strode purposefully to the podium.

"Susan Garrett was not the first victim of the law school system," she began. "But she *will* be the last!"

Cheers and cries of "Go get 'em Katrina!" erupted from the audience. Dean Strong gave an alarmed look to Murray Frobisher, seated with a dapper Frank Rooney. Rooney had spent the evening before at a nearby Blanchard's, buying elegant clothing on advice of counsel.

"We're not going to stand for any more brutality in the classroom!" Katrina continued. "We're not going to be humiliated by ego-tripping professors who justify their behavior by wrapping themselves in the Socratic method as if it were"—she looked directly at Sanford Clapp—"as if it were a terrycloth robe on a cold October night!"

The audience erupted again. Clapp wanted to crawl away and die.

"Are we going to take it?"

"No!"

"Are we going to take it?"

"*No!*"

"I can't hear you!"

"NO!!!" exclaimed the frenzied students.

"I'll tell you something about the faculty here," Katrina went on. "They don't listen to reason. They listen to threats. They listen to blackmail."

"Sounds like she's been listening to Frobisher," Dean Strong said aloud.

"We have to send the McKinley faculty a message! We have to send the McKinley administration a message! We have to send the entire legal community a message! We're sick and tired of being humiliated! We're sick and tired of being abused! We're sick and tired of law school the way it is today!

I'm not blaming any one person," she said, looking squarely at Clapp, who avoided her gaze.

"I'm blaming the whole system! The current system of legal education in this country is a joke! It's got to go! These professors don't educate. They don't give a damn about teaching, about their students, about you and me! All they care about is their prestige, their *Law Review* articles, their outside consulting jobs, and how many women law students they can screw in a semester! Is that the way it should be?"

"No!"

"Is that the way it should be?"

"No!"

"I can't hear you!"

"NO!!!"

A reporter and camera crew for a local television station were just pulling out of the law school parking lot when they heard the chorus of students answering Katrina's questions. They had filmed the Clapp speech and some opening remarks by the Dean, all of which, they felt, was fairly pedestrian stuff. The reporter looked at the crew. The driver backed the van into another space, and they ran with their equipment back into the auditorium.

"Nothing ever changes in law school, or anywhere else," Katrina was saying, "unless someone demands change. We're not going to let McKinley forget Susan Garrett or the other two students who took their own lives. We're going to demand changes! And we want those changes *now*! No more brutality or banality in the classroom! No more professors pushing us around! We want the curriculum scrapped! We want the Socratic method scrapped! And we want any professor who abuses, mistreats, or humiliates even a single law student— we want that professor scrapped, too!"

The audience went wild with cheering. The television crew got it all on videotape.

"I've just gotten off the telephone with the heads of the women's associations at the other four law schools in town," Katrina went on. "They've pledged that if we go out on strike, they will, too. If we blockade the entrance to McKinley, they'll blockade the entrance to every law school in the city! If the faculty can't get inside, they can't humiliate the students!

And if they don't promise to stop abusing the students, *they'll never get back inside*! Are we going to tell those other law schools that we didn't have the *guts* to stand up to our professors?"

"No!"

"Well, then, what are we going to do?"

"Strike!"

"When are we going to do it?"

"NOW!"

"What do we want?"

"STRIKE!"

"When do we want it?"

"NOW!"

"What do we want?"

"STRIKE!"

"When do we want it?"

"NOW!"

"Thank you very much!" Katrina Walfish, eyes shining, moved away from the podium to tumultuous applause. The students surged forward to surround her. The television crew pushed through the mob to interview Katrina. Sanford Clapp, fearing for his life, snuck out through a side door.

Meanwhile, Rebecca Shepard was in her car and on her way to the Grey Mountains Inn. She felt bewildered by the events of the morning—Sanford's accusation, her fight with the Saint, and her conversation with Dean Strong. It bothered her not to be present for the memorial service, but she was simply too overwrought to have attended. From Dean Strong's office she went directly to her car. She removed the Saint's suitcase and brought it back to her apartment. She simply had to get away and to be alone. She thought about calling someone at the law school to find out what was going on, but she decided that there was no point. "I'm sure the Dean said something dull," she told herself, "and then Sanford said something duller, and then everyone took off for a long weekend. Everything's probably back to normal already."

Rebecca was wrong. Bedlam spread from the auditorium and throughout the law school building as students surged in every direction, sealing off entrances and chasing out the few professors who remained after the memorial service. Some

students took over the print shop and began turning out plac-
ards reading "No More Brutality and Banality in the Law
School!" News of the strike quickly reached the city's other
law schools, whose student bodies, led by their women's law
student groups, promptly shut them down. The local radio
stations began to broadcast the story. They sent reporters, and
television stations sent camera crews, to each of the law
schools, but especially to McKinley, where Katrina Walfish
stood on the front steps giving an endless series of news conferences to arriving members of the press.

Katrina keenly regretted Rebecca's absence, whose advice
she gladly would have sought as events unfolded. She felt that
Rebecca was wrong to disappear when she was most needed.
Rebecca did not even return any of the telephone messages
Katrina left on her answering machine. To Katrina's own surprise, though, she found herself more than equal to the task of
leading the strike. Moreover, she found herself loving every
minute of it.

TWENTY-SIX

Ronald Blotchett, dripping wet, a bath towel wrapped lightly around his waist, emerged from the bathroom in Karen Conner's apartment. Karen, the Adjunct Professor of Wills at McKinley Law School and a fifth-year associate at the prestigious downtown law firm of Gregory and Peterson, lay curled on her futon, a rumpled pink flannel sheet pulled up just below her neck. Karen had blue eyes and auburn hair cut to a length she described as "new wave corporate." She had a reputation around her law firm for getting what she wanted. What she wanted, more than anything else, was to give up the practice of law and become a full-time member of the McKinley faculty. Five years of eleven-hour days at the office had taken their toll, and she had had enough.

The usual path for attorneys in private practice who have tired of the competitive struggle and weekends of work is to go "in-house"—to join the legal department of a corporation that is a client of the firm. Although the pay is not quite as high, the hours are nine to five, or thereabouts, and the daily pressure is much less intense. Karen wanted no part of going in-house—she wanted out of practicing law and into teaching it. She did not feel that she knew Dean Strong well enough to broach the subject directly. She had been casting about for an "in" with the Dean when Ronald Blotchett called, ostensibly to discuss estate planning. And now, here was Blotchett, his expression suggesting that he had been thinking deeply about

something while he was in the shower, and that a pronounce-
ment on that subject, whatever it might have been, was forthcoming.

"I didn't really intend to do this," he said, speaking slowly.

Karen smiled. "What didn't you intend?" she asked. "To
wash your hair?"

Ronald paused, realized that Karen was making a joke, and
shook his head. "No, I mean my being here. The whole bit."

Karen, somewhat concerned, shifted her weight under the
sheet. "What are you talking about?" she asked. "Didn't you
enjoy yourself? Or are you married? Bisexual? Do you have a
disease? Is there something you should have told me last
night?"

"No, nothing like that," said Ronald, who came and sat on
the edge of the bed and stroked Karen's ankle. "I had made a
kind of resolution. I was going to change my style."

Karen studied him. She feared that he was making fun of
her somehow, but she did not think him bright enough to do
so. "What do you mean, change your style?" she asked. She
rubbed her foot against his thigh. "I kind of like it the way it
is."

"Thank you," he said, but he looked more and more troubled. "But I really wanted to change my whole *approach*," he
said.

"Your approach? To what?"

"To women," he said soberly. "To you."

Karen sat up. "Your approach to women?" she repeated,
trying to understand.

"Sure," said Ronald. "I've got to explain. The other morning, one of my students, um, pointed out a few things I wasn't
aware of. In the way I relate to women students. And then
yesterday afternoon I came across a book in the drugstore
about relationships and how to love people. It's called *Hug-
ging*. I don't know if you've heard of it. Well, I read the first
couple of chapters before I picked you up for dinner last night.
I decided then and there that I wouldn't do this kind of thing
any more. I was going to take things slower. Especially with
you."

Karen grew more puzzled. "I don't know what you're talking about," she said.

"This," he said, pointing to the bed, irritated by her failure to catch on. "Us. Sex. Last night. This morning. The whole thing. I wanted to turn over a new leaf."

Karen's eyes narrowed. "You're a very strange man," she said.

"It was the most harrowing thing that ever happened to me," said Ronald, shaking his head slowly. "One of my clerkship interviews turned into a nightmare. She wiretapped me. I mean my couch. I mean, she was carrying a transmitter, and I admitted that I'd slept with some of the women I'd recommended for clerkships."

"Why did I ever agree to have dinner with you?" Karen asked.

Blotchett looked concerned. "You didn't like the food? I told you to order the piccata."

"The meal was wonderful," said Karen. "My fettucine was great. The wine you chose was terrific. I love chianti. Even the strolling violinist wasn't too pathetic. It's just *you*."

Blotchett took off his towel and slid under the sheet. He stretched, folded his hands beneath his head, and looked at the ceiling. "I feel as though I've just blown everything, that's all."

"Ronald," said Karen, eying him, "has anyone ever told you that you're not like all the other boys?" And they trust this man to teach law students, she thought.

"No," he said. "No one ever did. What do you mean?" Suddenly, without waiting for an answer, he rolled over and faced her. His expression was contrite. He took her hand. "Karen, I'm truly sorry."

She shook her head uncomprehendingly. "There's really no reason to apologize. Honestly. I just want you to know that you're turning what was a very pleasant experience into an episode from *The Twilight Zone*."

Ronald's eyes lit up. "You mean you're not angry? You don't mind that we went to bed together after one dinner?"

"It's unusual for me, I'll say that much," she said. "But of course I'm not *angry*. Look, *I* invited *you* to come inside when you were going to drop me off. You didn't have to break my door down. When you called me, I knew you didn't really want to talk about your will."

"You did?" Ronald was amazed.

Karen just laughed.

"I lied," Ronald admitted. "But that was the old Ronald Blotchett. The new me would never have done that."

"I think I would have liked the old Ronald Blotchett better," she responded. "At least I would have known where I stood with him. The new you is a little bizarre. Look, it's ten-thirty already. I've got to get dressed. I've got to go to the office."

Blotchett leaned on one arm. "You don't normally go in to work this late, do you?" he asked.

Karen laughed. "I told my secretary I might be in conference this morning. I can tell lies, too, you know."

"Wow," said Ronald. "So you were kind of planning on this."

"You might say that," said Karen. "You full-time professors have the life," said Karen, sitting up and putting on a nightgown that had fallen on the floor at some point. "You only have to show up to teach your classes. I'm so far behind in my work I could just scream."

Ronald thought this over. "Well, there's more to being a professor than showing up for class," he said, but he could not think of what other things he really had to do. "Oh. We have faculty meetings sometimes, and I'm responsible for clerkships. But I always thought that doing wills was a nine-to-five job," he said.

"Not if you're up for partner next year," said Karen.

"Oh, sure. Do you think you'll get it?"

Karen sighed. "It looks pretty good," she said, "but you can never really tell until the last minute. It's partly political, and it's got a lot to do with personalities. It's just like getting tenure, I suppose."

"That reminds me," said Ronald. "Rebecca Shepard's up for tenure this year, at McKinley. Do you know her?"

"We've had lunch a few times," said Karen, looking concerned. "What are her chances?"

"I don't really know," he admitted. "I haven't been paying a lot of attention."

"Haven't you heard anything?"

Ronald scratched his head. "Yeah. She's supposed to be good at her job, but she's not really a team player."

"That's no good," said Karen.

"No, I guess it isn't. I guess she won't get it, unless Ed Strong surprises everybody."

"You know something strange?" Karen asked. She looked serious. "Now that I'm this close to making partner, I'm not sure I want it."

"Why not?" he asked, rubbing his chin. "Everybody at a law firm wants to make partner."

"Well, not everybody. I'm just tired of the whole routine. I'm tired of the firm, and the clients, and the work, and the hours. I'm really pretty burned out."

"I'm surprised to hear you say that," said Ronald. "Although I guess I don't know why I'm surprised. I don't think I even knew who you were before last week."

Karen smiled again. "Do I look like a partner in a law firm?" she asked. "Or a potential partner, anyway?"

Ronald examined her, and smiled. "Most partners I've met had a little more clothing on. But if you don't want to be a partner at Gregory and Peterson, then what do you want to do?"

"Teach," she said unhesitatingly.

"But you do teach. You teach three mornings a week, right?"

"No, I mean teach full-time. Like you." She pulled herself close to him and looked directly into his eyes.

"Really?" Ronald looked thoughtful. "Have you told Dean Strong?"

"Not yet," said Karen, studying him.

"Why not? He's the person you have to talk to. He's in charge of these things."

"Of course he's in charge, he's the Dean," said Karen. "I just don't think I know him well enough." She was still watching him closely.

Ronald rubbed his chin. "I could put in a word for you, if you'd like. That is, if you think it might help."

Karen tried to conceal her delight. "Gee, Ron, I'd hate to impose on you this way. We just met, and everything—"

Ronald sat up straight. "Karen, I insist!" he said firmly. "I'll see him first thing Monday morning."

"Would you really?" She held her breath.

"Well, he's probably got his hands full with the suicides and everything. That reminds me. There was some sort of memorial service today. I was supposed to be there, I guess. But I'll mention it the first chance I get."

"In that case," said Karen, smiling mischievously and sliding back under the covers, "maybe I'm not in such a hurry to get to the office."

"You're not?" Ronald asked, his delight undisguised.

"No, I'm not," she said, kissing his left shoulder. "Come here, you great big handsome law professor. I'm not finished with you yet."

"Okay," said an agreeable Ronald Blotchett.

TWENTY-SEVEN

The McKinley graduate school cafeteria, located on the eighth floor of the business school and serving law, business, medical, and dental students, afforded a sweeping view of the slum neighborhood surrounding the campus. Rumor had it that McKinley University owned most of the decrepit buildings, many of which were rented out to students. The rest were homes to thousands of desperately poor people. In the shadow of McKinley they lived lives terrorized by drug users, drug dealers, and street crime. The McKinley security force did a thorough job of keeping them all off the campus.

Katrina Walfish, lunch tray in hand, spied the Saint sitting alone. She had turned over temporary responsibility for the strike to Marlene Feight, electronics expert and Katrina's second in command, so that she could grab some lunch. Katrina noticed that the Saint's expression was glum. He was neither reading nor talking as he ate, unusual for a law student.

She walked over. "Mind if I join you?" she asked brightly. "I hear you're in deep shit."

"Feel free," said the Saint. "And you don't know the half of it."

Katrina seated herself and poured some dressing onto her salad. "Oh, don't I?" she asked, not looking up. "Sanford Clapp figured out that you and Rebecca did the letter."

"Bad news travels fast," said the Saint, adding cream to his

232

coffee. "There's more. Rebecca's furious at me. She says it was all my fault."

"I'm sorry," said Katrina, between bites.

"We were supposed to go away together to the Grey Mountains for the whole weekend, but she went without me."

"Wow," said Katrina, eating quickly. "Did she tell you where she was staying?"

"No. She told me she never wanted to see me again."

"Amazing," said Katrina. "Pass that little thing of cream, will you?"

"Huh? Oh, sure," said the Saint, passing the cream.

"Thanks."

The Saint was taken aback by Katrina's apparent lack of sympathy. He reminded himself that he should have known better than to discuss any non-Katrina-related subjects when there was something that *she* wanted to talk about. "How's the strike?" he asked.

"Oh, it's the greatest," said Katrina, suddenly coming to life. "It's long overdue. We're going to bring the law school to its knees. No more brutality and banality in the classroom, or maybe it's 'No more banality and brutality.' I keep forgetting. I guess it's not much of a slogan, but we had to come up with it pretty quickly. We missed Rebecca this morning. She should have been there."

The Saint thought about how angry she was in the library. "I don't know," he said. "I think she needed to get away. She's been under a lot of pressure lately."

"I guess so," said Katrina, downing her coffee. "Well, I've got to get back to the barricades. You want to know something funny? You know what I was thinking about when I went up to speak at the memorial service?"

"What's that?" the Saint asked.

"The first time I got called on in Contracts."

"Really?" the Saint asked. "How come? What happened?"

Katrina shook her head and gave a rueful smile. "I'll never forget it," she began. "I knew the assignment inside out and backwards. I knew *everything* about that stupid case—it was the one about the millworkers' strike. I'll never forget it as long as I live. I was staring at Clapp, just *daring* him to call on me. Like Clint Eastwood—you know, 'Make my day.'

Well, Sanford must have noticed me because suddenly I heard him saying, 'Ms. Walfish?' And I'm sitting there ready to tell him how many commas there are on page 261 of the decision, and he asks, 'What is the procedural posture of the case?' Those were the exact words he used. I'll never forget *them* either.

"Well! I'd never *heard* the expression 'procedural posture.' I didn't know what the hell he was talking about. I found out later—I went straight to the library and looked it up. It just means what's happening with the case, is it on appeal, or is it still on trial, or whatever. That's all. But I didn't know that then, and I just sat there with a stupid grin on my face. He gave me a long look that really put me in my place, and then Manning raised his hand and said that the procedural posture of the case was that it was on direct appeal to the Supreme Judicial Court of Massachusetts. I nearly died. I mean, how the hell did Manning know what procedural posture meant?"

They both smiled.

"You might not have liked the way Clapp taught," said the Saint, "but he motivated you to study. And now you say that you'll never forget what that expression means, and you'll never forget about the Massachusetts millworkers' case."

"Yeah, but big deal," said Katrina. "I could have looked up 'procedural posture' in the law library, and I'd remember it just as well. And as for that case, it's from 1849! It's about as relevant as Hammurabi's Code. So what if I know it or if I don't know it? Do you think Bill Rehnquist knows about that case? I bet he doesn't."

"I bet one day you'll remind him about it," said the Saint.

She giggled. "I bet you're right. But look at Rebecca. She doesn't teach the way Clapp does, scaring everybody to death half the time. I had a blast up there, turning the tables on him at the memorial service. By the way, how'd you like my photograph of Sanford and Tony in the *Law School News*? Charming, huh?"

"Rebecca," repeated the Saint. "She told me to clear all my stuff out of her apartment by nine o'clock tonight."

"I didn't realize she was that upset at you."

"She bawled me out in front of a bunch of other students.

In the library. She pretty much told me that it was over between us."

"How do you feel? I know how much you care about her."

"How do you think I feel?" asked the Saint. "I feel awful. I feel like I let her down."

"By not talking her out of doing the Professor of the Year letter? I mean, she was angry at herself and she blamed you?" Katrina could be acutely sensitive about human nature when she felt like it.

"Exactly," said the Saint. "All I can do is hope that she changes her mind. She was a little harsh, but she's been under so much pressure, waiting to find out if she'll get tenure and everything. Just between us, I was getting a little frustrated myself. She hasn't been easy to live with."

"Boy, I had no idea she was upset," said Katrina. "She never said anything."

"She never does," said the Saint. "You sort of have to figure things out for yourself with her."

Katrina looked at her watch. "I've just got to get back. What are you going to do? I mean, are you going to take your stuff out of her apartment, and everything?"

The Saint grinned. "Of course not. First of all, it wouldn't be safe in my place."

"Where do you live?" she asked. "You're not living in the dorms any more, are you?"

"No, I'm in McKinley student housing. Out there." He indicated a clump of crumbling walk-up apartment buildings visible in the distance.

"I see your point," Katrina said diplomatically. "Do you think she'll change her mind?"

"I hope so. I'm sure she will." The Saint frowned. "Eventually."

"You know what?" said Katrina. "She's affected me more than any professor I've ever had. To my mind, Rebecca Shepard stands for the idea that you don't have to take all this crap from these people."

"Terrific," said the Saint. "To my mind, Rebecca Shepard is a woman who wants to cut me out of her life."

"How are you going to handle it?"

The Saint grinned. "I'll do what I always did in West

Africa when the *oba*—the chief in my village—got angry at me."

"What's that?" Katrina asked, her tone sardonic. "Pray?"

The Saint kept grinning. "Hell, no. I'm going to *hide*. Until she forgets all about it."

"Coward," said Katrina. "Well, you're welcome to the couch in my living room, if you want it." She looked at her watch again. "It's funny. If it weren't for the memorial service and the strike, I'd be in classroom D, listening to Blotchett muttering incoherently about the Bill of Rights."

"I hear he's teaching a seminar next year on the right against self-incrimination," said the Saint.

Katrina gave him a dirty look. "Nobody loves a wise guy, okay? Here's an extra key. I don't know what time I'll get home. Just make yourself comfortable, all right?"

"If you're serious—" the Saint began, pocketing the key.

"I'm completely serious."

"Thanks," he said. "I could use the change of scenery. Good luck with the strike. Wish me luck with Rebecca."

Katrina gave him a thumbs-up sign. "She'll come back," she said. "She loves you!"

"That's easy for you to say," said the Saint, looking up at her, his expression serious. "You didn't see her in the library."

TWENTY-EIGHT

Night came to the McKinley campus. University and city police, television cameras, newspaper reporters, and hundreds of students kept vigil over the strikers, who successfully prevented students, faculty, and staff from entering the law school building. For the second night in a row, Katrina got no sleep. She and her colleagues spent the early morning hours at the Blue and White Cafe drafting a manifesto and a series of demands. The fact that classes had been canceled through the end of the week even before the strike began in no way lessened its importance to the students running it or to the faculty members and staff people locked out of their offices. While the student leaders drank black coffee and made plans, the Saint, who found himself at loose ends without Rebecca, hung around the scene in front of the law school for a few hours and finally went to Katrina's apartment and fell asleep on the couch. Elsewhere, Sanford Clapp, Ronald Blotchett, Bob Stanger, Murray Frobisher, and Frank Rooney spent the evening playing poker in Clapp's apartment for a penny a point. Rooney was winning hand after hand, to the consternation of Sanford Clapp.

"Leave it to Frobisher to bring in a hustler," he complained. "Let me guess, Murray. You get ten percent of whatever he takes off of us."

"I'll thank you not to insult my client," Frobisher said stiffly. "Shut up and deal."

Jackson Ward and Dean Strong had dinner together in the Dean's apartment and discussed negotiation strategies. Tom Culpepper was a guest on *Nightline*. Tony Sloop's performance art group, Foaming at the Mouth, told its audience that the evening's proceeds would go to a legal defense fund for the Women's Law Caucus. The only McKinley professor unaware of the strike was Rebecca Shepard, who ate dinner in her room at the Grey Mountains Inn, read half of a mystery, and turned in early. She missed the Saint. Today, she decided as she drifted off, was probably the worst day of her life.

Rebecca awakened just after eight o'clock the next morning. She turned on the television to watch a morning news program. To her surprise, the first face she saw on the screen was that of a bleary-eyed Katrina Walfish. She stood among a group of McKinley students before the barricaded front doors of the law school.

"What's going on?" Rebecca asked aloud.

She listened in great surprise as the announcer reviewed the events of the last twenty-four hours. ". . . and there seems little chance that classes will meet today at McKinley, or at any other law school in the city, for that matter. Andrea?"

"Thank you, Charles. Charles Jones reporting live, outside McKinley Law School. We'll switch back to Charles as further developments unfold. In other law-related news, the Supreme Court—"

"I don't believe it!" Rebecca exclaimed. "Go, Katrina!"

She reached for the telephone and dialed first her number and then the Saint's apartment, but there was no answer in either place. The Saint was still sound asleep on Katrina Walfish's living-room couch. Dejected, she looked at the television screen.

"A Japanese team of scientists have announced that a computer program they've just completed could make law professors obsolete. With the story in Tokyo is Meredith Dean."

She was young and blond and she stood holding a microphone in downtown Tokyo. "If you're a law professor, you're not going to like what you're about to see. If you're a law student, sit back and relax. You might just love it."

Meredith Dean now stood in a laboratory among some

beaming Japanese scientists in white lab coats. "These men have just completed the final tests of an artificial intelligence program that, they claim, teaches law more effectively—and far less expensively—than conventional live professors.

"Artificial intelligence, or AI, is a branch of computer science, which, roughly put, teaches computers to reason like human beings. Research in artificial intelligence began in the 1950s both here in Japan and in the United States. AI scientists study people who are experts at a given task, like doctors, or aerospace engineers, or, now, law professors, and attempt to come up with computer models which mimic the experts' thinking patterns. These models, called 'expert systems,' already aid doctors in diagnosing patients in hospitals and help NASA plan space shuttle missions.

"Although many research teams have attempted to adopt artificial intelligence to the classroom, these scientists are the first to actually complete a software program that law students could use instead of going to class."

"And they would be much better lawyers, we think," said one of the scientists.

"Hideo Toshikawa is head of the research team that designed the program," said Meredith Dean.

"We believe," said Toshikawa, "that our program can train a mind for legal thinking in a much shorter period of time than in classrooms following the traditional Socratic method. In a lecture hall of one hundred students the professor can interact with only one student at a time. But with the expert system we have created, all of the students could be engaged critically with the 'professor'—all they need are standard personal computers and our software. To borrow an expression from our Chinese friends, our program will let a hundred flowers bloom, not just one," he concluded, looking terribly pleased.

Meredith Dean stood in Tokyo traffic once again. "The program will be available for sale in the United States by the end of next year. For *Wake Up, America*, I'm Meredith Dean in Tokyo."

"Thank you, Meredith. Now this."

Rebecca leaned forward and turned off the television. "Another blow at the Socratic method," she murmured. She got out of bed and began to throw her things into her suitcase. "I've got to get back there."

Meanwhile, Dean Edward Strong, wearing a warm-up suit, running shoes, and a towel over his shoulders, was riding his Exercycle in the living room of his apartment. Like Rebecca, he had been watching the report about the McKinley strike and the other law-related news story on *Wake Up, America*. It grieved him to see McKinley barricaded. The strike, which the Dean was utterly powerless to halt, was the single most frustrating event in his career. Unless it could be settled promptly and with a minimum of embarrassment to the law school, it threatened to become the most damaging event as well.

There were other frustrations. Students who ran with him along the river at lunchtime or who laughed so much at his stories during Evidence lectures would not speak to him now. Katrina Walfish would not even return his telephone messages. The Dean could not vent his frustrations through racquetball or running by the river, because the press kept a watch on both his health club and his normal jogging routes. He gazed absentmindedly at the television screen, his legs pumping vigorously, a metaphor for his determination to ride the whole thing out.

The intercom buzzed. Edward Strong dismounted and asked who was there.

"Murray Frobisher."

"Come on up," he said, looking around the apartment. The dirty dishes from his dinner with Jackson Ward were still in the sink.

"More bad news," the Dean said aloud. "I just know it." He toweled the perspiration from his forehead and boiled water for coffee. Murray Frobisher was the one who first called Edward Strong's apartment the "Deanship-in-Exile." There was much truth to the statement. Since the students had taken over the McKinley building, and since the press mobbed the Dean whenever he went outside, most of the administration's business took place in the kitchen and living room of the duplex apartment.

Frobisher entered and wasted no time.

"Here, did you see this?" he said, bearing a copy of a light blue journal. "It's the new issue of the *McKinley Law Review*."

"Give me that," said Dean Strong, all but snatching the journal from Frobisher's hands. "It's got Rebecca's article, doesn't it?"

"Yeah."

"How is it? And how'd you get a copy?"

"One of my spies on the *Law Review*," said Frobisher. "I called him last night and said that if I didn't have an advance copy of the new issue by seven this morning I'd boot his ass out of the law school."

"Sounds like you've been taking lessons from Sanford," said the Dean, flipping through the journal.

"That's the way I operate, okay?" said Murray. "Look, I got you the article, like you asked me to, didn't I? Aren't you even going to thank me?"

The Dean lifted his eyes from the journal, but only for a moment. "Thank you, Murray. Page 279. Here it is. 'The Socratic Method: The Unexamined Curriculum.' What did you think of it?"

Frobisher wiped his forehead with a handkerchief. He went into the kitchen and poured himself a glass of water.

"Pour me one, also," said the Dean, scanning the first few paragraphs.

"I already told you what I think," Frobisher snapped. "She's a reformer, and she wants to upset the status quo. I found this article truly alarming, Ed. If even one third of the things she suggests ever happened, law school as we know it would be gone forever."

"Murray, I don't know if you saw the news this morning, but the status quo *is* gone forever. Did you see what was on *Wake Up, America*? The Japanese have come out with a computer professor that teaches law better than we do. And this strike is still going on. I'm no alarmist, Murray, but I just don't see law school standing still much longer."

"Ed, you scare me when you talk that way." Frobisher

looked directly at the Dean. "You're not on Rebecca's side in this, are you?"

Dean Strong frowned and looked away. "It's not a matter of taking sides, Murray," he said. "It's just a question of facing the inevitable."

Frobisher's eyes narrowed. "You wouldn't give her tenure, would you, Ed?"

The Dean was silent.

"Ed, you wouldn't do it to us, would you? Don't you realize the effect you'll have on the law school? Do you know what will happen to the morale of the faculty?"

"I'm aware that the morale of the faculty might slide a bit, but there's also the morale of the students to consider." And my sagging career, the Dean thought.

Frobisher began to panic. "Ed, if you give her tenure, it just won't be as much *fun* around here any more! Can't you see that?"

"Murray," the Dean said, "the faculty's sense of 'fun' is what got us into this mess in the first place. Look. I'll read her article before I make up my mind about Rebecca. I promise."

Frobisher looked pained. He felt betrayed. "Don't you have to follow the recommendation of the tenure committee you appointed? That's me, Clapp, and Tom Culpepper. I don't know about Tom, but Sanford and I are both voting no. We figured you chose us *because* we'd vote no. And Sanford says she did that Professor of the Year letter, and you're *still* thinking about giving her tenure! What's going on here?"

"First of all," Dean Strong responded, "the committee's recommendations are just that—recommendations. They're not binding on me. I'm free to do what I want, what I think has to be done. And second of all, well, you're right. When I appointed the committee, I intentionally stacked it against her. But I've been having second thoughts, and third thoughts, and fourth thoughts, and I just need a little more time to think the whole thing through. In fact, Murray, if you'll excuse me, I've got to read Rebecca's article and I've also got to come up with some sort of strategy for dealing with the strike. You're coming to the emergency faculty meeting here at noon, aren't you?"

"Yes, but Ed—" Frobisher's eyes pleaded with the Dean, who escorted him to the door.

"Murray, I understand how you feel about Rebecca. But times are changing. And I promise you I haven't made up my mind. We'll kick it around at the faculty meeting, okay?"

"But Ed, aren't you aware of—"

"Murray, I'm aware of everything. See you at noon."

A dejected Murray Frobisher looked sadly at the Dean. "McKinley will never be the same, Ed. I never thought you'd be the one who did it in."

Frobisher left the apartment. Dean Strong closed and locked the door behind him. "I forgot to offer him coffee," said the Dean. He turned off the coffeepot and mounted the Exercycle, the latest issue of the *McKinley Law Review* in his hands. The Dean began to read Rebecca's article, but now he was pedaling slowly.

THE SOCRATIC METHOD: THE UNEXAMINED CURRICULUM

by Rebecca Shepard

Socrates, the Greek philosopher in whose name law students are needlessly tormented, said in his famous *Apology* that the unexamined life is not worth living. Socrates, himself an educator, would have agreed that the unexamined curriculum is not worth teaching. And yet the curriculum in our law schools today was engraved in stone—or so it seems—nearly a century ago, and has remained unexamined and virtually impervious to change, despite the vast changes since then in American society. It is fashionable to ask why our legal system fails to serve our nation. A much better question to ask is this: Why do law schools fail to serve the needs of our law students?

By now the Dean's legs had ceased to pump at all.

Students receive practically no exposure to the real worlds of American law and justice. They study Contracts, but they never see an actual contract. They study Civil Procedure—the rules governing lawsuits and trials—but never see even a single courtroom document. They study Evidence—the rules that govern the admission of testimony and other forms of proof in a trial—but never set foot in a courtroom. They study Criminal Law but never visit a jail, or meet a convict, or a victim. They study Property but they spend half the semester on obsolete inheritance laws from England. Little wonder that when law students reflect on their three years, many conclude that it was almost a complete waste of time. Since law students must memorize an endless sea of obscure facts about each case, they have no time to reflect upon the larger underlying issues. Any sense of right and wrong they may have brought to law school is quickly subverted, undermined, by the endless round of memorization in the library followed by brutalization in the classroom. No wonder so many students graduate hating everything connected with the law.

The Dean stepped off the Exercycle and sat on the sofa, reading all the while.

What does it mean for a nation when its lawyers graduate so poorly equipped for practice? The societal costs are enormous. For one thing, lawyers frequently comment that they learn on the job almost everything they know about the practice of law. They also say that little they learned in law school prepared them for their practices. Clients, therefore, from the biggest multinational corporation down to the poorest widower whose Social Security benefits have been terminated unfairly, subsidize the real cost of training our lawyers. But if the law schools do not train lawyers, what purpose do they serve? They provide one of the sweetest forms of employment known to mankind: the tenured law professorship. These fortunate souls who have attained the rank of full professor enjoy lifetime job security, some of the highest salaries in academia, a minimal course load, no required contact with students, and endless spare time to pursue prestigious and lucrative outside consulting and lecturing assignments. Law schools exist for the sake of the faculty, not for the students, and not for the society those students are ostensibly trained to serve. My quarrel is not with law itself, for the study of law encompasses every aspect of human experience. Its study can stimulate the intellect and the emotions, the heart and the soul. I say, simply, roll away the boulders that stand in the path of what could be the greatest education of all.

Dean Strong flipped through the rest of the article. "Forty-five more pages of this," he said to himself. "Talk about going down in a blaze of glory. I'd call this kamikaze scholarship." He skipped to the conclusions and scanned the list: Reduce law school from three years to two. Scrap the Socratic method. Scrap the case method. Require clinical experience of each student. Eliminate the "curved" grading system to reduce the sense of competition. Eliminate all large classes. Require large law firms that interview on campus to subsidize recruiting costs for public interest law firms. And on and on.

"Frobisher's wrong," the Dean said aloud, unable to finish even the conclusions. "Rebecca's not a reformer. She's a bomb-throwing radical. Well, I've got my revolution—if I have the stomach for it." The Dean left the unfinished article on the sofa, shook his head, and climbed back on the Exercycle.

TWENTY-NINE

As Dean Strong contemplated Rebecca's essay, a fatigued Katrina Walfish was sprawled in a chair in the back of the Blue and White Cafe. A large cup of black coffee, untouched, sat before her on the table. The Blue and White was Katrina's command post. Students guarded the entrances to McKinley Law School in keeping with a duty roster that Katrina had drawn up and posted on the cafe's front door. At Katrina's direction, Marlene Feight, law student and electronics expert, hooked up the cafe's stereo speakers to the PA system on the law school steps. City police met with Katrina at the cafe in order to learn of the students' plans. The Blue and White's owner, Andrew Kefalias, was delighted with the increased business and hoped the strike would last forever. For now, though, the moving force behind the walkout leaned her head against the back wall of the Blue and White and began to doze.

She was startled by the voice of Jackson Ward. "May I join you?" he asked.

Katrina snapped awake. "Professor Ward, if Dean Strong sent you, I just can't—"

"No one sent me. May I sit down?"

"Of course." Katrina rubbed her forehead. "I'm so tired. I thought I ordered coffee. Oh, here it is." She gulped it down. "I need caffeine," she explained. "Lots of caffeine."

Ward smiled. "I'll bet," he said. The waiter approached and Ward ordered hot tea with lemon.

"You know," said Katrina, "you're the first professor to come in here since the strike began."

"Is this the students' turf?" Jackson asked, smiling.

Katrina smiled weakly. "I guess so," she said. "I'm not really awake yet, by the way."

The waiter brought Ward's tea and Katrina indicated that she needed another cup of coffee. "What brings you in here?" Katrina asked.

"I was wondering if you've heard from Rebecca," said Jackson, looking concerned. "I haven't seen her since the strike began."

"Neither have I," said Katrina, regaining full consciousness. "She went someplace in the Grey Mountains. She was angry at the Saint over the Professor of the Year letter."

"Doesn't the Saint know where she is?"

"No, I asked him. She never told him where she was going. It's not like her. It's like she deserted us."

"I agree that it's out of character for Rebecca," said Jackson. "She must have been quite upset."

"I'm actually kind of angry with her, to tell you the truth. I mean, she *is* the adviser to the Women's Law Caucus, and we *are* leading the strike. The least she could do is be around to advise us."

Jackson raised his eyebrows. "Doesn't that sound like a conflict of interest?" Jackson asked. "After all, as a member of the faculty here, Rebecca may see the strike in slightly different terms than the students do."

"Don't ask me," said Katrina. "I haven't taken Ethics yet. Even so, it's not like Rebecca to disappear."

"I agree," said Jackson.

"Professor Ward, do you think that Rebecca's going to get tenure? They have to decide by next Friday, don't they?"

Jackson frowned. "They're supposed to decide—actually, the Dean is supposed to decide by next Friday. But the strike could delay matters."

"The Dean? I heard her tenure committee was Frobisher, Culpepper, and Clapp."

"That's true—but they only make a recommendation to

Dean Strong. He's free to ignore what they say. It's his decision."

"Well, what's going to happen?"

"It doesn't look good right now, to be honest. The committee you mentioned is almost certain to recommend against giving her tenure. I spoke to Murray about it the other day. He's unalterably opposed. I didn't speak to Sanford, but everything he's ever said or done in faculty meetings makes me think that he'd vote no also. I have no idea what Tom Culpepper thinks."

"He could surprise everyone and vote for her," said Katrina. "That would make the tenure committee vote two-to-one against. If Strong wanted to stack the committee against Rebecca, having a two-to-one vote is a pretty clever way to do it."

"Ed's a smart man," Jackson agreed. "But there are ways to get around even smart people."

"What are you talking about?"

"Never mind."

"How is Dean Strong reacting to the strike?"

"He's very unhappy," said Ward. "It hurt his feelings that the students would walk out without even talking to him first. He prides himself as being especially open with the students. He looks upon the strike as a personal failure. He called a Committee of Ten meeting for noon today, to talk things over."

"I never thought of it that way," said Katrina. "I never meant to hurt his feelings. But still, three suicides in a row is pretty unusual. You'd think he might have reined Clapp in after the first one."

"With all due respect, there's no proof that Sanford was involved in any of the suicides."

"No proof? But they were all in his class."

"That could be coincidence, you know. I don't love Sanford any more than you do. Frankly, I— Well, never mind. I will say that I disagree with his teaching style, but students don't kill themselves because of the way someone teaches a class."

"What about Susan Garrett?" Katrina asked. "A hundred people in her Contracts class saw how Clapp just walked all over her. She ran from the room in tears, and, well, the rest is history."

Ward frowned. "Katrina," he said, "Susan had emotional problems long before she came to McKinley. I think everyone knows that by now. I'm not saying that Clapp's treatment of her didn't hurt her very deeply, but it's dangerous looking for a cause-and-effect relationship between his teaching and her suicide. Or any of the suicides."

"Maybe you're right," said Katrina. "We were thinking about making Clapp's resignation a condition for ending the strike."

"That will never work," said Jackson. "Ed Strong would never go along with that. I don't think he's Sanford's biggest fan. But if you tie ending the strike to Clapp's resignation, you'd be forcing the law school to admit that Clapp was responsible for their taking their own lives. And that hasn't been proven, and it probably never could be."

"Hmm," said Katrina. "We had another idea, also."

"What's that?"

They both turned to see Marlene Feight staring reproachfully at Katrina.

"Why are you talking to a professor?" Marlene asked.

"Oh, Jackson's cool," said Katrina. "I need another minute, Marlene, okay?"

Marlene, disapproving, left the restaurant.

"It's actually two things," Katrina said. "Our demands, I mean. One would be to establish a committee of students, faculty, alumni, and trustees to reevaluate the entire McKinley curriculum. The other would be to demand that Clapp withdraw his charges against the Saint. You know, Daniel Conway."

Jackson nodded vigorously. "Now you're talking," he said. "The committee idea is excellent, because it's the kind of political solution that doesn't cost anyone anything. You can claim victory and so can Dean Strong. And the idea about Conway is also very good, because that would focus the heat on Clapp."

"How would you feel about mentioning these ideas to Dean Strong at the Committee of Ten meeting?" Katrina asked.

"I would be glad to," said Jackson, nodding. "I certainly will. Where can I find you if I need to talk to you?"

"Right here. So you really think there's no chance Rebecca will get tenure?"

"The way things are right now," said Jackson, "it doesn't look good. I had dinner with Dean Strong last night. He was very angry about the Professor of the Year letter. He thought it displayed poor judgment on Rebecca's part."

"Don't any of you men have a sense of humor?" Katrina asked. She rubbed her eyes. "I'm awake again. Almost. My head hurts."

Jackson removed two dollars from his wallet and left them on the table. "I've got to get to the faculty meeting, Katrina. Thanks for your company. I enjoyed it. I'll call you here later."

"But Professor Ward—"

"I'll call you," he said, and he was gone.

Katrina looked at her watch. "Nine-fifteen," she told the waiter standing nearby, who hadn't asked. "Time for me to be charming and dynamic. Wish me luck."

THIRTY

When Daniel Conway awoke on Katrina Walfish's living-room couch, it took him a few minutes to remember where he was and what he was doing there. Then it all came back: Rebecca confronting him in the law school library and then leaving for the Grey Mountains without him; the memorial service and the strike that followed; and the rest of the day, which found him unsure of what to do with himself. He looked around the apartment. Katrina's bedroom door was open and the light was on. The bed was untouched. She never came home, he realized. He showered, dressed, made some coffee, and left a note thanking Katrina for her hospitality. He then wandered toward the law school. A knot of students were milling in front of the main entrance, which was still barricaded. Students and police looked on, but the scene was quiet.

The Saint hoped to catch a glimpse of Katrina so as to thank her personally for the use of her couch, and to find out whether she had heard anything from Rebecca, but she was not to be seen. In fact, she was still in the Blue and White Cafe, discussing strategy with Marlene Feight—who again reproved Katrina for consorting with the enemy, in the form of Jackson Ward. Conway ran into a few classmates and he asked them what was going on. Nothing at all, they said, with a trace of disappointment. Katrina had read a message from Dean Strong about an hour before, in which the Dean said that the faculty and administration would respect the strike and

251

would not try to enter the law school building; at the same time, the Dean said, he welcomed the opportunity to discuss the underlying issues and negotiate a settlement. In other words, there would be no pitched battles on the steps of the law school.

The Saint stood and enjoyed the bright October morning and realized, for the first time since he entered McKinley, how much of his life he now spent indoors. He remembered how different things were in his village in Nigeria, where no one had ever seen a fluorescent light bulb, a desk chair, or a case-book. All of Conway's class materials were inside the shuttered law school building. Like it or not, today would be a day off, and he thought he might take advantage of the sunshine and the warm weather. He left the law school and crossed the McKinley campus without a particular destination in mind. Two blocks from the eastern edge of the campus was a park that overlooked the river. This was where Dean Strong ran with students at lunchtime, and this was where Rebecca and the Saint often took long walks at dusk. Without thinking about it he found himself in the park, absentmindedly examining the sunlight where it touched the leaves. He looked out at the river and the palisades on the other side. He watched a class of third-graders, walking two and three abreast to a playground a block away. He realized that he was thinking only of Rebecca.

He understood that his feelings toward her were rather complicated at the moment. He still loved her, or he thought he did, at any rate. He was quite angry, though, about what had happened in the library. It did not seem fair to him that Rebecca should blame him so vehemently for what was as much her decision as his own—sending the Professor of the Year letter. Second, the manner in which Rebecca chose to inform him that the relationship was over—announcing it in the library, in front of five other students—was terribly embarrassing to Daniel. The moment when he went to collect his books and papers after she stalked off was as demeaning as anything he had ever experienced. Sometimes it takes a crisis to point out what should have been obvious all along, he thought. He sat on a park bench and watched a tugboat make its way slowly down the river. He wondered whether the whole thing—his relationship with Rebecca—was pointless. Did he want to spend the rest of his life with a woman four years older than himself? With a woman capable of treating him as thoughtlessly as she did the day before?

And just as quickly, Daniel found himself taking her side. She was under more strain now than ever before in her career, more than she was likely to face ever again. A woman like Rebecca and an institution like McKinley could meet head-on, or not at all. The clash of identities was too great for compromise. And, after all, she probably would have gone elsewhere and not sought tenure at McKinley were it not for Daniel's insistence that she stay and fight. Surely he could find it in his heart to forget about the scene in the library, he told himself. We all say and do things we later regret.

There was still the matter of Rebecca's ultimatum. Nine o'clock last night came and went and the Saint's personal belongings—clothing, papers, books, souvenirs of Nigeria—were still in her apartment. He thought about it for a while and decided that the best thing to do was to go to Rebecca's place, put his gear in boxes, leave the boxes there, and see where things stood upon her return Monday. If she had changed her mind about ending things, he had only to unpack. If she remained firm that things were over between them, he could borrow a car and collect the boxes that night.

"That's it," he said to himself, slapping his thighs. "That's the plan." He stood, stretched, took one last look at the river, and walked back toward the McKinley campus. He tried a few different stores before he found all the boxes he could carry in front of Pete's Discount Liquors. He packed half a dozen, one on top of the other, and made his way to Rebecca's, where he dumped them on the living-room floor. He dragged two of the larger boxes into the bedroom and opened the door to the closet. He was about to take out the first thing he saw—his winter coat—when suddenly he stopped cold.

"This is ridiculous," he said. "I'm not going anywhere." And then he heard the front door open. "What the—" he began, running to the living room. There stood Rebecca, overnight bag in hand, as surprised to see him as he was to see her.

"What are you doing here?" they both asked. Neither knew

how to react to the presence of the other. They both spoke at once.

"I heard about the strike and I—" Rebecca began.

"I was coming to get my—" the Saint began.

"Hold it," she said. "What are all these boxes for?"

"You told me to clear my stuff out and I—"

"Saint, I'm so sorry about yesterday. I had no right to say the things I did. I hope you can forgive me."

"You are?" asked the Saint, dumbfounded. "I mean, you do?" He still was not over the shock of seeing her in the apartment. "What are you doing here?" he asked again. "You weren't supposed to be back until Monday."

"I know," said Rebecca. "I heard about the strike on television this morning, and I—I missed you."

Relief surged through the Saint's mind. He did not let on immediately, though. "You mean you didn't mean the things you said in the library?" he asked.

"No, of course not! I was miserable all day and all night! I tried to call you, but you weren't home." Rebecca was utterly contrite.

"You mean you *don't* want me to pack up and get out of your life?"

Rebecca looked pained. "No, of course not. I just took all my frustrations and everything out on you, and—" Suddenly Rebecca understood that the Saint was teasing her. "You creep! You forgive me, don't you? How could you let me go on like this?"

The Saint grinned. "You're beautiful when you apologize," he said. "I wish I had a camera."

"I wish I had a frying pan," said Rebecca, "because I'd hit you over the head with it!"

They held each other close and kissed.

"I missed you, too," he said, stroking her hair.

"Daniel, I felt absolutely awful about yesterday, and the way I've been since the semester began. I promise—tenure or no tenure—that's all over with."

"You really promise?" he asked, grinning slyly.

"How can you even *ask* me that?"

"Well, in that case," he said, kissing her lips, "I love you."

"Well, in *that* case," she said quietly, "I love you, too."

When they came up for air this time the Saint's expression was mischievous. "So," he began, "once they reject you for tenure, where are we going to look for jobs?"

His words stung Rebecca. "How can you even *joke* about that when—" Then her tone softened. "Did you say 'we'?"

The Saint, serious now, nodded.

"Do you mean—" she began. "Are you asking—"

"Marry me," said the Saint.

She looked up into his eyes. "Okay," she said.

"Okay?" the Saint repeated. "Is that the best you can do? I just asked you to marry me! All I get is an 'okay'?"

"Uh-huh," she said. "That's all you get. And if you really love me—"

"Oh, but you know I do!"

"Then would you mind getting these boxes out of my living room?"

The Saint laughed and shook his head. "Just kiss me," he said, and she did.

THIRTY-ONE

"We'll wait five more minutes for Rebecca Shepard," said Dean Strong, still in his warm-up suit, "and then we'll get this meeting under way. I don't think Ms. Kennecutt was able to track her down and tell her about the meeting."

The entire McKinley Committee of Ten, except Rebecca, was gathered in the Dean's living room. It was just past noon. As it happened, Murray Frobisher was not the only one who had tracked down a copy of Rebecca's article on the Socratic method. Sanford Clapp, Aaron Mountain, and Robert Stanger each had gotten their hands on advance copies of the new issue of the *Law Review*.

"When I saw her article this morning, I couldn't believe they printed it instead of my piece," Aaron Mountain was saying. "Of course, my article is coming out in the next issue."

"How'd you manage that, Aaron?" asked Sanford Clapp. "Bribery? Cocaine? Call girls for the entire editorial board?"

"You're a fine one to talk, Sanford," said Mountain. "Anything I learned about abusing students I learned at your feet."

"Gentlemen, please, this is no time for—"

"You just keep your mouth shut, Aaron," said Clapp.

"What didn't you like about Rebecca's article?" asked Stanger.

"It wasn't scholarly enough," responded Mountain.

"What do you know about scholarship?" heckled Clapp.

"Sanford, please," said Stanger. "Tell me, Aaron, why do you say that the article wasn't scholarly?"

"I guess I don't mean that exactly. It's just that she doesn't appreciate the importance of Conflict of Laws. She called it 'an archaic discipline which should no longer be taught in law schools,'" Mountain was quoting from an already well-thumbed copy of the article, "'because judges have not followed any Conflict of Laws rules for the last twenty-five years.' She said judges do whatever they want and then get their law clerks to find justifications for their actions."

"Well, that's true, isn't it?" asked Murray Frobisher.

"Of course it's true," said Aaron Mountain. "But just because something is irrelevant is no reason to stop teaching it."

"I didn't think much of her article at all," said Clapp.

"Why's that?" asked Frobisher.

"I admit it was well written, and everything," Clapp began, "but she has no regard for her colleagues. She wants to kill the goose that laid the golden egg. I happen to believe in the Socratic method and in the case method as proven ways of educating lawyers. It certainly helped me in my practice of law, and I make reference in class to those days all the time."

"I know you do," said Stanger. "I always hear from the students about your war stories from your many years in practice. The students must think you practiced law for a century. How long did you practice for, Sanford?"

"Well, I, well, that was a number of years ago and I don't recall the exact length of time."

"Nine months, Clapp. You practiced law for exactly nine months," Stanger said, "and then you were let go for incompetence. How exactly—"

"I told you that in confidence!" Clapp fumed. "How dare you repeat that here!"

"Sanford, it's in the Stud book for all to see," said Stanger, referring to the American Association of Law Professors' alphabetical index of professors, their publications, and employment histories. "I want to know how exactly the Socratic method helped you practice law."

"I—I—well, it taught me to—to—to think on my feet."

"Judging from your performance right now, I find that hard

to believe," said Stanger, and the living room shook with laughter.

"Sanford," Stanger continued, "I didn't practice law for nine months in the boonies in the Pacific Northwest the way you did. I practiced law for fifteen years right here in the big city. I made partner at one of the most prestigious dog-eat-dog corporate law firms in the nation. I've seen dozens—no, hundreds—of young associate attorneys come and go. Top graduates of the top law schools. And I didn't see one whom the Socratic method made a better lawyer.

"Now," Stanger went on, "you may not know this about me, but I believe that tradition and precedent are extremely important." Tony Sloop nearly burst out laughing. Stanger glared at him. "And I understand that the Socratic method is a time-honored tradition in law school that predates any of us here."

"Even me," added Thomas Oliver Andrew Culpepper.

"Even Tom," said Stanger. "But when I read that young lady's article this morning, the scales fell from my eyes. I read it not as a professor with a vested interest in the status quo but as an ex–law firm partner, an ex-president of a corporation dependent on lawyers. And I said to myself, Bob, you're staring the future in the face! Everything she wrote is true! Her article represents, in my opinion, the writing on the wall."

Pandemonium ensued.

"Gentlemen, please," said the Dean.

"Bob, I think this time you've gone too far," Frobisher said. "It's easy for you to talk, because when Blanchard's cut you loose they gave you a half-million dollars as a going-away present. But what about the rest of us who have to scrape by on the salary of a law professor?"

That was too much for Sanford Clapp. "Oh, Murray," he said, "you're a fine one to talk! What were you telling us last night about a fifty-thousand-dollar retainer from the guy who shot the President—"

"He didn't shoot the President," said Frobisher. "He shot *at* the President. There's a big difference."

"That's right, Murray. A difference of a million dollars, from which you intend to extract a hundred thousand, and that's before your legal fees! So don't let me hear you complaining about making ends meet. And I swear that guy cheats at poker."

"Okay, so maybe I'll make a few bucks off the guy," Frobisher admitted. "Big deal. But look at the rest of you. Some pipsqueak of a woman writes an article and every one of you is ready to go sucking up to her. Oh, Rebecca, what a lovely article you wrote! Oh, Rebecca, you're right! Law school is *so* nasty! We have to change everything immediately, just for you! Well, damn it, I don't think we have to change anything. I think we're doing just fine the way we are. We're a top-ranked law school with a national—with an international reputation. Our graduates go on to the best clerkships, the best firms, they make partner, they become judges. We've even had graduates on the Supreme Court. I'm not saying we can rest on our laurels, but I think this self-flagellation is a pointless exercise! We do good work and we turn out a good product, and we should be proud of ourselves!"

"Hear, hear," said Aaron Mountain.

"I respectfully dissent."

All eyes turned toward Culpepper.

"I've been following the discussion quite closely, and I'm not sure I can agree with everything you say, Mr. Frobisher. Certainly we have many fine graduates who have made their mark in many different areas of the law, and to the extent that we're responsible, well, yes, we ought to pat ourselves on the back.

"Now, I haven't read this young lady's article, but I take it that she finds fault with the way we teach law—not just here at McKinley, but the way all law schools go about things today, with the Socratic method and the case method. Now, I've never mentioned this to anybody, because nobody ever criticized the Socratic method, at least not until lately. But I've never been that comfortable with it, and to tell you the truth, I've never employed it."

The room was hushed.

"I'm older than anyone else on the faculty, not smarter, just older," Culpepper continued. "I was graduated from the McKinley Law School back in 1935. In those days there were still alive and teaching some of the men who had been law professors in the days of the revolution in legal education, before the turn of the century. Of course, they were old men by the Thirties, but they still remembered Dean Christopher Columbus Langdell at Harvard. The Socratic method and the case method—why, they were all his idea. And I used to sit in this very room with some of those old-timers and they told me how they thought that the two methods of instruction were nothing but an excuse for the faculty to embarrass the students in class and to have a good time doing it.

"And those old-timers knew they were old men and they knew they wouldn't be teaching forever, and to a man—to a man, I say—the only thing they regretted was that they hadn't tried to stand up to Langdell and his case method, because if they had, then maybe law school wouldn't have become such a terrorizing institution. 'We stopped teaching,' they used to say, 'when we started asking students to state the facts of the case.' Well, all I can say is, I hope those old-timers are listening, wherever they are, because it sounds like someone down here has finally started listening to them."

Silence.

Frobisher, overcome, blew his nose. "That's beautiful, Tom," he said.

"It's just a passing thing," Ronald Blotchett said quietly.

"What do you mean, Ron?" asked the Dean.

"It's just a fad, that's all," Blotchett said. "I read Rebecca's article. It's not the first time someone has criticized the Socratic method. A lot of people aren't crazy about what goes on in law school, and articles like Rebecca's get written all the time. And sometimes people make a big deal out of them for a while, but most of the time the articles are just ignored, and then they go to collect dust and die on the shelves of law school libraries. Come on, guys, we've seen this happen a dozen times."

"I hate to admit it, but Ronald may be right," said Dean Strong. "I've heard it said that changing a curriculum is harder than moving a graveyard. As much as I like and respect Rebecca, I have to agree with Ron. Her article is not the first attack on the Socratic method, and I'm sure it won't be the last. The only reason we're so worked up over it today is that it's the most recent. It hasn't had a chance to be forgotten about. And if it weren't for Rebecca being up for tenure, and if it weren't for the strike, I'm sure we'd never have even read her article. The new issue of the *McKinley Law Review* would have found its way into our offices and would have just gotten lost among all the stacks of things we intend to read but we know we'll never get to."

"I agree with Ed," said Murray Frobisher. "I hadn't really thought about it in those terms. We really are getting worked up over nothing at all. The article might get a little attention today, but by nightfall no one will even think twice about it."

"I was really excited when I read it," said Tony Sloop, "but I have to go along with Murray, Ed, and Ron."

"Is there anyone here who hasn't read the article yet, aside from Tom?" asked the Dean.

Silence.

"Well, that's the last bit of evidence for her tenure question," the Dean said. "I'd like to do something a bit unusual right now. Rather than wait for the recommendation of Rebecca's tenure committee, I'd like to do something slightly different from standard practice. I, of course, will make the final decision as to whether Rebecca should get tenure, but I think it only fair that each of you get a chance to express your opinion here in a faculty meeting. If there are no objections, I'd like to go around the room and see how each of you feels. As I said, the final decision remains with me. Any objections?"

Silence.

"As long as Rebecca isn't here right now, I'd just like to hear how each of you feels. Again, I don't want any speeches. I just want to know if you're for or against. "Murray Frobisher?"

"Against."

"Tony Sloop?"

"For."

"Sanford?"

"Against."

"Bob Stanger?"

Stanger paused. "For," he said.

"Jackson Ward?"

"For."

"Tom Culpepper?"

"I'm for her, Dean Strong."

"Thanks, Tom. Ron Blotchett?"

"Against."

"Aaron Mountain?"

"Against."

"Four votes to four," said the Dean. "A lot of help you guys are."

"What are we going to do, Ed?" Murray asked. "Sanford and I voted no. Your tenure committee voted two to one against."

"I'm aware of that, Murray," said Dean Strong. "I still think this would be an excellent time to offer tenure to a woman candidate."

"I'll bet you do," said Jackson Ward, his anger rising.

"I beg your pardon?" asked the Dean.

"Never mind," said Ward.

"How are you going to find one?" asked Frobisher. "Will you call Sears and order one from the catalog?"

The Dean glared at Frobisher.

"She's not the only woman on the faculty," said Ronald Blotchett.

"Who else is there?" asked Sanford Clapp. "Miss Pander? The librarian? She already has tenure. And why is it so important all of a sudden to give another woman tenure?"

"It just is," Frobisher said heatedly. "Okay?"

"Take it easy, Murray," said Clapp. "I was just asking."

"I agree with Murray," said Dean Strong. "There's a lot to be said for offering a woman tenure. Who did you have in mind, Ron?"

"I was actually thinking of Karen Conner," he said, trying to sound casual.

"The Adjunct Professor of Wills!" said Frobisher. "I never thought of her! Great idea, Ron!"

"She'd love it," said Blotchett. "She'd accept in a minute. I'm sure of it."

"How do you know so much about what Karen Conner wants?" Clapp asked Blotchett. "You haven't done her up on your clerking couch, have you? I thought that couch was reserved for students."

Blotchett laughed. "You're just jealous, Sanford."

"Gentlemen, please." It was the Dean. The idea of offering Karen tenure had never crossed his mind. He seized on it instantly as a way out of his dilemma, if only a partially satisfactory one. "Ron, do you really think that she might accept tenure?"

"I *know* she would. She just told me that she hates her job and that she'd give anything to be a full-time academic."

The Dean appeared immensely relieved. "What if we were to put this to a vote right now?" he asked. "All in favor of offering tenure to Karen Conner—"

"Just a minute!" interrupted Jackson Ward. "Ed, I'm not going to sit here and let you railroad this through!"

"What's eating you, Jackson?" asked Frobisher.

Jackson glared at him. "I'll tell you *exactly* what's eating me. Karen Conner has taught exactly four semesters at this law school. To my knowledge she has never published a scholarly article. I'm sure that some of the people in this room have met her. Now, I know how important precedent is to many of you. In all of my years here we have never offered tenure to an adjunct professor. Ed, is there any reason for your sudden interest in women's rights? It never used to bother you that we had no tenured women teaching here."

"No, Jackson," said the Dean, alarmed. "I'm not sure I know what you mean."

"I'm surprised at myself for doing this," said Jackson, "but you leave me no choice. Ed, could it have something to do with a consent decree?"

The Dean's face turned red. "How do you know about that?"

"What's Jackson talking about?" asked Ronald Blotchett.

"Nothing, nothing at all," said Murray Frobisher. "He's just full of hot air. Let's get back to the vote for Conner. Look, Jackson, if you don't like her, then just vote no. Don't make it a federal case."

"Dara Sample already did," said Jackson, rising to his feet. "I wasn't aware of it until just the other day. It happened before I came here. But when you turned down Dara Sample for tenure, she went to court and claimed that McKinley discriminated against her because of her sex. The court records were sealed, but I've done a little, well, detective work."

"Jackson, how could you?" said the Dean.

"It seems that the law school made a large settlement," Jackson continued. "Somewhere in the low six figures. We bought Dara off, in other words. And we entered into a consent decree with the court to the effect that if we gave tenure to a woman within five years, the record of the sex discrimination case would never be made public. Gentlemen, this is the fifth year."

Pandemonium erupted. There were shouts of "Why didn't you tell us, Ed?" and "Who else knew about it?"

Jackson continued. "I hoped it wouldn't come to this, but this business about Karen Conner just seals it for me. If Rebecca doesn't get tenure, I'll go public. I'll tell the media why we gave tenure to an adjunct professor. I'll embarrass this law school to within an inch of its life, so help me."

"But Jackson!" exclaimed Dean Strong. "That's—that's unethical! It's blackmail!"

"Nobody's perfect, Ed," said Jackson, reddening and looking at his shoes. "In fact this goes completely against my nature. That's life, I suppose. Now I'm going to make it a package deal. Rebecca gets tenure, Sanford drops the charges against Daniel Conway, the students get a curriculum review committee, everyone forgets about the Professor of the Year letter, and I guarantee that the strike will end within twenty-four hours. Or I go to the reporters. Not that they'll be that hard to find. They've been camping outside the law school since yesterday morning. Take it or leave it, gentlemen."

Murray Frobisher spoke first. "You sonofabitch," he said. "I never thought I'd see the day that Mr. Ethics turned into Mr. Slimeball."

"Coming from you," said Jackson, "that's high praise."

"Gentlemen, please." The Dean tried to restore order.

"I never dreamed that you'd stoop to a cheap tactic like this," said Sanford Clapp.

"I feel the same way," said Jackson. "Half of me is disgusted with myself for doing this. But the other half of me is loving it."

"Jackson," said an admiring Tony Sloop, "you've got more guts than I ever gave you credit for."

"Ed, is this true?" Clapp asked. "Did you really sign a consent decree without telling us?"

The Dean was trapped. He closed his eyes and nodded. "I was just trying to protect the reputation of the law school," he said.

"And your own career," said Clapp, pointing a finger at the Dean. "I never liked you, Ed. I never liked your ambitiousness. I want you to know that."

The Dean sighed.

"I might confess to being surprised myself, Ed," said Tom Culpepper. "I never would have dreamed that you'd try to keep something this important from the faculty."

"I'm sorry, Tom," said a contrite Dean Strong. "Look. Four or five years ago I never dreamed that we'd have this much trouble finding women to teach here. Rebecca's been the only one in all this time. I don't know. I was just trying to balance too many competing interests. On the one hand, I thought Rebecca deserved tenure, just going strictly on the merits. On the other hand, a law school faculty is a delicate thing and I can't give tenure to someone who makes other people unhappy. Sanford, do you really find Rebecca that objectionable?"

Sanford Clapp looked away. "Not really, Ed," he said, defeated. "I just don't like it when people make me look like a chump, that's all."

"Well, what about you, Ron?" Dean Strong asked. "Why did you vote against her?"

"I don't really know, Ed," said Blotchett. "I figured if Murray didn't like her, there must have been a good reason. I didn't really focus on the issues."

"What about you, Aaron?" asked the Dean. "What were your objections to Rebecca getting tenure?"

Mountain remained silent. He wanted to see which way the consensus was forming before he committed himself to a position.

"Is it just because she's a woman?" asked the Dean. "Or is it because we disagree with some of her ideas?"

"With *all* of her ideas," muttered Sanford Clapp.

"I admit that it was wrong of me not to inform all of you about how the Sample case affected Rebecca's tenure decision," the Dean continued. "It was a mistake of judgment on my part. I hope that you can forgive me. I really did have the law school's best interests at heart. I'm sorry. But look. We've got a strike to settle and a lot of issues to decide. Jackson, can you guarantee that the students will end the strike if we meet the conditions you mentioned?"

"Absolutely," said Jackson Ward. And then, on second thought: "Well, probably. How's that?"

"Murray," the Dean asked, "would you really leave McKinley if Rebecca were given tenure?"

Frobisher sagged in his chair. "I suppose not," he said, his disappointment undisguised. "I wouldn't like it, though. I'll get used to it. Somehow."

"Well, what about the rest of you? Would giving Rebecca tenure result in *anyone's* departure?"

Silence.

"If the students want a curriculum review committee," Dean Strong reasoned, "we can give them a committee. That's easy enough. And it seems as though any opposition to Rebecca has melted away. The only remaining obstacle to settling the strike are the charges against Daniel Conway."

The Dean faced Sanford Clapp. "How about it, Sanford? How about dropping the charges? For the good of the law school. If you do, I might just forget about your little adventure in the dormitory the other night."

Sanford Clapp hung his head. "Well, I guess I've got no choice. Maybe I did overreact a bit to what Conway said about me, and to the whole Professor of the Year thing. But Ed, when you make it to the Supreme Court, you'd damned well better pick all of your clerks from my students."

"You've got a deal," said the Dean, shaking Sanford's hand and clapping him on the shoulder. "Jackson, I don't know who you've been talking to on the students' side, but my telephone is on the counter."

"Thanks, Ed," said Jackson. "Crime pays," he said to himself as he put through a call to the Blue and White Cafe.

"Meeting adjourned. Thank you, gentlemen," said a relieved Dean Edward Strong. The McKinley professors, except for Jackson Ward, filed out of the apartment, shaking their heads and talking quietly.

"I'm more than a little bit grateful, Jackson," said Dean Strong, after the others had departed. "If it weren't for your —your underhandedness, I might never have done the right thing."

"Well, in a backwards sort of way, that's what ethics are all about," said Jackson. "Just a minute, Ed. Hello, is this the Blue and White? This is Jackson Ward. Give me Katrina Walfish.... Hello? Katrina? It's Jackson. I've got good news.... Yes, they've agreed to everything.... Yes.... What's that? I can't hear you. . . . The strike is over? Of course I'll tell the Dean! Goodbye!"

"Did they accept?" Dean Strong asked.

"They did!" said a jubilant Jackson Ward.

"Oh, thank goodness," said an equally jubilant Edward Strong. "But where's Rebecca?"

THIRTY-TWO

That evening, Rebecca Shepard, the Saint, Katrina Walfish, Jackson Ward, and Dean Strong gathered at the Blue and White to celebrate the good news. Andrew Kefalias, the owner, treated them to champagne. "You should go out on strike more often," he said, popping the cork. "This is the best week I've had since I opened the place."

"Congratulations, Rebecca," said Katrina Walfish.

"It's your party, too, Katrina," said Jackson.

"I'd like to make a toast," said the Saint. All present raised their glasses. "First, to Rebecca, for becoming a tenured member of the faculty at McKinley. And for another reason we're not ready to talk about. Next, to Katrina, for her role in leading the student strike—and, incidentally, for getting me off the hook with Sanford Clapp. And finally, to Professor Ward, for excellence in public speaking. From what I've heard today, Professor Ward was single-handedly responsible for convincing the faculty to approve Rebecca's tenure and to settle the strike."

They clinked glasses and sipped the champagne.

"Jackson," said Rebecca, "you still haven't told us what you said at the Committee of Ten meeting. It must have been the greatest example of legal oratory since Clarence Darrow."

"Come on, Professor Ward," said Katrina. "Tell us how you did it."

"It was hardly legal oratory," said Dean Strong. "It was more like legal blackmail."

"What do you mean?" asked Katrina, taking another sip of champagne.

"Let's just say that it wasn't my finest hour as an Ethics professor," Jackson allowed.

"Rebecca, you still haven't told us how you feel about getting tenure," said Katrina.

"That's right," said the Saint.

"What upheavals are in store for us now?" asked Dean Strong. "On the one hand, I'm awfully excited about your ideas on legal education. On the other, I'm scared to death of what might happen to McKinley."

Rebecca laughed and sipped her champagne. "No upheavals, I promise," she said. "At least not right away. Look, the whole thing hasn't even sunk in yet. And I'm hardly the first woman to win tenure at a law school."

"You are at McKinley," said Katrina.

"Except for Miss Pander," said the Saint.

"She's not a woman, she's a librarian," said the Dean. "Oh, for crying out loud, now *I* sound like Frobisher."

Rebecca cleared her throat. "I wanted to make it here because I think it's important for women students to have a role model. And I think law school could be the most exciting intellectual experience instead of—"

No one was listening. All present stared with great surprise at someone standing directly behind Rebecca. She turned to look.

It was Murray Frobisher. His expression was uncharacteristically sheepish. "Somebody told me I'd find you in here," he said, looking away from Rebecca. "I just came to say that I was pretty much leading the opposition to your getting tenure, until Jackson wised us up as to certain matters at the faculty meeting—"

"You needn't go into details, Murray," Jackson interrupted.

"Oh, come on," said Murray. "You didn't do anything all that terrible. I'm—I'm sorry I called you Mr. Slimeball. It just slipped out. Look, Rebecca," Murray continued, touching the back of her chair. "I think it'll work out fine, and I'm sorry I— Oh, nuts, you know what I'm trying to say."

Rebecca put her hand on Murray's arm. "Really, Murray, there's nothing to apologize for," she said.

"Well, there's something else, too," said Murray. "Sanford couldn't be here because he had a consulting job in Toronto. At least he *says* he's got a consulting job in Toronto. Sanford asked me to, um, to welcome you to the tenured faculty of McKinley. He says he never should have given you a hard time the way he did. Why do I spend half my life apologizing for Sanford Clapp?"

"Murray," said Rebecca, "thank you for giving me the message. Now come on, have some champagne."

Murray brightened as Katrina poured him a glass. "To our new lady law professor," he toasted. "I never thought I'd see the day."

"I'll drink to that," said Dean Strong.

"You know what, Murray?" Katrina began. She was feeling the combined effects of sleeplessness and champagne. "Maybe you're not the total asshole I always thought you were."

"Katrina!" said Rebecca, somewhere between shock and laughter.

"No, no, it's okay," said Murray, pulling up a chair next to Katrina. "I'm not a total asshole. But I admit I come close."

"I admire your honesty, Murray," said Katrina, looking him over. "But that's about all I admire."

"Come on, you two, this isn't the time," said Dean Strong.

"Jackson," Rebecca asked, "did Murray really call you Mr. Slimeball at the faculty meeting?"

Jackson nodded. "I think that was the precise term, yes," he said, his expression melting into a grin.

"I don't know what you did," Rebecca told him, "and I guess I don't want to know. But I'm grateful. It sounds like I owe my job to you."

"I wouldn't say that at all," Jackson replied. "You could never have gotten tenure unless you deserved it. But sometimes even deserving candidates need a little— Let's call it a little push. And I learned something today. Something I never would have guessed, even after twenty years of teaching Ethics."

"What's that?" the others asked.

"Being—what did Murray call me?—being Mr. Slimeball can be a lot of fun."

EPILOGUE:
THE
FOLLOWING
SPRING

THIRTY-THREE

"Engagement of the Year." Sanford Clapp stood before his mailbox at the McKinley Law School and reread the unexpected engraved invitation. "The Women's Law Caucus cordially invites you to a reception in honor of the marriage of Rebecca Shepard to Daniel Conway. May 1st at eight o'clock in the Thorne Lounge."

"You'll be there, won't you?" asked Rebecca, opening her own mailbox. As Sanford turned to face her, Rebecca thought that she noticed a glimmer of regret in his eyes.

"I wouldn't miss it for the world," he said gallantly.

She gave him a warm smile. "Good," she said, touching his arm. "A celebration wouldn't be the same without you."

He blushed at the not-so-oblique reference to their "victory" lunch last October. "I hope there's a little more foundation to this party than there was to mine," he said. "Samantha and I will be delighted to attend."

Rebecca smiled again and departed. A lot had happened in the six months since she had been awarded tenure. For example, Dean Strong won considerable attention in the national media for his adept handling of the student strike. His picture appeared on the cover of *Newsweek* under the headline "Law Schools on Trial," and he was invited to universities all over the country to discuss his methods of peaceful resolutions of student unrest. That he was little more than a bystander in the actual negotiations at McKinley and that the deal was forced on him at the last minute was nowhere reported.

Murray Frobisher successfully defended Patton Pictures in the pandering trial. Randolph Patton was delighted with the result because it allowed his production company to go ahead with a full shooting schedule. Frobisher was disappointed with the victory. He was hoping to lose at trial and on appeal so that he could argue the case before the United States Supreme Court.

Peter Chesnut accepted a low salary/high stock option compensation package and went to work as chief financial officer of Patton Pictures in February. He rapidly made plans to take the company public.

Randolph Patton submitted *Backstage at the Rock Concert* to the Cannes Film Festival, where it won the oak-leaf cluster for Best Foreign Documentary. Randolph is currently contemplating a hostile takeover of Delta Airlines.

Frank Rooney was sentenced to two years in the prison wing of a Bethesda, Maryland, mental hospital. He received an advance of four hundred and fifty thousand dollars for the hardcover edition of his memoirs, which were tentatively titled *From Rocks to Riches*.

Tom Culpepper announced his retirement. He told the *Law School News* that "with fine young teachers like Rebecca Shepard, McKinley is in good hands." Four hundred and fifty students presented him with a petition asking him to reconsider his decision, and he agreed to teach for two more years.

The Museum of Modern Art invited Tony Sloop's group, Foaming at the Mouth, to perform at its annual Christmas Performance Art Festival. The undisputed highlight of the festival was Sloop's own "Homage to the Toaster-Oven," which consisted of making grilled cheese sandwiches for everyone in the audience. The curators of the museum added a videotape of his performance to its permanent collection.

The trustees of the McKinley Law School announced the endowment of a new Professorship in Law and Banking. One and a half million dollars was donated, anonymously.

After two and a half months on the living-room couch, a

chastened Sanford Clapp was permitted to sleep in his own bedroom again.

Jackson Ward published an article in the March issue of the *Harvard Law Review* entitled "The Better Part of Valor: Sometimes Legal Ethics Can Be Safely Ignored."

The Curriculum Review Committee, an outgrowth of the student strike and composed of students, faculty, alumni, and trustees, met regularly over a period of three months and adopted as its findings the conclusions of Rebecca Shepard's tenure essay. Dean Strong, needing some time to regain his nerve, announced that he was taking the report "under advisement."

Ronald Blotchett, who had been seeing Karen Conner exclusively for six straight months—his longest relationship since his marriage—was the first professor to agree to teach his class in accordance with Rebecca's methods, but only on condition that it did not require any extra work on his part. The law firm of Gregory and Peterson announced that Karen Conner would become a partner as of January first. After some hesitation, she accepted.

Aaron Mountain's article on Conflict of Laws appeared in the December issue of the *McKinley Law Review* and was universally ignored by others in the field.

All of the editors of the *Law Review* won judicial clerkships.

Katrina Walfish was offered a judicial clerkship in Denver, and her boyfriend Paul proposed, over the telephone. She turned down both offers. Instead, she and Paul decided that they would live together in New York for a year after they graduated from law school, and then they would decide about their future together. Meanwhile, Katrina spurned bids from five top New York corporate law firms and took a job with the Women's Law Cooperative, a small public interest firm that litigated women's issues and represented the indigent and the homeless.

Daniel Conway and Rebecca Shepard were to be married on the first Saturday after Finals Week, so as to maximize the number of McKinley students who could attend. The joint officiants at the ceremony would be Dean Strong and the *oba,* or chief, of the Nigerian village where Conway had served. The *oba* would make his first trip to America courtesy of McKinley University, where he would present a series of lectures on Nigerian law, history, and culture.

Jackson Ward agreed to be the best man.

ABOUT THE AUTHOR

Michael Levin studied ancient Greek and English literature at Amherst College and is a graduate of Columbia Law School. His writing has appeared on the Op-Ed page of *The New York Times* and in the *Jerusalem Post*, and has been anthologized in a college textbook on writing. He has worked for CBS News in New York, doing research and writing for *60 Minutes* and the *CBS Evening News*. His first book, *Journey to Tradition*, a non-fiction study of secular Jews who embrace Orthodoxy, was published in 1986. *The Socratic Method* is Levin's first novel. He lives in Marblehead, Massachusetts.